Midnight Secrets

PARKER'S LANDING
BOOK ONE

ASHLEY A QUINN

TCA PUBLISHING

CHAPTER 1

Claire

"Pebbles! No!" I looked up at the still dark sky and groaned before dashing out the door after my Yorkie. Pebbles had darted past when I opened it to pick up the paper and was now halfway down the front walkway, barking frantically at the stray cat we startled. My hot pink mule slippers slapped against the concrete as I ran after the pup. It was too early for this.

My dog reached the end of the walk and turned right, now headed down the public sidewalk. I picked up my pace. I didn't want Pebbles to run into the street. It was early yet and traffic was light, but that didn't mean a car couldn't come around the corner.

"Pebbles!"

The little pooch ignored me and kept running. I tightened the belt on my robe and ran as fast as my impractical shoes would let me. In the growing light, a running figure turned the corner ahead, stumbling over the little dog.

"Whoa!"

I heard the deep rumble of a man's voice. Squinting into the twilight as I neared, I could more clearly see the figure that had stopped and now approached my dog. In gray sweats, and a white long-sleeved tee, the man cut an imposing figure. Muscles strained the fabric of his shirt. If I hadn't been so concerned about Pebbles, I'd have taken more than a moment to appreciate his physique. I mean, I was a single, hot-blooded woman, after all, and this man checked all the boxes for tall, dark, and handsome—just my type.

Pebbles barked and backed away, but the movement tucked her up against the Winslow's picket fence. In one quick move, the man stepped forward and plucked my dog from the ground. Pebbles barked and squirmed in his arms, but she was no match for his size.

I hurried toward them.

"I take it this little devil is yours?"

Huffing and puffing from my early morning sprint in my slippers, I stopped in front of him and nodded. "Yes. Sorry." I reached for Pebbles. "She slipped past me when I opened the door to get the paper. Thank you for catching her."

He handed her over. "No worries. She's had her rabies shot, though, right?" He eyed the growling beast now in my arms.

I frowned. "Of course she has." I pet my dog's head, trying to calm her down. "She's just worked up."

"Good. Wouldn't want her to pass on some deadly disease when she bites someone." He touched two fingers to his forehead and tipped them forward. "Have a good day."

I spun, watching him run off with a scowl on my face. How dare he insinuate my dog was mean? Pebbles was the sweetest animal on the planet.

I snuggled her close to my face. "You're not mean, are you?" I crooned. "You just like to let people know you exist." Glaring at the handsome stranger's retreating form, I started back toward my house. His attitude almost made me not appreciate his firm tush as he ran. Almost.

Shaking my head, I returned home, locking the front door behind us. I set my dog down on the hardwood floor. "Now,"

I shook a finger at the animal. "Behave while I finish getting ready."

Pebbles wagged her little tail and dashed into the living room to attack her stuffed monkey. I chuckled. At least one of us liked mornings.

Picking up the paper I dropped when she escaped, I went into the kitchen and opened it. I knew it was a bit old-fashioned to still get a physical newspaper—especially at my age—but I liked having the hard copy in my hands. I processed the information better.

Looking through the headlines while I drank a glass of lemon water, I noted nothing too untoward had happened in Parker's Landing yesterday, which was great. There had been a rash of burglaries lately, and I was glad to see there weren't any to report.

With my water finished, I laid the paper on the bar and retreated upstairs to take a shower and get dressed. After showering and drying my hair, I donned a short-sleeved, fitted cobalt-blue dress and a pair of black pumps, then put on my makeup. A gray linen blazer completed the ensemble.

"Come on, Pebbles," I called as I descended the staircase and rounded the banister. As far as I could tell, my Yorkie hadn't done her business on her mad dash down the sidewalk, so she needed to go outside.

Collar and tags clinking, my little dog ran toward me, her tiny toenails tapping on the floor.

"Let's go outside." I led Pebbles to the back door and opened it. Immediately, she dashed outside, barking.

I rolled my eyes and stood on the stoop to make sure she went potty. Pebbles ran around the yard, nose in what was left of the last snowfall, but refused to pee.

"Pebbles, would you just go potty? I'm going to be late if you don't hurry up." I had an early meeting. Otherwise, it wouldn't bother me to be a little late. I was the boss, after all.

It's not like I could fire myself for not being in the office right at eight o'clock.

My dog ignored me and continued to sniff. I looked at my watch and sighed. I had my morning routine timed down to the minute. Chasing after my ornery Yorkie put me behind, and this was not helping.

"Pebbles! Go pee!" I tapped my foot, waiting. When she ignored me, I took my phone from my dress pocket and got online to order coffee. Normally, I ordered it when I reached the coffeeshop, but I was already running late. I couldn't go without my morning jolt, though.

Two minutes later, Pebbles finally squatted and relieved herself. I heaved a sigh. I was only ten minutes behind now.

I rolled my eyes. "Thank you. All right, let's go inside." Pebbles stuck her nose back in the snow. I growled through clenched teeth. "Pebbles, come."

She lifted her head, considering.

"Pebbles, it's time to go. Come." Finally, she trotted toward the door. I opened it for her, then quickly stepped inside and shut it. I didn't want her to dart out again. Urging the feisty animal to stay in the kitchen, I set the baby gate in the doorway, then picked up my things from the island, where I laid them last night. "All right, sweetie. You be good."

Pebbles barked once, her daily protest about being left behind, then walked to her bed in the corner and picked up a stuffed teddy bear. She tossed her head with it in her mouth, then plopped down to snuggle.

I smiled. The little stinker tried my patience some days, but her cuteness made up for it.

Double-checking that I had everything, I left the house through the garage door.

CHAPTER 2

Claire

"Good morning." I held open the door to The Cozy Cup and smiled at Mrs. Tewksbury as the older woman exited the building, a steaming vanilla latte in her hand. How did I know that's what the woman carried? Because Mrs. Tewksbury had ordered the same drink every Monday for the last five years. Ever since the coffeeshop opened.

"Well, good morning, Claire. You're running late today."

"Yeah. Pebbles was being a stinker. Put me behind a bit." Usually, I was in the coffeeshop, chatting with the owner—my best friend—by the time Mrs. Tewksbury arrived. There would be no chatting today, though.

"Well, I hope the rest of your day goes more smoothly."

"Me too, thank you."

"Bye, dear." Mrs. Tewksbury waggled her fingers and strolled away, off to meet her friends for their morning walk.

I stepped inside the coffeeshop, letting the door swing closed. The bell overhead rang, announcing my arrival.

"Hey, you. Good morning." Mina Kensington, my best friend, waved from behind the counter.

Waving back, I walked over to the pickup counter. "Can't stay and chat. Got an early meeting."

Mina gave me a thumbs-up. "Stop by later? I have something to tell you."

"Oh?" I paused, my interest piqued.

Mina laughed. "It's nothing that important. Just an idea I had. We'll talk later."

"Oh." I glanced at my watch. I really wanted to know what Mina had to say, but I would be late—later—if I didn't get a move on. "Okay. I'll try to come back around lunch."

"Sounds good."

With another wave, I left. Juggling my purse and breakfast, I pushed the button on the door handle to unlock my car, then got in. The plush brown leather seat enveloped me, and I set my coffee in the cup holder. Tossing my purse and the bag with my muffin on the passenger seat, I closed the door and started the car. With a quick glance in my mirrors, I backed out of my parking space and headed around the corner to my office.

Homes by Holmes's office was a quaint single-story white bungalow converted to office space probably thirty years ago, long before I bought it. Before I moved my real estate business in, it had been an insurance agency, and before that, a dentist's office. But I liked the small building with its black shutters and black and white awnings. It was a little vintage and retro and a whole lot inviting. Deep red vases I kept on either side of the door all year-round spilled over with greenery. I'd removed the poinsettias and holly after Christmas, but it was too early to add spring flowers.

We were firmly in the doldrums of a southern Alaskan winter, but in just a couple of months, the warmth would return. We'd seen shades of it the last couple of days, actually. For February, it had been warm. Low to mid-forties with more rain than snow, though we'd seen a couple of skiffs, including one last night. In fact, it had been warm enough, lately, I'd taken several strolls on the beach just beyond my back fence. There was something awe-inspiring about watching the steel-gray waters of the Pacific in the winter.

Next week, though, they were calling for a return to more seasonable temperatures and another significant snowstorm. I'd be back to digging paths through the yard, so Pebbles didn't disappear into the snow as soon as she stepped outside.

Tugging on the door, I let myself in. "Morning, Tamara." I smiled at my receptionist, Tamara Martin.

"Morning, boss."

"What are you doing here?" One of my realtors, Savannah Smith, poked her head out of her office. "I thought you had to go meet the staging crew at that house on Autumn Creek Road?"

"I do, but I wanted to drop off the contracts for the Spring Street sale so Tamara can make copies and get it all filed." I shrugged one strap of my large purse off my shoulder and reached inside, removing a folder. I passed it across the desk to Tamara.

"I'll get it taken care of." Tamara took the folder with a smile.

"Thanks, Tam. Could you also call Will Davis and see if he has room on his schedule for a closing this Friday?" One of my properties was moving through the sale process faster than expected, so we needed to move the closing date up a week. "And put this in my office?" I set my coffee and my muffin on the desk. It would only take me fifteen minutes to open up the Autumn Creek house. Then I could come back and start my day at a slower pace.

"You got it."

"Great, thank you. Okay." I spun on my heel. "I'm off." Throwing a hand in the air, I waggled my fingers and left again.

Back in my car, I maneuvered out of my small parking lot and pointed my vehicle toward the middle-class neighborhood of Willow Den and my new listing on Autumn Creek Road. My homeowners had signed the contract Friday and were eager to sell, so I'd sent pictures to the head of my staging crew, Lynne Young, and asked her to meet me at the house with whatever she thought she'd need to make the house more attractive to buyers. I had the key to let her and her crew inside.

Pulling up behind Lynne's box truck, I hopped out, keys in hand. The driver's door of the truck opened and Lynne got out.

"Morning."

"Hey. Sorry I'm late. Pebbles was a pain."

Lynne waved a hand. "I've only been here a couple minutes."

"Good. I'm glad I didn't keep you waiting." My heels clicked on the concrete driveway as I headed for the front door. "I'll get this unlocked so you can get started."

"So, what did Pebbles do today?"

I huffed. "Ran out the front door after a stray cat when I opened it to pick up the newspaper. I had to chase her down the sidewalk in my robe and slippers."

Lynne laughed. "You need to take that dog to obedience school. Maybe then she'll listen."

"She does. When she wants to." I chuckled. Pebbles most definitely had selective hearing.

I slipped the key into the lock. "Anyway, I'm just thankful some guy running came around the corner when he did. He corralled her against the Winslow's fence." I frowned as the memory of his attitude toward my dog came back. "He wasn't too enamored with her charms, though." I stepped over the threshold.

Lynne smiled. "Maybe he hadn't had his morning coffee yet." The older woman followed me inside.

"Maybe." I shrugged. "So, do you need help bringing things in?" I hoped not. That coffee and muffin called my name, but I hadn't seen any of Lynne's crew outside and didn't want to leave her alone to unload everything by herself.

"No. Sammie should be here soon. You weren't the only one with animal trouble this morning. Something got into her trash last night and left a mess on her patio."

My nose wrinkled. "I'll take chasing my dog down any day over that."

"Me too."

"Okay, well, do you want to walk me through what your plan is, then?"

"Sure." Lynne pointed behind me. "I brought an entryway table to put in here and some trinkets to display. In here"—she pointed to the living room to the right—"I brought some décor to spruce things up. A mantle display and some blankets. And this really cool—" She stopped. "Claire. Did you leave the door open the last time you were here?"

"What?" I turned to look at the French doors leading to the backyard. One was open a crack. "No. Why is that open?" I walked toward it, looking at the lock. Maybe it was broken. Reaching for the handle, I stopped, remembering the spate of burglaries we'd had lately. "Crap." I looked at Lynne. "We should probably check the house. Make sure nothing's been stolen."

Lynne wrinkled her nose. "Yeah. You go up, and I'll look around down here?"

I nodded. "Don't touch anything."

"Don't worry." Lynne pulled her sleeves down and tucked her hands inside. "I won't."

With a nod, I left the room and went upstairs. Hopefully, I didn't find anything missing. Maybe someone forgot to lock the door—whether it was me or the homeowner—and it blew open. Filing a police report and calling my homeowners to explain a break-in was not on my agenda for today.

Reaching the landing, I paused, frowning as I realized I

would have to touch the doorknobs to check the rooms. They were all closed. Well, except for the master bedroom. That door stood open. Which was weird, because I know I closed all the doors the last time I was here. It was an odd quirk I had when I showed houses. It was how I made sure no one was still in the home after an open house. When everyone was supposed to be gone, I would walk through and check every room, then close the doors as I went. It had become such a habit that I did it when I showed homes privately and when I took listing photos as well. And I know I closed that door after doing my walk-through to take pictures for Lynne.

The plush cream carpet quieted my footfalls as I traversed the hall to the master suite. With a knuckle, I nudged the partially open door inward.

Rumpled bed clothes hung half off the black metal-frame bed. A lamp laid on the floor, having fallen from the night-stand. Clothes hung out of the dresser and littered the floor.

Eyes huge, I stared at the mess. "What on Earth?" Walking deeper into the room, I headed for the closet. There was a floor safe hidden behind some long dresses. I wanted to check that it was still there.

I rounded the end of the bed.

For half a second, I wondered at what I was seeing. Then it registered.

A scream bubbled up my throat, but got stuck and came out as a strangled cry. I stumbled backward, tripping over my heels to land on my butt on the floor. Like a crab, I scrambled back, then pushed to my feet and stared at the space between the bed and the closet, horror making my stomach do somersaults.

There, on the floor crumpled into a heap, was Mrs. Hammond, one of the homeowners. Eyes open, sightless and slightly cloudy, her gaze fixed at a point under the bed, she lay in a pool of deep red blood.

Dead.

CHAPTER 3

Ozzie

Murder wasn't the first case I expected to have once Chief Riggs let me off my chain and out into the world by myself. But here I was, pulling up to a fresh murder scene.

Blowing out a breath, I shut my cruiser off and got out, walking up to the first officer I saw.

"Garnett."

The twenty-year veteran turned. When he saw me, one eyebrow rose. "Chief sent the newbie by himself?"

One side of my mouth slid up. "Yep. He cut the apron strings." My expression sobered. "What do we have?"

"Nastiness. I don't like this one."

I studied the older man as I digested that. "Murder is never good. What makes this one worse?"

Sergeant Garnett tipped his head toward the house. "Come on. I'll show you."

Curious now, I followed him toward the front door. My gaze caught on the blonde woman sitting on the porch steps. "Who's that?"

"Claire Holmes. She found the body—she and her

colleague, there." He nodded to the box truck in the driveway.

"They know to stay put until I talk to them, yes?"

Garnett's head bobbed. "Yep. I posted Turner out here too. He's directing traffic and keeping an eye on them. They can't get out, anyway. He blocked their vehicles in." His gaze flicked to the navy-blue Land Rover in the driveway.

My eyebrows winged upward. That was a nice car. Especially for this area. "What do we know about her?"

"She's a real estate agent."

"This house is for sale?" I didn't notice a sign in the yard when I drove up.

"Not yet. But that's why she and her colleague are here. The deceased is one of the homeowners."

"Got it."

We approached the porch. I expected Ms. Holmes to look up, but she kept staring out at the yard, her expression blank. Shock, it seemed, had set in.

Passing her, we went inside. After donning shoe covers, Garnett led me upstairs to the master bedroom, where the crime scene unit was busy processing the scene.

Grant Iverson glanced up from his position on the far side of the bed. "Hey."

I gave him a nod of acknowledgement. "Is it okay to come through?" I motioned to where he crouched.

"Yeah. Just watch your footing. There's quite a bit of blood back here."

Rounding the bed, I stopped near the end. A woman lay face down on the beige carpet, her head turned so she stared under the bed. Her deep red skirt and jacket blended in with the pool of blood spread out around her. One black heel hung off her foot, hooked only by her toes. The other was on the floor beside her legs.

"What do we know about her? Garnett said she's one of the homeowners."

"Her name is Marie Hammond. She's forty-one. Married," Grant answered. "One of my techs found her purse. She's a teacher at Parker's Landing Academy. That's all we've got so far. No kids, as far as we can tell."

I reached into the cargo pocket on my pants and produced a small spiral notebook, then grabbed the pen I kept clipped to my collar and jotted that down. "What about cause of death? Do you have any ideas about that yet? Other than exsanguination?" I gestured to the copious amount of blood staining the carpet.

"No. We were just getting ready to roll her." Grant looked up at his colleague, Maya Gossard. "You ready?"

She nodded and picked up a thick plastic sheet, holding out one end to him. Grant took it, and they unfolded it, spreading it on the floor beside Mrs. Hammond.

"Okay. On three." Grant wrapped gloved hands around the woman's ankles. Maya put a hand under her right arm. "One… two… three." Together, they rolled Mrs. Hammond onto her back onto the plastic sheet.

I tipped my head, studying the front of her body. "I don't see any burn marks. And those don't really look like bullet holes."

Grant picked up his camera and snapped several photos. "I agree. They look like stab wounds." He took several more pictures from different angles and with a ruler.

Finally, he was ready to open her jacket. It was unbuttoned, but blood had made it sticky. Carefully, Maya folded the fabric back while Grant took more pictures. The slashes through her blouse were much more evident than those through the jacket.

"She was definitely stabbed." Grant glanced back. "The medical examiner's office will be able to tell you more once they conduct her autopsy."

Mouth flat, I nodded once. "Has anyone contacted her husband?"

Garnett smirked. "That's your job."

I rolled my eyes. "Gee, thanks."

"Welcome."

"Before I go making phone calls, are we sure he's not somewhere on the property, also deceased?" If it was a home invasion gone wrong, that was a distinct possibility.

"We checked when we arrived," Garnett said. "No sign of him. There's only one vehicle in the garage, but from the discoloration on the concrete, I would say there's normally two."

"Okay. I'll see about tracking him down, then."

The radio on my belt crackled to life.

"PL-one-ten for PL-two-twelve, over."

Unclipping it, I answered. "PL-one-ten, PL-two-twelve. Go ahead, over."

"I've got the RP out here with some information you should know, over."

It sounded like the realtor's shock might have worn off. "Copy that. I'll be out shortly. PL-two-twelve out."

I turned to Garnett. "Let's find some contact info for the husband, then I'll talk to Ms. Holmes."

CHAPTER 4
Claire

An icy breeze blew over my face, tousling my flaxen hair. The change in the weather the forecasters assured us all was on the way had arrived.

Or maybe that was the chill blanketing my body from finding Mrs. Hammond dead in her bedroom.

I shivered and huddled deeper into my coat. Cold seeped through the skirt of my dress from the concrete porch beneath me. It added to the numbness slowly claiming me from what I'd seen. All that blood and Mrs. Hammond's lifeless body. How could this happen? Mrs. Hammond wasn't even supposed to be in town. She and her husband were supposed to be off looking for a new home in Boston.

Her husband! Eyes wide, I shot to my feet. Where was he? If the wife was here and dead, where was Mr. Hammond? Was he dead too?

I glanced around, looking for the young cop who'd arrived in response to my frantic 9-1-1 call and was surprised to see that others were now on scene. When did they get here? I shook my head. No matter. Any of them would do.

Hurrying over to the first officer I saw, I waved my hands to get his attention. "Officer?"

The man turned, a curious dip in his brow. "Yes, ma'am?"

"Hi, Officer"—I glanced at his nametag—"Turner. I'm Claire Holmes. I found the—I found Mrs. Hammond. I had a thought. She and her husband were supposed to be out of town, house-hunting in Boston. If she's here, where is he? Have your colleagues started a search of the property? He could be here." I didn't want to think that he was dead, too, but it was a possibility.

Officer Turner's frown turned serious. "We have officers canvassing, yes. Are you certain they weren't supposed to be here?"

I nodded. "Yes. That's why my stager and I were here." I pointed to Lynne, who sat in her van, the driver's door open. "It was the perfect time to prep their house and take listing pictures."

"Okay. Let me get Detective Quartermaine on the radio. I'm sure he'll want to talk to you." He lifted the radio mic off his shoulder.

I frowned as the officer's words registered. "Wait. Is he already here?"

The man nodded.

My frown intensified. "How did I miss that?"

Turner shrugged. "Not sure." Pressing the talk button on his mic, he had a short conversation with someone inside.

Hooking the small black square back onto his shoulder, he propped his hands on his gear belt. "He shouldn't be too long. Would you like to have a seat in my patrol car to wait? I probably should have offered that sooner. It's chilly out." He gestured to the vehicle a few feet behind him.

"Oh. No, thank you. I'll just—" I fluttered a hand and sighed. I didn't know what to do.

"I think you should sit down. Come on." He reached a hand behind my shoulder, not touching me, and guided me toward his car. "I'll leave the back door open so you don't feel like a criminal."

"That's appreciated." I offered him a tight smile.

"Of course." He opened the rear passenger-side door.

I eyed the vinyl seat with trepidation. "Is it clean?"

He chuckled. "We wipe them down after every suspect. I can't promise it'll smell the best in there, but it is clean, yes."

Lovely. Well, hopefully with the door open, it wouldn't be too bad. I lifted a foot and placed it in the car, folding my long body into the seat. My knees bumped the seat in front of me. It was times like this I cursed my five-foot-ten-inch height. "Boy. You guys don't give your suspects much space, do you?"

"No, ma'am. It's safer if they can't move around too much. Why don't you swing your legs out? It might be more comfortable."

I did as he suggested. The door frame cut into my leg, but it was infinitely preferable to being squished. Folding my hands in my lap, I tried to force my mind not to wander. I didn't want to think that Mr. Hammond could be lying dead on the property somewhere. One dead body was enough.

Thankfully, the detective was true to his word and soon emerged from the house.

"Here he comes." Officer Turner motioned to the front porch.

I looked past him. The man striding toward us was not what I expected.

Not at all.

For one, he was handsome as sin. Thick dark hair waved atop his head. A head that topped most of those around him by several inches. Dressed in black tactical pants and a black department polo shirt under a black coat emblazoned with the state patrol logo, he had a handgun strapped to his right hip. The whole package exuded male magnetism and confidence.

And danger.

A shiver went down my spine. I wouldn't want to mess with him.

As he neared, I got a better view of his face. Fine lines bracketed dark brown eyes, set off by his tan skin. This was a man who spent a lot of time outdoors. Though some of his coloring appeared natural. There was an exoticness about his features that said he had some Mediterranean heritage of some sort. And despite the lines, he was younger than I expected. Early-thirties at most. There was something familiar about him too. It was in the way he moved. But I couldn't put my finger on it.

"Turner." The detective nodded at the officer. "This my witness?"

The moment he spoke, things clicked in my brain. "You." I stood up.

He frowned. "Yes? I'm Detective Quartermaine."

"You're the man from this morning."

He blinked. "I'm sorry, what?"

"My dog. You helped me catch her." It might have been too dark this morning for me to get more than a general impression of his handsome face, but I would know that voice anywhere. It was like gravel over whiskey. That little bit of rasp turned an everyday baritone into something I would no doubt hear in my sleep every night for the foreseeable future.

His eyes widened. "You're the hot-pink slipper lady?"

A blush roared to life, and I was sure I was red to the roots of my hair. Of course, he would remember my attire.

I straightened to my full height and pretended not to notice the heat flaming on my face. "I am." I held out a hand. "Claire Holmes. I found Mrs. Hammond."

"Right." His large palm enveloped mine for a quick shake. "What were you doing here, Ms. Holmes?"

"I'm a realtor. The Hammonds contracted me to sell their house. I was here with my stager, Lynne Young, to get it ready for listing." I gestured to Lynne, who still sat in her van, then shoved my hands into my pockets.

Quartermaine glanced at the van, then back to me. "Okay. Walk me through what happened. What time did you arrive?" He took a notepad from his pants pocket and a pen from the collar of his shirt.

"Oh, um, about eight-fifteen, I think. Maybe a few minutes after. I was running behind because—well, you know why."

"Your dog?"

I nodded.

"All right. What happened after you arrived? Was Ms. Young already here?"

"Yes. She said she only beat me by a couple minutes."

"Did you see anything out of the ordinary before you went in?"

"No. We walked up the drive and went to the front door." I motioned to the house. "I unlocked it with my key, and we went in."

"The front door was locked?"

"I can't say one hundred percent. I didn't check it before I put the key in. But it was closed. Unlike the French doors off the living room. They were open."

He nodded once and wrote something in his notebook. "What did you do after you discovered the door open?"

"We've had that rash of break-ins lately, so Lynne and I decided to split up to see if anything was missing. She checked downstairs while I went up."

One dark eyebrow winged upward. "You just decided to traipse through what could be a crime scene? Why didn't you call the police the moment you saw the open door?"

I bristled at his chiding tone. I wasn't an idiot. Or a child. "We thought it was possible the wind blew the door open. The weather here isn't exactly calm."

"Were there leaves or dirt on the floor near the door?"

I frowned. "What? Why would you ask that? Do you think the killer brought that in on his shoes?"

"Uh, no. If the door blew in from the weather, it stands to reason leaves and dirt would blow in too. Even with the snow we've had, stuff still floats around."

"Oh. Right. Of course." I gave a nervous laugh, quickly cutting it off. "Sorry. I'm a little out of sorts." Finding dead bodies would do that to a person. I cleared my throat. "Anyway, I didn't want to trouble the police if nothing was missing and there were no other signs of an intruder. I'd have just relocked the door and gone about staging as planned."

The tiny frown that had been present almost since he walked up intensified. "You wouldn't have called the police?"

I shook my head. "It's not the first French door I've seen blow open. I've had it happen while I'm standing in the room. The frames shift and they don't latch properly anymore. Sometimes not even if they're locked. I would have assumed that's what happened here."

"Never assume."

"Huh?"

"Never assume. Because assumptions can be and are often wrong."

"Oh." He had a point, but I doubted I'd have done anything differently. As I said, I'd seen it several times.

"All right. So, you and your colleague split up. What happened then?"

"I went upstairs. When I got to the landing, I realized I'd need to touch the doorknobs to check the rooms, and I hesitated. I didn't want to smudge any prints if it was indeed a burglary. That's when I noticed the master bedroom door was open."

He tipped his head, a slight furrow between his brows. "You sound like that's unusual."

"It is. I have this habit where I close doors at my listings. It started as something I did after an open house to make sure no one was hiding in any of the rooms. I do it after showings and when I take listing photos, too, so I know I didn't miss anything. And I know I shut that bedroom door when I left Friday. Since the Hammonds were out of town, it made me wonder why the door was open. No one else should have come through the house."

"Why were you in the house on Friday?"

"To take pictures for Lynne. She couldn't meet me here that day to do a walkthrough, but we wanted to get the staging set up as soon as possible, so I took pictures for her Friday night. The Hammonds left earlier that afternoon for Boston, right after they signed the papers contracting me to sell the house."

He nodded. "Okay. Continue. What did you do after you noticed the open door?"

"I went inside. The room was a mess. Covers half off the bed, a lamp on the floor. Clothes—everywhere." My hands fluttered.

"How did you find Mrs. Hammond? She was on the far side of the bed, not visible from the doorway."

"After I saw the mess, I wanted to check the closet. I noticed a floor safe when we did our first walkthrough, and I wanted to make sure it hadn't been tampered with." I swallowed hard and moisture gathered in my eyes. "I didn't make it that far. I saw her and—" I broke off and closed my eyes, sucking a breath in through my nose.

Forcing the thoughts away, I looked at the detective. "I left the room and called 9-1-1."

He made a note. "What happened after that?"

"Lynne and I left the house to wait outside like the dispatcher asked us to."

Again, his head bobbed. "Okay. I think I have what I need from you for now. I'll—"

I held up a hand. "What about Mr. Hammond?"

Detective Quartermaine paused. "We haven't spoken to

him yet. Wait." He narrowed his eyes, then glanced around the yard. "Did you find him dead too?"

I could see a healthy dose of skepticism in his expression, but also a smidge of doubt.

"No. I didn't leave the front porch after I called the police. But I am wondering if he's dead somewhere on the property. They weren't supposed to be here, and they were supposed to be together in Boston. Have your officers looked for him?"

"They have, Ms. Holmes. There is no one else on the grounds."

My shoulders slumped. "That's a relief." But another thought hit me, making me tense again. "But if he's not here, then where is he?" My eyes widened. "Do you think whoever killed Mrs. Hammond kidnapped him?"

Officer Turner coughed. He raised a fist to cover his mouth and cast a quick look at Detective Quartermaine. I narrowed my eyes, studying the officer's face, then looked at the detective. A smirk played with his firm lips.

A frown took over my expression. "You think I'm nuts, don't you? Some airheaded blonde who's spouting wild conjecture?" I crossed my arms and glared at Detective Quartermaine. "Who's assuming now, hmm?"

Turner covered a laugh with another cough. Detective Quartermaine returned my glare.

"I have your statement, Ms. Holmes. Don't worry about Mr. Hammond. I'll track him down, I assure you. In the meantime, if you hear from him, let me know and have him call me." He took a card from another pocket and held it out to me.

I took the white rectangle from his fingers. "May I leave now?"

"Yes. But stay available in case I have more questions." He said the last as he backed away, his attention turning to Lynne, who was no doubt next on his list of people to interview. I hoped he was friendlier to her than he was to me.

I pressed my lips into a tight line and nodded. Not that he saw me. I wanted to say more and call him out on his rudeness, but I didn't figure that would endear me to him. Plus, I really did just want to leave. "Officer Turner?" I turned to the younger man. "Would you be so kind as to move your squad car so I can get my vehicle out?" I gestured to my Land Rover.

"Oh, yes. Of course. Sorry."

"No problem. I know you're just doing your job. Thank you." As he hurried away, I took a deep breath and blew it out, trying to settle my nerves. Striding to my car, I debated just going home. My concentration was shot. All I could think about was Mrs. Hammond lying on the floor in a pool of blood. I didn't even know how the woman died. Was it a stabbing? Gunshot? And where was Mr. Hammond? I hoped he was okay.

Shaking my head, I unlocked the car and got in. For a moment, I just sat there and stared at the house. How was I supposed to work the rest of the day?

Oh, come on, Claire. You're a professional.

Damn straight, I was.

Squaring my shoulders, I pushed the button to start the engine. As a professional, I had obligations. And besides, working would help control my thoughts. If I went home, I'd just spend the day worrying and wondering.

With a nod to myself, I put the car in gear and backed out of the drive. Work it was.

CHAPTER 5

Claire

"**K**nock, knock."

Mina's sing-song greeting and the quick rap of her knuckles on the door brought my head up.

"Mina. Hi." My shoulders sagged as I realized why she was here. "I'm so sorry. I forgot about lunch." I glanced at the clock on the wall. It was just after one-thirty.

"I figured, so I thought I'd come down and bring you an afternoon pick-me-up." Mina held up the two paper cups in her hands, an oversize purse hanging from the crook of her elbow as she walked in and sat down across the desk. "One white chocolate mocha with a shot of caramel."

"Oh, bless you." I accepted the cup and took a sip. "Mmm, yum. Thank you." My adrenaline—and caffeine—high from this morning had worn off, and now I struggled to stay awake. Who would have guessed finding a body could make a person so tired.

"Okay, what's that look?"

My forehead wrinkled. "What look?"

"The one that says you've had a terrible day. The last time you looked like this, Adam Nielsen dumped you and you lost out on a sale to Miranda Bennett in the same day." Mina tipped her chin down to pin me with a look. "I know there's no man in your life to dump you, but Miranda? What did she do?"

I sighed. "It wasn't Miranda." I actually hadn't had many dealings with the other realtor lately, thankfully. I couldn't stand that woman. "You really don't know why I look like I had the worst day ever?" I raised a hand and drew a circle in the air by my face with one finger.

Mina shook her head, a curious frown now lighting her face. "No. Should I?"

My eyebrows lifted, and I nodded. "Yeah." I figured the gossip mill would have been in full swing by now. "So, I went to the Hammond house on Autumn Creek Road this morning to meet Lynne for staging."

"Right. I remember you mentioning that over the week-end," Mina said, lowering her cup after taking a drink. "I take it that's why you blew out of my coffeeshop like a house afire. Did something happen? Was Lynne not there?"

"No, Lynne was there, but something did happen." I felt tears press at the backs of my eyes again and took a quick breath. "I don't know how you don't know about this, but I found Mrs. Hammond on the floor in the master bedroom. She'd been murdered."

Mina gasped. "What? Oh my gosh! After the morning rush, I closeted myself in my office to get some work done. I had no idea."

It still surprised me she didn't know. Gossip flew through The Cozy Cup faster than a peregrine falcon.

"You're sure she was dead?"

"Considering she was in a pool of blood, her skin was the color of chalk, and they brought her out in a body bag, yes, I'm sure." I pressed a hand to my belly, willing the nausea away as I remembered Mrs. Hammond's appearance.

Mina winced. "Sorry. I'm just surprised. Do the police have any leads?"

"I don't know. I gave my statement, then left. I haven't talked to the detective since then."

"Hmm." Mina stuck a nail between her teeth and looked to the side, then dropped her hand. "Who's handling the case?"

"Detective Quartermaine." I rolled my eyes. "I hope he's a better detective than he is people-person."

"Quartermaine? He's the new guy. I don't know much about him, other than he likes his coffee as black as his hair and makes every woman in my shop stop and stare when he comes in—me included."

"Yes, well, handsome doesn't mean nice."

"What do you mean? He's always polite when he comes into the shop."

I lifted a shoulder. "Then maybe it's just me. He wasn't very pleasant to deal with." I took another drink of her coffee, trying to keep the frown off my face.

It was Mina's turn to shrug. "I don't know. He's always been nice. Maybe it was the situation."

I hummed, not buying it. He'd been rude this morning too. "Could be." I didn't want to dwell on Detective Jerkface, though.

"So, are you okay? That had to be a shock. Why are you here and not at home?"

"I'm okay. I needed to stay busy, so I came in to work. It's helped keep my mind off things. Helped the spinning, you know?" I twirled a finger near my ear.

"Understandable. You sure you're all right, though?"

"I'm fine, Mina. Just wondering what happened. And where Mr. Hammond is. He's not answering his phone. I've tried his cell and the number they left for their hotel."

Mina snorted. "Maybe that's because he did it."

I frowned. "What do you mean? You think Mr. Hammond killed his wife?"

Mina's eyes widened. "You don't? Claire, spouses are the

first suspects in homicides. You watch enough crime dramas, you should know that."

"I know. I mean, I do, but…" I trailed off and shook my head. "I just can't see him doing it. He seemed so nice."

"Ted Bundy seemed nice too."

I rolled my eyes. "Mr. Hammond is not a serial killer. I don't think he's a killer of any kind. He and his wife seemed pleasant toward each other when we met to discuss selling their property. Maybe a little strained, but what they were planning was a huge life change." I frowned, thinking more about their attitudes toward each other. I truly didn't remember any animosity between the couple. "I am curious about what happened to him, though. I hope he's okay. That he's not hurt somewhere."

"Do you have any other numbers you can call to reach him?"

I started to shake my head, then stopped, my brows dipping. "Wait. Maybe." Shifting, I pushed the contracts I'd been reviewing to the side and pulled my keyboard closer. "I have their banking and employment history on file. I could call his office and see if anyone has heard from him. Or knows how to reach him." I paged through the scanned records until I found his paystub. The name and phone number for his company were at the top.

Lifting the receiver on my desk phone, I dialed the number.

The receptionist picked up after the second ring. "Hello, Crandall and Crandall Investments. This is Alicia."

"Hello, this is Claire Holmes from Homes by Holmes Realty. I'm trying to reach Warren Hammond."

"Oh, he's not in today. He and his wife went to Boston. May I take a message?"

Clearly, Detective Quartermaine had not been to Mr. Hammond's office to break the news of Mrs. Hammond's death. "It's rather urgent that I speak to him. Do you have a way to contact him other than his cell phone? He's not answering."

"Hmm, did you try his wife?"

"I did. She's not answering, either." I was not about to tell this woman she was dead. The police could do that. "I tried their hotel as well. The Four Points in Newton?"

"Oh, actually, they're staying at The Whitney Hotel in Beacon Hill."

My eyebrows knit together. "Oh, I must have the wrong information, then. Do you have a room number?"

"I'm sorry. I can't give out that information."

"Oh, right. Yes, of course. I'll just call the hotel and have them connect me. Thank you for your help."

"Of course. I hope you reach him."

"Thank you. Goodbye."

"You're welcome. Bye."

I set the phone down and stared at it for a moment, then looked at Mina.

"What?"

"The Hammonds lied about where they were staying. They told me they were at The Four Points, but the receptionist said they're at The Whitney."

Mina's eyebrows rose. "That sounds like an expensive place." She took her phone from her pocket and opened her internet browser.

"I know. I wonder why they lied."

"Or how they could afford it." She let out a low whistle. "I was right. It's not cheap." She looked up. "Autumn Creek Road isn't the ritziest part of town. This is definitely not a hotel I'd expect someone who lives there to stay at."

I hummed, thinking. "They both work. And he is a financial investor. I've seen their finances. They mostly live off of her income. Most of his gets socked away into their savings."

Mina raised a finger. "That's the way to do it when you get married if you can swing it."

"Yeah. And they don't have children, which makes it even easier."

"How old are they?"

"Early forties."

"Wow." Mina shifted uncomfortably in her chair, her frown returning. "Makes you think, doesn't it? We're not far off from that, and I don't think I have the kind of savings they do."

It did. I grimaced and nodded. "Yeah, me either." I picked up the phone again.

"Who are you calling now?"

"The Whitney Hotel."

"Wait." Mina leaned forward and put a hand over the keypad. "Do you think that's wise? What if he's there and you get him on the line? What are you going to say to him? He might not know about his wife yet. I know if it were me, I wouldn't want someone—especially someone who's not law enforcement or someone I know well—telling me my spouse is dead. And definitely not over the phone."

Crap. Mina was right. Scrunching my nose, I replaced the receiver. "Yeah."

"Maybe you should just call Detective Quartermaine and tell him what you found out."

I scrunched my nose harder. "Do I have to?"

Mina gave me a look.

I sighed. "Fine." Reaching into my desk drawer, I rummaged inside my purse for his card. Finding it, I picked up the phone and dialed.

It rang six times, then rolled to voicemail, which made me happy. I didn't have to talk to him and listen to him tell me to stay out of things.

"Hi, Detective, it's Claire Holmes," I said after the beep. "I wanted to let you know that the Hammonds were supposed to stay at the Four Points Hotel in Newton, Massachusetts, but the receptionist at Crandall and Crandall, where Mr.

Hammond works, said they were staying at The Whitney in Beacon Hill in Boston. No, I didn't call the hotel. I just wanted to see if anyone had spoken to him today. I'm worried. I also didn't tell the woman on the phone that Mrs. Hammond is dead. Anyway, that's it. Bye."

I replaced the receiver and looked at Mina. "Happy?"

She grinned. "Yep."

"Good. Now tell me what you wanted to talk about."

"Oh, that." She set her coffee on the desk, then leaned sideways and dipped a hand into her bag, producing a folder. "Read this and tell me what you think." She set it in front of me.

With a curious frown, I slid the folder closer and opened it. After the first few lines, I could tell it was a business plan.

I glanced up at her, shock making my eyes round. "You want to expand the coffeeshop?"

Giving me a bright smile, she nodded. "Mr. Shuman is moving out of the space next door. I want to turn The Cozy Cup into a café."

Quickly, I read through her plan. It was sound. "I like it. You're sure that's the price you can get for his space?"

"Yes. He contacted Miranda Bennett to give him a selling price." She wrinkled her nose in distaste. "I wanted to tell him he should call you, but I didn't want there to be any argument of favoritism shown, so I kept my mouth shut."

I chuckled. "Good move. I can't say for sure without seeing the space in more detail, but this price seems fair for that location. Do you want me to represent you as your buyer's agent?"

"Yes, please."

"All right. I'll get a contract drawn up. Is this what you want to offer him?" I pointed to the number on the page.

"Yes."

"Okay. I'll get on it."

Mina clapped softly. "Awesome. I'm ready. I have so many plans. I'm going to completely revamp the coffeeshop space."

"What's wrong with it?" I liked the way it looked. "Can't you just keep the theme and add tables for the café?"

"I could, but it's a little dated. I want to lighten it up a bit. Make it more farmhouse cozy instead of the nautical cozy it's got going on right now. You know I didn't do much to it when I bought it five years ago."

"I know. But you realize this is an ocean town, right?"

"Yes. But I think a lighter color palette and a lot of greenery will go over well with the patrons. And I want to ditch the driftwood decorations."

I frowned. "You're keeping your counter, though, right?" Her hand-hewn checkout counter was gorgeous.

She gave me a horrified look. "I'm not crazy. That thing is a work of art."

A smile crossed my face. "Good. I think the townsfolk would riot if you did. And I'd lead the charge."

Mina laughed. "You would."

Grinning, I closed the folder, then tapped it with one hot-pink fingernail. "Can I keep this for now?"

"Yep. I was hoping you'd jump onboard. That copy is for you."

"Perfect. I'll work on the paperwork later this afternoon."

"Great." Mina gathered the handles on her bag and picked up her coffee. "I'll let you get to work. I know you're behind because of what happened this morning."

My nose wrinkled at the reminder. "Yeah. I just hope they find Mr. Hammond safe and sound, and that he had nothing to do with his wife's death."

Mina shrugged. "The spouse is always the most likely suspect."

"I know. But I just didn't get that vibe from them, you know?" I lifted a shoulder and blew out a breath. "I don't know. It's all crazy."

"It is. But please do what Detective Quartermaine suggested and let him handle it?"

I held up my hands. "I'll behave." But mentally, I crossed my fingers. I had no intention of sticking my nose into the middle of the investigation, but if information happened to come my way, well, I would be more than happy to ask a few questions.

CHAPTER 6

Ozzie

My breath fogged, sweeping past my face as I ran through the darkened streets of Parker's Landing. Icy fire seared my lungs as I inhaled deep breaths of the cold air, but I didn't mind. It helped to clear my head.

I'd lain awake for hours last night, mulling over details of the Hammond case. I couldn't find the husband. Every phone number I called either went to voicemail or there was no one at that location by that name. I'd called both hotels in Boston that Claire Holmes mentioned in her message. Neither had a guest registered under Hammond's name. There wasn't even a booking for the couple.

To cover my bases, I emailed a picture of Warren Hammond to the heads of security for both places. They said they'd keep an eye out, but I didn't hold out much hope he was there.

If Hammond didn't murder his wife and then run, he was dead somewhere. Or running from someone who wanted him dead.

I sucked in another lungful of icy air, willing the returning thoughts away and forcing my mind onto something else.

I cycled through my morning to-do list. Number one was

making sure Marie Hammond's body left the county morgue and headed to Anchorage for autopsy. After that, I planned to book a flight there for a couple of days from now so I could observe the procedure. Once I had my travel squared away, I would file requests for the Hammonds' financial information and phone records. If the warrants were ready. I filed for them yesterday afternoon, and they should be through. Then I needed to go to the school where Marie Hammond taught and interview her colleagues.

Or that might happen before I put in the records request. It all depended on those warrants. Things moved more slowly here than in North Carolina. It wasn't because of less urgency. There just weren't the personnel to get things done any faster. As a special detachment of the state police, I was the only detective on the small police force here. Most of the legwork for this case I would do alone. Though the chief said I could borrow an officer when needed. If I needed more expertise, I could call Juneau's police department or bring in the big guns from the other state offices in Juneau or Anchorage. It was a much different way of policing than I was used to.

My jogging route carried me around the corner toward Claire Holmes's house. Her windows were still dark, which didn't surprise me. I'd set out a little earlier this morning since I'd been unable to sleep.

I still couldn't believe the put-together professional I'd met at the Hammonds' was the same hot-pink slippered, bathrobed woman I encountered running down the sidewalk after her little Yorkie in the dark yesterday. The two images just didn't jive.

Both were appealing, though.

Claire Holmes was a beautiful woman, no matter what she wore.

But she's a witness, my internal voice reminded me.

I rolled my eyes at myself.

Like I was really looking for a relationship.

I'd been in town a month. And I hadn't moved here to find a woman. There had been plenty of those in North Carolina. I was here to build a deeper adult relationship with my brother. We were the only family each other had left after our Mom died last year. Ellis had another couple of months until his stint in the U.S. Coast Guard was over, then he planned to take over a commercial fishing vessel from a friend.

I couldn't imagine him as a full-time fisherman. Right now, he was a machinery technician and spent his days repairing ship engines and hydraulics. It would be interesting to see him go from that to catching fish.

Jogging past Ms. Holmes's house, I continued around the block to the path that took me along the water through a local park.

It sure was beautiful here.

At this hour, there wasn't much to see. Some lights glistening off the rippled water of the bay. But once the sun came up, I knew the sea would be alive with fishing vessels of all colors and sizes. That eagles and gulls would swoop overhead, looking for an easy meal. I loved the salty smell that permeated the air and the sound of the birds squawking. I'd been a mountain boy all my life, but living on the ocean felt right.

It helped that I hadn't sacrificed the mountains for my new home. They ringed the entire region, so close I felt like I could step out my door and hike up one.

Maybe in the summer I would.

Meandering through the park, I turned toward home, ready to get back where it was warm. My nose felt like a popsicle. The rest of me was fine. It was just my nose. I needed to invest in a treadmill before next winter. When I first arrived, I'd been too busy to do more than lift weights and maybe take a quick sprint on the treadmill at the police gym. Once the weather warmed some, I started running outside.

The first week or so, I kept the runs short. It was just too chilly for my southeastern U.S. blood. But I gradually acclimated and the weather had warmed enough I could go more than a mile or two. I was up to five, which is what I typically ran back home.

My nose still froze, though.

Reaching my house, I let myself inside, savoring the heat that enveloped me. In my living room, I did some stretches, then went to the kitchen, guzzling a bottle of water before heading upstairs to shower.

Clean and dressed in the department's standard uniform, I made breakfast, then headed out to my car for the short trip to our small police station.

The engine of my gray four-by-four, heavy-duty truck roared to life. Cold air blasted from the vents, but I knew it would soon warm up. This car had been a great purchase. Before I left North Carolina, I sold the small SUV I had, knowing that one, the cost to ship a vehicle was ridiculous, and two, I would need something more robust up here. Something I could put a kayak in or a load of wood. This truck was a few years old, but the mileage was low, and it ran like a dream.

Making my way along Glacier Highway, I drove the two miles to work. I could have run, making it part of my morning exercise routine, but there was one shower at the station, and the water never got past lukewarm. Plus, the weather here could be unpredictable. Not to mention the risk of stumbling over wildlife. Animal encounters weren't unusual even near people's homes, but I had to pass through about a mile of vacant land to get to the station. I preferred to stick to the neighborhoods near my house, where I was less likely to encounter a moose.

Water splashed under my tires as I drove through a puddle turning into the station's parking lot. I found a space near the backdoor, then headed inside.

The scent of cinnamon and coffee hit me the moment I walked in. Even though I'd eaten, my stomach rumbled. Riggs's wife liked to bake. At least once a week—usually more—she sent him in with a pan of something.

I followed my nose to the small break room. Gabe Turner stood near the coffeemaker, a paper bowl in one hand and a plastic spoon in the other.

"What is that?" I moved closer, eyes locked on the crock pot on the counter. "It smells divine."

"Apple cobbler."

"Yum." Knowing I wouldn't get any later if I didn't take some now, I reached for the stack of bowls beside the slow cooker.

"Not yum. Yummy. Divine. Earth-shakingly good." Gabe shoveled another bite into his mouth.

A smile tilted one side of my mouth as I picked up the spoon and lifted the lid off the pot. A wave of cinnamon-appley goodness smacked me in the face.

I scooped up a healthy spoonful and plopped it into my bowl. Picking up a plastic utensil, I took a bite.

Flavors burst over my tongue. "Holy cow."

"Right? Divine." Gabe scraped the bottom of his bowl, getting every last morsel.

I didn't blame him. I planned to do the same.

"You need any help on the Hammond case?" Stepping over to the trash can, Gabe dropped his bowl in.

"Not yet. But I probably will once I get their financial and phone records." I scooped up as many apples as the plastic spoon would hold. It was a good thing I ate a hearty breakfast before I came in. Otherwise, I'd be eating a second helping of this.

"When you get to that point, give me a call. I'm happy to help."

My head bobbed as I finished the last of my treat. Turner was a good cop with a level head and an eye for detail. I would be glad to have his assistance. "Sounds good. Hey, do you know who I contact to arrange travel?"

"Riggs is the one who approves it, but his admin, Nina, will help you book it." He grinned backing toward the door. "I hope you like small planes."

I didn't, but I would survive.

Turner left, and I finished my cobbler, then headed for my desk. After checking with the morgue that Marie Hammond's body was scheduled to fly out to Anchorage for autopsy, and the state medical examiner's office to find out when she would be on their schedule, I made my way to Riggs's office to see Nina.

She looked up from her computer and gave me a sunny smile when I walked in. "Well, good morning. Do you need to talk with Danny?"

"Actually, I came to see you." I returned her smile.

"Oh?" Her smile turned sassy. "Go on."

Chuckling, I motioned to the chair in front of her desk, silently asking if I could sit.

She nodded.

I perched on the gray cushion. "I need to go to Anchorage for Marie Hammond's autopsy. I'm told you're the person to help me with that."

"I am. Did you clear it with the chief?"

"Yes. Last night." I hadn't even asked. He told me to make sure I booked the flight and overnight accommodations.

"Alrighty, then." She turned back to her computer. "When do you need to be there?"

"Thursday. She's on the schedule for that afternoon."

"Perfect. I can get you on an early flight that morning and then an early one home the next day. Does that work?" She glanced up from the screen.

"Yes."

"Okay. I'll get it taken care of and send you the itinerary."

"Thanks, Nina. I appreciate it."

She gave me another sunny smile. "You're welcome. Now, shoo." Making a quick flicking motion with her hand, she glanced at the door. "We both have work to do."

Chuckling, I got up. "Yes, ma'am."

Leaving her to it, I went back to my desk just off the main squad room. With a few strokes on the keyboard, I logged in and went straight to the warrant database. Fingers crossed, I searched for the ones I filed.

In seconds, they popped up, both showing an active status.

"Awesome," I muttered. Saving the files to my computer, I went about requesting the Hammonds' financial and phone records. It would be a day or so before those came back. But that was fine. I planned to interview her co-workers today. I needed to talk to Warren Hammond's work colleagues as well. He was still missing.

Their house had yielded scant clues. Many of their belongings were already packed away and with a moving company, ready to be shipped to Boston. What was left in the house were everyday items, like clothing and just enough dishes to get them through. All the art on the walls was gone, and they had nothing stored in the house. It was like walking into the most basic model home you could find. If there were clues to her murder, it wouldn't come from their house.

Picking up a legal pad, I clipped a pen to my collar and headed out.

The drive to the school wasn't long. Within twenty minutes, I pulled off the main road and into the parking lot.

Parking near the main entrance, I got out and went into the vestibule. A camera and intercom system on the wall near the inner doors had a label underneath that read, "Press button for front desk."

I pushed the button.

It rang, then a woman's voice came over the speaker.

"Yes?"

I held up my badge to the camera lens. "I'm Detective Quartermaine from the state police. I need to speak to your principal."

"Oh. Is this about Marie?"

"It is." I wasn't surprised she knew. We hadn't notified the school, but it was a small town. The news was probably all over by lunch yesterday.

The door buzzed. "Come in."

I pulled it open. Looking left, then right in the hallway, I spotted the office to the right. Through the glass-walled entrance, I saw a woman peering at me from behind a desk.

Letting myself in, I gave her my most charming smile, hoping to put her at ease. "Good morning."

Her cheeks flushed. "Good morning. If you want to have a seat, I'll let Pat know you're here." She picked up the phone on her desk.

I eyed the black, hard plastic chairs pushed against the far wall. "I'll stand, but thank you." I crossed my arms, notepad in hand, while she made the call.

A trill came from behind a closed door down the short hallway behind her. It stopped a moment before the secretary spoke.

"There's a detective here to talk to you about Marie." The woman kept her voice soft, but in the small space, there was no privacy.

"Okay." She hung up and looked at me. "She'll be out in a moment."

"Thank you."

True to her word, a blonde woman in her fifties emerged about twenty seconds later. Rounding the desk, she held out a hand with a polite smile. "I'm Pat Byron."

"Oscar Quartermaine." I shook her hand. "It's nice to meet you, though I wish it were under more pleasant circumstances."

Her expression turned pinched. "Me too. Let's go in my office, shall we?" She motioned down the hall.

Following her down the short corridor, she led me into a well-appointed, though tight, space. I sat on the comfortable, upholstered brown chair in front of her desk and laid my notepad down.

She sat down in her black leather desk chair. "How can I help you, Detective? What happened to Marie is just dreadful. We're all in shock."

"Tell me about her." I sat back, assuming a relaxed posture. Over the years, I'd learned that asking a broad, open-ended question often led to more information.

"Well, she was nice. Always willing to help out with things around the school. She liked to joke, but wasn't mean about it, you know?"

I nodded but stayed silent.

"The kids liked her. So did the parents. She kept her class engaged and did well with problem students." Her composed expression crumpled slightly. "I just don't know why someone would do this." She turned a frown on me. "I heard Warren's *missing*." She rolled her eyes.

That was interesting. She liked Marie but not the husband.

I stayed silent several beats, hoping she'd continue, and was quickly rewarded for my patience.

"I don't know what she saw in that man. His money, probably. He didn't treat her well."

"Oh?" The single word prompted her to continue that line of thought.

She nodded, grimacing. "I don't know as if he hit her. But I guess if he stabbed her, he probably worked his way up from beatings. I know he belittled her, though. I've heard him do it. And he drinks a lot."

I raised an eyebrow.

"We do the standard holiday get-togethers, you know? At this year's Christmas party, we played some party games, like the candy cane run and pin the star on the tree. Silly stuff. She kept dropping candy canes, and he told her she was worthless and said how he couldn't believe she wasn't doing it on purpose. That no one was that bad at the game." She shook her head, clearly disgusted.

"You said he drinks a lot. Was he drunk then?"

"Yes. We held the party at a restaurant with a banquet room. He was several drinks in by that point, and was slurring his words some."

"What did Mrs. Hammond do?"

"She finished the game, then left the room."

"But not the party?"

Mrs. Byron shook her head. "No. She was gone about fifteen minutes. When she came back, she sat at a table with another teacher from the high school and ignored her husband until they left."

I pulled the pen off my collar. "What's the teacher's name?"

"Grace Alonso."

Sliding my notepad forward, I wrote her name down. "Is she here today?"

"Yes."

"I'd like to speak with her before I leave. Tell me about Mrs. Hammond's relationship with the rest of the staff."

"It was good. She never created waves. Everyone liked her."

"Was she particularly close to anyone? Other than Ms. Alonso."

"Kaya Strand. She's another high school teacher."

I wrote her name down as well. "Tell me about Mrs. Hammond's attitude lately."

Mrs. Byron frowned. "What do you mean?"

"Has she seemed… off?"

She glanced away, thinking. "Not really. I mean, she might have been a little quieter than usual, but nothing drastic."

"And no problems with any students or their parents?"

"No—" She stopped, frowning. "Well, there's been one." Sitting forward and folding her hands on the desktop, she rolled her bottom lip in, running her tongue over it as she stared at a point over my shoulder. "She's had a student skipping class. Just hers."

"What does she teach?"

"History."

"Okay. Go on."

"It's strange. It's just been her class. The student goes to every other class without incident. We contacted the parents, and they've refused to do anything about it, going so far as to tell us they'll be ignoring all messages on the subject. That their child has a reason and it's none of our business." Her mouth pursed. "We've taken action and issued the student detention more than once. They're verging on suspension if the behavior continues."

My eye twitched. Obviously, there was a reason this student felt the need to skip class. But no one wanted to truly dig to get the answer, preferring to punish first and ask questions later. "Has anyone tried following the student?"

"We don't have the resources for that."

"Really? This kid is gone for what? Forty-five minutes to an hour?"

She nodded.

"I'm sure *you* could take that much time out of your day to tail the kid and find out what's going on."

She bristled. "I have quite the busy schedule, I assure you."

I hummed and decided to drop it for now. I wasn't here to get involved in school problems. "I need to talk to this student and their parents."

"If the parents agree, sure."

I motioned to her phone.

She frowned. "You want me to call them? Now?"

"I'd prefer it, yes. And put the call on speaker."

Her gaze hardened. "I would prefer to call and ask first."

"Ma'am, this is a murder investigation. And I am not interested in why the child is cutting class. I want to know if they had anything to do with Marie Hammond's death."

She huffed, some of the obstinance leaving her features. "All right." Reaching for her computer mouse, she clicked through a couple of screens, then picked up the phone. "I'm not sure they'll answer. They've been letting school calls go to voicemail."

"Do they know your number?"

"I've called a couple of times, yes. But most of the calls have been from Mrs. Hammond." She dialed, then pushed the speaker button and set the phone in the cradle. A soft, electronic whir filled the room as it rang.

"Hello?" A woman answered.

"Hello," Mrs. Byron said. "This is Pat Byron at PLA."

The woman sighed and didn't let her say more. "I'm sorry. I don't have anything—"

"This is Detective Quartermaine with the state police," I interrupted.

The woman went silent.

"Mrs. Byron made me aware you and your student have had some issues with Marie Hammond."

"You called the *cops* on us?" The woman's incredulity came through the line loud and clear as her voice rose.

"She didn't, ma'am. Mrs. Hammond was murdered yesterday. I'm investigating her death."

More silence came over the line, then, "Why are you calling me? I didn't have anything to do with it."

"Ma'am, may I have your name, please? And before you say no, it would be in your best interest to cooperate."

There was a short huff. "Bethany Cable."

"Thank you." I added her name to my notepad. "Why has your child been skipping Mrs. Hammond's class?"

She stayed silent.

I held back a sigh. Some people needed some extra encouragement. "Ms. Cable, I am not here to get you or your child in trouble. I just want to rule your family out as suspects in her death."

"Suspects? Because Misha skipped class a few times? He was just helping his nana." The woman let out a soft groan of frustration. "My husband and I have had to pick up some extra work shifts lately. Grocery prices…" She trailed off, blowing out a breath before continuing. "Anyway, my mother isn't in the best of health, and she can't drive. Misha's been leaving school to take her to her dialysis appointments."

Mrs. Byron gasped. "Oh my. Why didn't you say something? We have resources—"

"Because it's no one's problem but ours. We don't need or want your help."

"It is our business, because Misha's missing school," Mrs. Byron said.

"He's fine. It's his senior year. And what's he going to use history for? He'll be a mechanic when he graduates. He only took the class because he needed an elective credit."

Mrs. Byron opened her mouth to respond, but I cut her off. "Ms. Cable, Mrs. Byron tells me you've been refusing to respond to calls and messages about your son missing school. Has anything beyond that occurred?"

"Like what?"

"Contact with Mrs. Hammond in other ways."

"Oh. No. I just delete all her emails as soon as I read them. And send her voicemails to the trash. We tried to tell her he had a good reason. She wouldn't listen. So we stopped listening to her."

I met Mrs. Byron's gaze and shook my head. While I understood the family's need to keep sensitive medical information private, a little explanation could have gone a long way.

But that was Mrs. Byron's problem to deal with, not mine. "You haven't talked to Mrs. Hammond beyond that?"

"No."

"What about your son?"

"I doubt it."

"Do I have your permission to speak to him?"

"No. He's still a minor, so you need me or my husband there to interview him. Even if I wanted to do that, I'm not leaving work. Now, if you'll excuse me, I need to get back to that." She hung up without waiting for a response.

I pressed my lips in a flat line. "Well, at least you got an answer to your problem."

Features tight, she nodded.

"Could you call Ms. Alonso and Ms. Strand to the office so I can talk to them, please?"

"It'll have to be one at a time. I'm the only one available to cover their classes." She pushed away from the desk. "You can stay here. I'll send Grace in momentarily."

"Thank you."

With a nod, she left.

While I waited, I sent a message to one of the county social workers, asking about transportation for elderly patients. The Cables might not accept help from the school, but maybe they'd take it from a different source.

A quiet knock on the open door had me looking over my shoulder. A dark-haired woman in her mid- to late thirties entered, offering me a soft smile.

I stood, greeting her. "Hello. I'm Detective Quartermaine. You must be Grace."

She took the hand I offered. "Yes. What can I do for you? Pat said you wanted to speak to me about Marie." The smile faded from her face as a sadness stole over her expression.

"I do. Have a seat." Getting up, I pulled the principal's now vacant chair around the desk, hoping to set a more informal tone than having us on opposite sides of it.

Grace sat, folding her hands in her lap.

I settled next to her. "Mrs. Byron said you and Marie were friends."

"Yes. I wouldn't call us besties or anything—well, I guess maybe we were work besties—but we did things together outside of school."

"Such as?"

"Lunch on Saturdays sometimes, or maybe coffee. And we'd go shopping."

"Tell me about her."

"What she was like, you mean?"

I nodded.

"She was fun. Always joking and smiling. And smart. Man, was she smart. It made her a tough teacher, but the kids didn't seem to mind. They liked her and her classes. She made learning interesting and fun, you know?"

I did. Several of my teachers through the years were like that. They'd been my favorite classes too. "Have you noticed any changes in her personality in the last few months? Or changes to her routine?"

Grace pursed her lips. Glancing down at her folded hands, she picked at the cuticle on one thumb with the nail from the other. "I wouldn't call it a change, really." She looked up. "She just seemed... down? I mean, she still joked around, still had the same enthusiasm in class with her students, but—" She stopped, looking away in thought. "I don't know. Some of the sparkle was gone from her eyes."

"Did that have something to do with her husband?"

She looked at me. "Pat told you about the Christmas party, didn't she?"

Again, I nodded.

"He's a jerk. I would not be surprised if he's the one who murdered her. She planned to leave him, you know."

I tipped my head. "Really?" That was news to me. There

was nothing at the Hammond's home to indicate they were on the outs.

"Yep. After they moved to Boston."

"Why wait?"

"Because it's expensive to move from here. Everything has to be shipped. Her family lives in Virginia. She wanted Warren to foot the bill to get back to the East Coast."

I was well-acquainted with how pricey it was. The department had offered partial relocation assistance, but I'd still forked out over a thousand dollars to move up here. And that didn't count my travel expenses.

"Do you know why they were moving?"

"Warren got promoted. That's how they came here too. She said he called the move up here a stepping stone. I guess it was, because he's supposed to be the new vice president of acquisitions at the firm's office in Boston."

I jotted that down, then returned to what really interested me about what she said. "Tell me more about the problems they were having."

"Like I said, Warren is a jerk. He drank too much, but even when he wasn't a drunk asshole, he wasn't very nice to her. He liked to point out how she wouldn't have such a comfortable life without him." Grace snorted. "They lived on her salary. His all went into *investments*." She rolled her eyes.

"You don't think they were investing his salary?"

"I'm sure they did some of it, but not all of it. He spent money on himself. But not on Marie." She shook a finger. "Every time I saw him, he had on a fancy suit, a watch that cost more than my house payment, and his car was never more than a year or two old. And it was a BMW. Marie drove a ten-year-old Honda Pilot, and all her clothes came from the local department store."

"Did you ever ask her about it?"

"No. It wasn't my business. She seemed content. When she was away from him, anyway. He didn't come to many school functions. I don't know how or why she got him to come to the Christmas party."

Nodding slightly, I shifted in my seat. "Tell me about that night."

Grace blew out a breath, ruffling her bangs. "Warren, as per usual, had too much to drink. He said some rather rude things to Marie, so I hustled her into the corner and made sure her back was to him the rest of the night. Then I glared at him every time he thought about coming over. He stayed away until they left."

"What did the two of you talk about while you sat together?"

"That's when she told me she planned to leave him. She said she was done being treated like dirt. I asked her why she married him if he acted that way."

"Let me guess, he didn't use to?"

Grace nodded. "She said the money from his job changed him. And he resented her for not wanting to go back to school so she could be an administrator and make more money."

I tipped my head as a thought occurred. "Was she the reason they lived on her salary alone? Did she not want to splurge?"

"That was part of it. I think she knew if they lived on both their incomes, or on his, they'd never save any money. Like I said, Warren liked to buy things."

That reshaped the way I viewed the man's spending habits. It could be Grace's perception of the couple's money issues were wrong, and it wasn't that Warren didn't want to spend money on his wife, but that Marie didn't want him spending money on lavish things for her, so he didn't. "Were there other reasons she planned to leave him? A mistress, perhaps?"

Grace lifted a shoulder, her gaze turning away for a moment as she glanced toward the hallway. "Maybe. I'm not sure. She never mentioned one, but knowing him, it's possible."

I made a note to look closely at his credit card and bank statements for signs of a mistress. "Was Warren aware of her feelings?"

"I don't know. But I would say probably not. I can't see him paying to move her back to the mainland. He'd insist she do it herself."

"Okay. Is there anything else you wish to tell me about either of them? Have there been any other strange occurrences in the last several months?"

She chewed on one corner of her mouth, looking away for several moments. "No." She met my gaze again. "Not that I can think of."

"One more question. Are there any places Warren would go to hide out or people he might feel comfortable contacting for help?"

"I can't say. I didn't know him well, and Marie never talked about his friends."

I clicked my pen closed and set it and my notepad on the desk. "Okay." Having gotten as much from her as I believed I could for now, I stood and reached into my pocket for a business card.

Grace rose from her seat.

"If you think of anything that might be pertinent, please call me. My email is on there, too, if you'd rather contact me that way."

She took the white rectangle I held out. "I will, thank you."

I nodded once. "Thank you, Ms. Alonso."

With a tight smile, she turned toward the door. At the threshold, she glanced back. "Find who did this, Detective. My friend didn't deserve to die."

No one ever did. "I will do my best."

Holding my gaze for another second, she left.

I returned to my chair, picking up my notepad and pen to summarize our conversation while I waited for Ms. Strand. Grace Alonso had given me some things to think about.

Several minutes later, movement in the hall drew my attention. I glanced up to see a woman close to my age appear in the doorway.

I stood, offering her a smile and my hand. "Ms. Strand?"

She shook my hand. "Yes. Mrs. Byron said you wanted to talk to me about Marie."

"Yes. Please, have a seat." I motioned to the chair Ms. Alonso had vacated.

The woman perched on the edge, clutching her skirt in her fingers. Her eyes were red-rimmed.

Knowing the conversation could be tough—and not wanting to make her cry—I relaxed in my chair, hoping to create a calm atmosphere. "Mrs. Byron said you and Mrs. Hammond were friends."

Kaya pressed her lips together and nodded. "Yes."

"Close friends?"

The woman lifted a shoulder. "Not terribly. We didn't really do anything together outside of work."

"But here you spent time together?"

Again, she nodded.

"Did Mrs. Hammond mention to you any of the problems she was having in her personal life?"

A frown formed between Kaya's brows and a bit of the sadness faded from her face. "Problems? No. What sort of problems?"

"With her husband."

"Oh." The woman's gaze turned hard. "You mean, *the jerk*?"

I quirked an eyebrow up. This was becoming the theme of the day. "What makes you call him that?"

"Because he was." She clutched her skirt again, then forced her hands open and smoothed the wrinkles she'd created. "All I know is what I saw at the functions he attended."

"Like the Christmas party?"

"Yes. He was rude. Not just to her, but to everyone. He just seemed to think he was better than all of us."

"Did she ever talk about his work or his friends?"

"No. She never talked about him, period."

My other eyebrow rose. "Never?"

"Nope. Which is why it always surprised us when he showed up with her to work functions. It's like they were trying to put on a normal front." She scoffed. "They failed. Every time. He was condescending and drank too much, which turned him into an even bigger prick. She ignored him the entire time. Then they'd leave in silence."

I wasn't surprised Marie wanted a divorce after hearing Grace and Kaya's takes on Warren, but I couldn't help wondering why they were married in the first place. Was this attitude toward each other something that had grown over time? Or did they simply have a marriage of convenience? If the latter were true, why? Especially if they hated each other. Why would they marry if they couldn't stand each other?

I asked Kaya several more questions about what Marie was like at school and if she'd noticed anything out of the ordinary, but much like Grace, she said everything appeared normal except Marie had seemed slightly depressed lately.

As I walked the woman to the door, my mind spun with the new information about the Hammonds' relationship.

Maybe Warren Hammond wasn't missing.

Maybe he was on the run.

CHAPTER 7

Ozzie

Teeth clenched and my knuckles white as I held onto the armrest, I said a quick prayer the small plane I was on wasn't about to go down.

We bounced again, only the seatbelt keeping me in my seat, as we descended into Anchorage. This had to be some sort of joke. Nina was having a jolly good laugh at my expense. I'd seen the bigger planes heading to Anchorage. Why did she stick me on this puddle jumper?

The ground rushed up to meet us as the pilot brought the plane in to land. With a soft bump and a shudder of the airframe, we touched down.

Closing my eyes, I let out a long breath, thankful to be safely on the ground. Tomorrow's flight wasn't far enough away.

Taxiing to the terminal, I watched through the small window as an airport employee drove over with a luggage cart. As soon as the pilot cut the engine, the young man wasted no time opening the cargo hold.

"Welcome to Anchorage, folks." The pilot unbuckled and got out of his seat. "If you have a connecting flight, please check the board inside for your next gate. And if this is your final stop, and you have bags, your luggage will be right outside." He reached for the door and unhooked the latch. Swinging it open, a blast of cold air hit.

"Watch your step on the way out." The pilot unfolded the stairs and descended.

I unfastened my seatbelt and moved into the aisle, eager to be off the tiny plane.

On the ground, I found my carry-on and headed inside. Nina had arranged a rental for me. If it wasn't a two-day drive home, I'd use it to get back to Parker's Landing.

Fifteen minutes later, I was ensconced inside a white Ford Escape and on my way to the state medical examiner's office. The autopsy wasn't scheduled for another forty-five minutes, but I couldn't check in to my hotel until three, and I wasn't about to eat lunch before watching the M.E. cut into Mrs. Hammond's body. It would be a pointless endeavor, because it would all end up in the trashcan in the corner.

Parking in the lot, I walked up to the building. After giving my name to the front desk, I was shown to a waiting area.

With time to kill, I opened my texting app and fired off a message to Turner to see what, if anything, he'd discovered from the Hammonds' credit card records. Yesterday, I tasked him with cross-referencing charges and tracking down where they were from.

Almost immediately, he responded.

Nothing much. Warren liked to eat out. A few of the charges look like they might be for more than one person. I'm going to check them out later. See if anyone remembers seeing him with someone.

That could be promising. Especially if we could get him on camera with a woman.

Before I could text back, he sent another message.

I checked business and property records this morning and found a plot of land in the middle of nowhere registered to an LLC

Hammond set up a couple of years ago. We might need to charter a bush plane to get out there.

I let out a long sigh. More small planes—and an even tinier one than I'd been on today. Great.

Okay. I texted back. *I'll call you later to go over autopsy results and see what you find out about those meals. Thanks for your help.*

Anytime, Turner responded.

Switching to my email, I cruised through my inbox. The Hammond case wasn't the only one on my plate. I had several theft cases and an assault to worry about.

Nothing significant had popped on any of them, though. One suspect had a bail hearing scheduled for tomorrow, another had been remanded into custody after violating the terms of his bail. I was still waiting on fingerprint and fiber evidence for the assault so I could hopefully make an arrest.

"Detective Quartermaine?"

I looked up.

In the doorway, a woman in blue scrubs, clogs, and her dark hair tucked up under a surgical cap smiled expectantly.

"Yes?" I rose.

She moved into the room, a hand outstretched. "I'm Dr. Rebecca Campos, the M.E. performing the autopsy on Marie Hammond."

I shook her hand, briefly. "It's nice to meet you."

"You too. Come on back." She motioned for me to follow her.

Entering the exam area of the facility, she led me to a prep station, where she gave me a blue gown, shoe covers, and a mask from the metal shelving.

"Put all that on. There's some chest rub on the shelf there if you want to put some under your nose." She nodded toward a shelf on the wall by the sink to my right.

I glanced over and saw the small blue container. "Great, thank you." Tucking the gown and mask under my arm, I put the shoe covers on. With them in place, I donned the gown, then utilized the chest rub before putting on the mask. Marie Hammond's body was fairly fresh, so the smell wouldn't be terrible, but there would still be an unmistakable odor of death about her. It was a sour smell and just… off.

"All set?" Dr. Campos's expectant smile returned. She'd donned similar attire while I got ready.

I nodded. "Let's do this."

She pushed through a swinging door to the lab.

Two tables over, a white sheet hid the outline of a woman's body.

Stopping beside a rolling table, she picked up some protective eyewear and slid the clear glasses onto her face. Next, she put on two sets of purple gloves.

"I completed my external exam before you arrived." She drew back the sheet, exposing Mrs. Hammond's naked corpse. "There are four stab wounds to the chest." She pointed to each one in turn. "This one appears to be closest to the heart." She gestured to one that went through the inside of the left breast. "We'll know more once I open her chest."

She moved to the woman's hands. "She has some minor defensive wounds to the ulnar aspect of the hands." Turning Mrs. Hammond's hand, she indicated some discoloration and scrapes to the side of one hand below the base of the pinkie.

"Did she fight back?" I asked.

"They don't look like marks I would expect to see if she hit someone. I think it was more that she put her hands up to ward off the attack." Setting Mrs. Hammond's arm down, Dr. Campos raised her own, pinkie side out, and guarded her face and upper chest.

I nodded, understanding.

"There's no sign of sexual assault. The rest of her external exam was unremarkable. No bruising except what I noted."

"Not even to her face?" I tipped my head, studying Marie's appearance. I'd always found it hard to tell what discoloration on a body was from lividity and what was from faint bruising. They were too similar for my untrained eye.

"No. Whoever stabbed her didn't hit her first." Dr. Campos reached for a scalpel. "Are you ready?"

I steeled myself for what was to come. "Yep."

She didn't wait. As soon as the word left my mouth, she put knife to skin and cut.

A thin pinkish line appeared on Mrs. Hammond's chest, only the faintest beading of blood welling from the incision as Dr. Campos pressed down and pushed it from the tissues.

Narrating into a recording device as she went, the doctor finished her Y-incision, then picked up a set of bolt cutters.

I closed my eyes and looked away, trying my best to tune out the sound of ribs snapping like tree branches. That sound, and the whirring buzz of the bone saw cutting through the skull were the two worst sounds in an autopsy. Since there wasn't any blunt force trauma to the head, I hoped to escape the latter today, but wouldn't hold my breath.

Glancing back over, I saw Dr. Campos set the cutters down and lift off the section of ribcage and sternum she'd cut out. It went onto a table behind her.

"There is a large amount of coagulated blood in the thoracic cavity." She flipped on a suction device and used it to clear the chest. The clot squeezed through the clear, half-inch tube to collect in an attached reservoir.

"There are coordinating stab wounds to the lungs and heart." She glanced up, piercing me with her dark gaze. "Your victim's death was swift. Her heart stopped likely within moments of the injury, and she exsanguinated within minutes."

I stepped closer to see the internal wounds. "Did the knife penetrate the sternum?" If it did, it could tell me something about the blade. A basic pocketknife likely couldn't pierce the thick bone.

"No. It was intact. Judging by the wound in the heart

muscle, the knife came in at an angle." Using one finger, she mimed the way the knife entered the chest. "Your attacker was right-handed. Or at least held the knife in their right hand."

"Can you tell me approximately how long the knife was?"

Dr. Campos poked at the hole in the heart, then turned, picking up the piece of the chest wall she'd removed and setting it back in place. Easing the skin flap down, she slid a thin metal rod into the wound. Grasping it at the skin level, she pulled it out and held it up. "At least that long." She reached out and picked up a metal ruler, laying it against the rod. "Six and a quarter inches." She lifted her head and met my gaze. Setting the rod down, she measured the width of the stab wound. "The blade was an inch-and-a-half wide."

"Okay." I chewed on the corner of my mouth under the mask. Knives that long weren't uncommon around here. Fishermen and hunters used boning knives that size and larger. The question was, did the Hammonds own a knife that size? And if they didn't and Warren didn't kill his wife, who owned a knife like that and had motive? Who had motive at all besides the husband?

Dr. Campos removed the section of ribcage again. She held it up, inspecting the bone. "No knicks. Whoever it was either knew what they were doing or got lucky and slipped right between the ribs." She set the bone down on the table, then picked up a magnifying glass and leaned closer to the body, inspecting the fatal wound. "It's a clean cut. No jagged edges." Straightening, she set the magnifier down. "You're looking for a smooth blade, no serrations, and sharp on just one side."

I'd bet my badge it was a boning knife. "Noted."

With the chest wide open again, she set to work removing the heart. Once dissected, we were able to see that the knife went through the left ventricle and the septum and just pierced the inner wall of the right atrium. The hole through the septum wasn't as wide as the hole through the skin and outer wall of the heart, lending to my theory it was a boning knife.

The rest of the autopsy was uneventful. I learned Marie had an IUD in place and remnants of a turkey sandwich and grapes in her stomach. Her last meal coupled with lividity and body temperature put the time of death at Friday afternoon. Claire Holmes found the body Monday morning.

Her killer had nearly a week's head start.

CHAPTER 8

Claire

Snow flurries danced in the air as I hustled down the sidewalk toward my favorite pet bakery. Pebbles needed more of her favorite peanut butter and yogurt bones.

My prissy little dog, nestled under my arm, had her nose in the air, sniffing as we walked. I always brought her with me when I visited Wags of Wuv.

But first, coffee.

Turning the corner, I spied the front entrance for The Cozy Cup. As I approached, the rich, warm scent of coffee assailed me. A smile lit my face.

Yes, coffee was exactly what I needed.

This week had been one for the books. It was all over town that I found Marie Hammond's body, so Monday and Tuesday, reporters tied up my phone lines, and one enterprising soul even showed up at my office after I rebuked his request for a comment over the phone. Tamara put on her bulldog cloak and sent that poor sap packing with his proverbial pen shoved where the sun didn't shine.

I treated her to lunch that day.

Tuesday, and part of Wednesday, I spent negotiating the sale of the space next to The Cozy Cup. Miranda tried to slip in some language that could have endangered Mina's pocket-book if the inspection came back with unsatisfactory results. Mina wasn't opposed to paying for repairs, but she wanted the option to ask the seller to fix them or to come down in price to offset some, or all, of the cost.

I really didn't like Miranda Bennett.

This wasn't the first time she'd tried such a thing. And I wasn't the only agent she tried it on. Most of us had wised up to her, though. But she still tried. Every time.

Pushing in the door, I stepped into the coffeeshop. The aroma here was ten times stronger, making my mouth water.

Mina, stationed behind the counter, spotted me and waved.

Smiling, I waved back as I got in line.

Pebbles gave a little bark when we reached the front, vibrating in my arms. Mina had a treat from Wags of Wuv in her hand.

"Who's Auntie Mina's good girl?"

Pebbles barked again.

Chuckling, Mina handed over the treat.

"She's so spoiled." I shook my head, grinning.

"That is not entirely my fault."

"True."

Amusement dancing in her eyes, Mina slipped Pebbles another treat.

"What can I get for you?"

I eyed her latte menu. "Let's go with the toasted marsh-mallow mocha." A little s'mores action sounded good.

Mina lifted a cup off the stack and wrote my name and drink order on it with a black marker. "You want a muffin?"

"No, but I'll take a cookie." The plate-size chocolate chunk cookies were calling my name.

She added that to the order on the screen, then read off my total.

I added a tip on the screen facing me, then slid my debit

card into the reader and entered my PIN. Mina bagged up my cookie and handed it to me, then moved to the espresso machine to start my drink.

I stepped to the side and waited.

With my back to the counter, I perused the small café. In the far corner, two men caught my attention. The one facing me looked familiar, but I couldn't place him.

He looked my way. I quickly averted my gaze, looking at Pebbles and scratching her behind the ears.

I chanced a look at him again.

He was still staring.

Feeling like a creeper, I shifted so my line of sight was out the front windows and not toward that corner. It also had the added bonus of being able to watch Mina make my drink. She was nearly finished.

But it wasn't soon enough.

"Good morning, Ms. Holmes."

I knew that voice. It had played as a soundtrack on several dreams this week.

I turned and looked up into a pair of rich brown eyes. Behind him, stood the man I saw at the corner table, a curious smirk on his handsome face.

A face that looked remarkably like Detective Quartermaine's, just slightly older.

"Detective." I offered him a nod. My gaze traveled past him to his companion.

He got the hint, turning to look at the man. "This is my brother, Ellis. Ellis, meet Claire Holmes. And her dog." He turned back to me with a quizzical frown. "I'm sorry, what was her name again?"

"Pebbles."

"That's right."

Behind him, Ellis chuckled.

"Pebbles. The escape artist." Detective Quartermaine lifted a hand, aiming to pet the dog, but she growled.

I rolled my lips in, smothering a smile. Pebbles remembered the man who stopped her morning jaunt through the neighborhood.

Ellis laughed harder. "What's the matter, Oz? Afraid of a five-pound ball of fluff?"

The detective aimed a glare at his brother. "The little ones are the kind you have to watch out for the most. Ankle biters," he muttered.

"Pebbles is sweet." I curled a hand around my dog's head and scratched her ear.

Detective Quartermaine scoffed. "She's a menace."

I covered Pebbles's ears. "Don't listen to him. He's just mad you're cuter than he is."

Ellis's bark of laughter drew out the smile I'd been fighting.

"Oh, I like you. Ozzie, you didn't tell me she had a wicked sense of humor."

He'd talked about me with his brother? I wasn't sure that was a good thing.

Grumbling under his breath, the detective glanced up and gave a slight shake of his head. "I'm going to murder Piper for giving me that damn nickname," he muttered.

A small frown formed between my eyebrows. Who was Piper?

Ellis snorted. "If you were, you'd have done it last year. I've called you Oz since we were young. Ozzie isn't that different."

"Makes me sound like a rocker."

"You don't like rock music?" I asked.

He turned those dark eyes on me. Thick, black lashes framed them, making him appear as though he wore eyeliner. I knew women who'd kill for the look he had naturally.

"I think it's fine," he answered. "But I'm a cop. Not a musician. I can't sing or play an instrument to save my life."

"It's true," Ellis chimed in.

I shrugged a shoulder. "It's still a fine name. Strong. Oscar feels a little formal, especially for someone your age."

"Exactly. I'm a young detective. I need the cred that comes with my name."

"I would say your actions speak louder since you're in the position you are already."

Ellis gave his brother's shoulder a shove. "See? She gets it."

Detective Quartermaine rolled his eyes. "Whatever. Have you been keeping your word, Ms. Holmes, and staying out of trouble?"

"Yes. I've been too busy to get in trouble."

"Though she might make an exception and strangle Miranda Benett if the woman doesn't knock off her shenanigans." Mina leaned over the counter with my coffee.

I turned her way, taking the coffee with a frown. "What did she do now? I thought we had everything squared away?"

"We do. I'm just being proactive. Until it's a done deal, I'm not holding my breath she won't try something else."

My mouth flattened. That was the truth.

"Who's Miranda Bennett?" Ellis asked.

"Another realtor," Mina answered. "She's a real piece of work. Wholly unethical, unlike my best friend." She held out a hand, gesturing to me.

"You're a real estate agent?" Ellis cocked his head, eyeing me with interest. "Ozzie didn't mention that. He just said you were a witness."

"I am. Are you in the market for a house?"

"I am," he parroted, a smile forming.

"You have a house." Detective Quartermaine turned to look at him.

"A rental, yeah. Since I'm staying, I want to buy."

I bent down and set Pebbles on the floor to free up a hand. Hooking her leash over my wrist, I reached into my handbag and took a business card from my wallet, then held it out to Ellis. "Here. Give me a call, and we'll set up a time to meet and discuss what you're looking for."

Ellis took the card. "I'll do that. Thank you." He offered me a disarming smile. I couldn't help but wonder what the same smile would look like on his brother.

But judging from the scowl on Detective Quartermaine's face, I doubted I would find out anytime soon.

"How's the investigation going?" I asked. "Have you found Mr. Hammond?"

The scowl intensified. "No."

"Did you check all their property? He has a cabin near Hoonah."

He narrowed his eyes. "How do you know that? I thought you were staying out of trouble?"

"He asked me to sell it too."

"Have you?"

"Sold it?"

He nodded.

"No. I haven't even listed it. They wanted to put the house up first and get it sold. Rural property like that is harder to sell in the winter because it's harder to get people out there to see it."

"Makes sense. Do you know what he used the cabin for? From what I've learned about Warren Hammond, he doesn't strike me as the hunting type."

"Me either." I'd been surprised when he disclosed the property to me. Both of the Hammonds were city people, through and through. "But that's what most people do in the bush, so I asked him if the hunting was good there. He said he didn't hunt, and that the cabin was just a place to get away. I looked it up on a map. It's not far from Hoonah. An hour or two by ATV or a short hop with a bush plane."

Detective Quartermaine's eyes narrowed. I could practically see the gears spinning in his mind as he mulled over that information.

"That's good to know. Thank you," he said, almost as an afterthought.

Pebbles barked and propped her tiny feet on my leg. I glanced down, and she wagged her tail. My spoiled dog was tired of being where she couldn't see.

Scooping her up, I aimed a smile at the detective. "You're welcome. If I can be of further assistance, you know where to find me." I glanced past him to Ellis. "Give me a call next week. We'll find you the perfect place."

"I'll do that." He lifted his hand, my business card still in his fingers.

"Great." I offered him a sunny smile. "If you'll excuse me, I have some errands to run." With a quick glance at the man's still brooding brother, I waved at Mina, who was back to filling orders, then hurried out of The Cozy Cup and away from *Ozzie's* intense, expressive gaze.

CHAPTER 9

Ozzie

I really needed to find Warren Hammond.

My thoughts in a blender, I mulled over what Claire said.

Why did a city dweller like Hammond need a mountain getaway? I understood how some people liked to take a wilderness retreat here and there for the solitude, but to buy a cabin in the Alaskan bush seemed a little extreme. Especially when it was someone who dressed like they worked in downtown New York.

Claire exited the coffeeshop and moved past the front windows, turning my thoughts in an entirely different direction. She was another city slicker, but unlike the Hammonds, there was a heartiness to her clothing that said she understood the harsh climate in which she lived. Her stylish sweater and jeans belonged on the pages of a fashion magazine, but the high-quality winter boots on her feet said she could easily add some snow gear to her getup and be right at home in the backcountry.

"Why didn't you tell me your witness was hot?"

I turned a glare on Ellis. "What bearing does that have on my case?"

"None. But you know I'm always on the lookout for the next ex-Mrs. Quartermaine."

Rolling my eyes, I walked toward the door, leaving him to trail after me. Ellis had been married a grand total of once, and after a bitter divorce, vowed to never do it again.

That didn't mean he didn't still love women, though. "Leave Claire alone," I growled. "She's not your type."

"A hot blonde isn't my type?"

I let go of the door, and it swung back, nearly hitting him in the face. Smothering a smirk, I kept walking. "Nice. She's nice." She and I hadn't spoken for more than a few minutes, but the way she carried herself and the way she treated the few others I'd watched her interact with told me a lot about her character. Claire Holmes was kind. And classy. Even if she was nosy.

"The women I date are nice."

"They're nice to get what they want. Claire is nice just because she's nice. And she's not the type of woman you can use and throw away."

"I don't 'use and throw away' women. We mutually agree to a short-term, pleasurable relationship. Maybe she likes to keep things casual. You don't know."

I let out a quiet grunt. He was right there, but my people reading skills rarely let me down, and Claire didn't seem like the type to parade a string of men through her bedroom. "I can guess."

"You're a cop. You're not supposed to guess."

That made me chuckle. "Only on cases, El." I glanced over as he caught up.

"If you want her for yourself, just say so."

I stopped, my jaw working as a slow burn of anger simmered in my belly. "Let's get something clear. Claire Holmes is a witness in my homicide case. She's off-limits, so even if I found her attractive, it wouldn't matter. But I'm also not going to engage in a battle of who saw her first. If you want to ask her out, be my guest. Keep in mind, though, if you break her heart, I might break your nose." And maybe a few fingers. Just the thought of Ellis dating Claire made me sick to my stomach. Not because I thought he'd treat her poorly—my brother was a serial dater, not a jerk—but because, despite my words, something about Claire appealed to me. And I didn't want Ellis to be the one who got to know her better.

The smirk on Ellis's face at the start of my spiel quickly faded. A more serious and contemplative expression took over. "You've changed, Oz."

"Yeah, well, seeing the worst humanity can do to another person will have that effect. I'm not the innocent kid you left when you joined the Coast Guard. I've grown up and learned that casual relationships often have disastrous consequences."

Ellis let out a snort, some of the lightheartedness returning to his expression. "More than ever now I want to find you a woman."

"I'm good."

A set of deep blue eyes flashed through my mind.

Firmly, I pushed thoughts of Claire away. I meant what I said. She was a witness.

Even if she wasn't, I didn't have time to date. Not while I was still trying to prove myself in my new department.

Ellis hummed. "Sure you are."

I aimed a glare at him, silently telling him to drop it.

He held up his hands. "Fine. I'll let you become a miserly old man. Where are we going?"

A grimace crossed my face at the thought of my destination. "To see a man about a plane." Getting to Warren Hammond's cabin had become priority number one. I needed to talk to Chief Riggs.

"You're going to find that cabin, aren't you?"

I nodded.

"Fine, but I'm coming with you."

Once more, I stopped walking to face him. "You can't."

A skeptical look pulled his eyebrows together. "Why the hell not?"

"It's police business."

"It's also Alaska, Oz. Your department isn't going to send anyone with you. They don't have the manpower. Hoonah *might* be able to spare an officer to accompany you, but I doubt it. You can't go walking into the wilderness after a potential killer by yourself. Especially since you don't know the area. That in itself is dangerous. This isn't the Appalachians. The bears here don't run up trees and hide, and moose will trample you just because you had the gall to breathe near them. And let's not forget about the weather. It can turn on a dime. You need someone to watch your back."

I raised an eyebrow. "And you're the one to do that?"

"Of course I am. I'm your brother."

"Which is why I hesitate to bring you. I don't want you to get hurt. Hammond could be armed."

Ellis turned a dark look on me. "That's supposed to make me back down? You're only strengthening my case."

We reached my truck, and I pushed the button to unlock it. "What about work?" I rounded the hood and opened the driver's door, getting in.

He hopped into the passenger seat. "I can take a couple days. It's not like I have much on my plate right now, anyway. All my duties are winding down since I only have a couple of months left."

I blew out a breath as I started the engine. It would be nice to have someone who understood the Alaskan wilderness. "I'll float it past the chief. But I can't promise anything."

Backing out of my parking space and onto the main road, I smirked and glanced at him from the corner of my eye as a thought occurred. "You know, if you go with me, that means you'll have to put off your meeting with Claire."

Ellis barked a laugh. "Absence makes the heart grow fonder, Oz."

With a chuckle, I shook my head. My smile turned teasing. "I don't know about that. I'm kinda wishing we were still thousands of miles apart."

His fist connected with my bicep.

"Ow." I rubbed the spot, exaggerating a pout.

"Asshole." Ellis laughed.

"Me?" My brows winged upward. "You're the one who punched me."

"You deserved it."

Probably. "Be careful, big brother. I'll put you between myself and that moose.

CHAPTER 10

Claire

Cold soaked through the thick wool socks on my feet as I stepped onto the back stoop, peering into the darkness for my dog. "Pebbles!" She'd been outside for several minutes to do her business before we went up to bed. It was time to come in.

Drawing my robe more tightly around my middle, I hid my hands in the thick, velvety fabric. The cold snap the weatherman promised had arrived.

I glanced at the sky. Heavy, leaden clouds, highlighted by the streetlights, hovered, promising to spit snow before morning.

All the more reason to go back inside and snuggle into my nice warm, comfy bed with a book.

"Pebbles!" I moved down a step. The little stinker was going to make me go put on shoes. She was probably back in the bushes again, chasing after the rabbit that liked to taunt her from the other side of the fence.

When she didn't appear after another thirty seconds and me calling her again, I huffed and traipsed back inside, where I shoved my feet into my boots. Snagging a flashlight from the cabinet in the mudroom, I went back outside.

"I swear, dog, you're going on a chain every time you go out from now on. I fenced the yard so you could have some freedom, but you've taken a little too much liberty a little too often." What was left of the snow from the other night crunched under my feet as I stomped across the grass toward the hedges that lined the back of my lot.

I flipped on the light and scanned the bushes. "Pebbles! Where are you?" Bending slightly at the waist, I peered into the branches.

After walking the entire fence line—twice—I straightened with a huff and glanced around the yard, concern replacing my ire. Where the heck did she go?

Not seeing any sign of my dog in the yard, I let myself out through the gate, hoping she was still close by. I regularly checked the fence, because I knew even the smallest opening was enough for my tiny dog to get through. In fact, I'd just checked it last week.

Walking the perimeter, flashlight aimed at the area where the fence met the ground, I looked for any breaks in the chain link. Along the back of the yard, about five feet past the beginning of the hedgerow on the other side, I spotted a hole in the fence.

"Crap." Crouching down, I frowned as I got a better look. With a finger, I touched a broken link. The edge was smooth.

It had been cut.

I turned, surveying the area beyond the fence, the roadway past that, and on down to the beach. There was no sign of anyone lurking in the darkness.

Or of Pebbles.

Did someone cut it so they could take her? Why else would they? The hole was much too small for a person to wriggle through.

I stood, calling for her again, a fearful, frantic note in my voice now.

Watching my footing, I hurried away from the fence, sweeping the ground with my light.

Tiny doggie paw prints in the patchy snow led off to the left.

She'd escaped!

Hope surged, weakening my knees. Forcing my joints to function, I followed them.

"Pebbles!"

Snow crunching, I stumbled a couple of times as I walked along the edge of the road. Occasionally, I flicked the light toward the beach. I could only pray Pebbles hadn't crossed to it. If she made it down to the rocky shoreline, one larger wave could knock her off her feet and sweep her into the sea.

For a solid five minutes, I followed the irregular pattern of prints, sure I'd stumble upon her soon. I mean, how far could a little dog get with only a few minutes' head start? I'd let her out while I loaded the dishwasher.

Tears pressed against the backs of my eyes as I continued to walk. I'd been *right there*. How did she slip away without me noticing?

Glancing back, I realized I'd walked almost two blocks.

I chewed on the corner of my mouth, sweeping my light toward the next patch of tracks. If I didn't find her soon, I probably needed to call for help.

But who?

I could call Mina. Except she was probably asleep. The Cozy Cup opened early, so she was almost always in bed by eight-thirty or nine o'clock. It was nearly eleven.

Times like these were when it would be nice to have family close by. With my mother long gone, and my dad living in California with my stepmom and my teenage half-brothers, I was all by myself up here.

I stumbled into a bare strip of ground and stopped, shining my light over the snow on the other side, trying to pick up Pebbles's trail.

But there were no more tiny paw prints.

I spun around, my light shining over the prints I'd followed.

Where did she go?

I aimed the light between the houses. It was bare all the way to the driveway, where the grass ended. She could have turned left and gone that way and not left any trail at all.

Or she could have gone right and crossed the road to the beach.

Turning, I pointed the light toward the embankment. The ground that way had more snow, but it was patchy.

That thud of fear in my chest returned.

I swept the area on the other side of the bare strip with the light once more, but it was as void of paw prints as it was the first time.

Which meant she turned.

So did I go right and check the beach? Or left and continue along the road out front?

My gut said left. Pebbles didn't spend much time walking along the road behind the house that ran along the shore. We crossed it to get to the beach when we walked there in warmer weather sometimes, and that was it. She was much more accustomed to the sidewalk out front of our house and on our road.

Decision made, I jogged between the houses, checking every patch of snow for Yorkie-size prints.

But there were none.

Cursing under my breath about ornery little dogs, I checked up and down the street, calling her name. Out here by the curb, there was even less snow to leave a trail in. It had melted off the road and most of the sidewalks.

Teeth clenched, I tried to put myself in Pebbles's head. If she turned, did that mean she wanted to go home? Or did she just not like running in the yards?

I took a leap of faith and turned right, toward home. My best guess was she'd been chasing something and lost it. Or she decided to explore, then figured out she was far from home and wanted to go back inside where it was warm.

While I walked, I continued calling her name. I'm sure the neighbors were peeking out their windows, wondering who I was and what I was doing walking down the sidewalk in my robe and boots. But hey, at least I didn't have my pink slippers on this time.

I was so engrossed in my search I didn't hear the car approaching until it tooted its horn. I glanced over and saw a gray pickup pull up to the curb beside me facing the wrong direction.

Trepidation skated down my spine with icy fingers. Parker's Landing wasn't known for its major crime, but I was still a woman walking alone late at night.

I put my hand in my pocket, ready to activate the emergency call feature on my iPhone.

The truck window rolled down.

Pebbles's head popped into view, and she barked.

My mouth dropped open, and I hurried forward before I even saw who was in the driver's seat. I didn't care. They'd found my dog.

"Lose something?"

Detective Quartermaine leaned closer, emerging from the shadowed interior with an amused smirk on his face.

"Where did you find her?" I reached out and scooped her from the vehicle. She squirmed in my arms and licked at my face.

"The security light came on in my yard. When I looked out the window, I saw her sniffing at the ground. I knew right away whose dog it was. That little bow on her head is unmistakable."

I smiled. "Where do you think she gets her name?"

A small frown puckered the area between his brows for a second before it smoothed out and he chuckled. "The Flintstones. Makes sense. Is there a Bam Bam running around too?"

A chuckle slid past my lips. "No. One dog is plenty for me. Thank you again for catching her."

"You're welcome. Just be careful opening your door. I think she's figured out she can slip past you."

"She didn't. Not this time. I let her into the backyard. It's fenced. Someone cut a hole in the chain link behind my hedgerow."

The levity on his face disappeared and a dark frown took its place. "You're sure?"

I nodded. "The first thing I did when I realized she wasn't in the yard was to check the fence perimeter. I found her trail and the hole. It's not bent like an animal forced its way through and the links haven't untwisted. It's been cut."

He tipped his head toward the passenger side of his truck. "Hop in. I'll take you home and you can show me."

Really? He wanted to look now? I just wanted to go to sleep. "That's not necessary, Detective. It's late, and—"

He held up a hand, cutting me off. "First, I think since rescuing your dog is becoming a bit of a habit, and we're neighbors; you can call me Oscar. Second, you're right—it is late. So please just get in the truck." Exasperation colored his rich tone.

I scowled at him, keeping my feet rooted to the sidewalk.

He sighed. "Look, it's cold and you're not wearing the best clothing to be out here." He gave my attire a once-over. "If I drive you back, you get out of the cold faster, and I can make sure your house is safe. We'll both sleep better if I do."

My resolve wavered. I *was* chilly. And it would be nice to know someone wasn't waiting in the wings for me to return.

A shiver that had nothing to do with the icy breeze coming off the ocean went through me. I hadn't given much thought to why someone would cut a dog-sized hole in my fence except to steal her.

But his words made me wonder.

What if it wasn't about Pebbles, but about me?

That thought set my feet in motion. I hurried around the front of the truck and climbed inside.

Warmth enveloped me as I settled into the cloth seat. My nose was frozen. So were my fingers.

"Buckle up."

I blinked. Was he serious? "We're going a hundred yards. Maybe."

"Most accidents happen within a mile of home." But he put the truck in gear and pulled away from the curb.

Thirty seconds later, he turned into my driveway and cut the engine.

I opened the door and slid out of the seat to the ground. It wasn't quite as tall as some I'd ridden in, but it was up there, even for someone my height.

His over six-foot frame had no trouble getting out, though.

I frowned as I watched him. The few inches really shouldn't make that much difference. Maybe it was just his legs; they were probably longer than mine.

Shaking off the silly thought, I rounded the hood, then waited while he took a flashlight from his back seat. With it illuminating our path, we headed for the backyard.

Traipsing along the exterior of the fence, I stopped a few feet past the start of the hedgerow and pointed to a spot near the ground. "There."

He aimed the light at the ground near the fence and walked forward a couple steps before crouching in front of the hole. "It was definitely cut." He touched an edge, then stood. "She didn't get cut, did she?" He nodded to the dog. "That hole isn't very big."

"I don't think so." Concern pinched my features as I ran a hand through Pebbles's fur. "I don't feel anything." I'd take a closer look later, just to be sure, but for now I was satisfied she was fine.

"Good. If you want, you can head inside. I'll take a look around out here and make sure nothing else has been tampered with." Oscar nodded toward the house.

"You're sure?"

"Yes. I'm guessing you've been out looking for her for a while. Go warm up."

"Okay." My nose and hands thanked him. "Can you come knock when you're done?" I didn't want to sit up, wondering if he was still out here looking for anything amiss.

"Yes."

With a soft smile of thanks, I hurried away, ready to be warm. Next time, I'd grab my coat before wandering through the neighborhood.

"But there better not be a next time," I muttered, dropping a kiss on Pebbles's head.

Inside, I set her on the floor, then immediately went to the coffeemaker. I needed something to warm me up from the inside, and I had a whole bag of decaf in the cupboard.

Adding enough grounds to the carafe side of my dual-brew machine to make two cups, I hit start, then went to the window to watch Oscar search.

It felt weird to think of him by his given name. But he had a point. It seemed we were neighbors, and Pebbles was determined we got to know each other.

And really, was that so bad?

Maybe he was gruff the first time because it was early, and who expects to get accosted on a run at that hour by a Yorkie?

As far as his staying out of trouble comments went, I had a feeling that didn't have much to do with me. He'd been very quick to leap to the conclusion I would stick my nose where it didn't belong. Someone somewhere in his past had done so. I'd bet my real estate license on it.

The coffee machine gurgled, expelling the last of the coffee through the filter. I returned to the kitchen and took a mug from the cabinet to pour myself a cup. Oscar could have the rest if he wanted it.

Wrapping my hands around the mug, I wandered back to the window to wait.

And to wonder more about why someone would cut a hole in my fence. If the goal was to take Pebbles, or even to lure me out and harm me, they'd have to lay in wait. There was no guarantee Pebbles would go through the hole or that it would happen quickly. That hole could have been there for days.

Oscar's flashlight bobbed outside the fence as he walked toward the gate. I watched him come through, then search the yard. There weren't many places to hide back there. I had a shed and some lawn furniture. And the bushes, of course, but those weren't big enough to conceal a person. I deliberately kept them low so they didn't obstruct my view of the bay.

Pebbles, who'd snuggled up on her plush bed by the couch, suddenly raised her head and let out a little bark.

"It's just your rescuer, sweetie." I shushed her, and she settled.

A minute later, he approached the back door. I opened it for him, then stepped back so he could come inside.

Redness from the cold tinged his cheeks, and the wind had mussed the dark waves of his hair.

He looked good enough to eat.

I raised my coffee cup and took a sip, hiding the scowl that formed as I admonished my errant brain. Those kinds of thoughts were not helpful.

Lowering the mug, I cast a quick look at the kitchen. "I made coffee, if you'd like some to warm up. It's decaf."

"Actually, that sounds nice." He rubbed his hands together, then blew on them. "It's chillier than I expected. You get a breeze from the ocean. My house is more sheltered."

"But my view is spectacular." I flashed him a quick smile,

then went into the kitchen and poured the rest of the coffee into a brown, hand-thrown ceramic mug. "Here."

"Thanks." He took it, cradling it in his large hands to warm them. "I didn't see much. Near that hole, it looks like there might have been some food. I found—"

Pebbles let out a series of barks, rising to her feet and spinning in a circle.

"Pebbles..." I let out a sigh.

"What's she barking at?"

"I have no idea. I thought it was you, but you're inside, and she's not paying any attention—"

A thump overhead silenced my words.

What the heck was that? I glanced at the ceiling.

Pebbles let out another flurry of barks and ran for the stairs.

"Pebbles!" I took off after her, depositing my mug on an end table. I made it just past the couch when a strong hand encircled my wrist, bringing me to a halt.

I looked back and right into a pair of intense, fierce, dark-brown eyes.

"Stay here. I'll check it out." He let go and moved swiftly around me to run up the stairs after a still barking Pebbles.

A series of thumps and bangs on the side of the house sent my heart into my throat, where it raced at a frantic beat.

What was going on?

"Hey!" Oscar's deep shout echoed downstairs. "Stop! Police!"

Pebbles's barks accompanied him.

Eyes wide, I moved closer to the staircase. Who was he talking to?

I looked up to see Oscar appear at the top, running at full speed and taking the steps with fast feet.

"Call 9-1-1. Tell them I'm in pursuit of a burglary suspect." He flew past me to the front door.

"Burglary?" My feet grew roots, and I stared at him, eyes round and jaw slack.

"Just call." He threw open the locks and let himself out.

The frozen air that came through was enough to snap me out of my state of shock. In just a few strides, I was standing in the doorway, watching him run down my driveway after a figure cloaked all in black.

CHAPTER 11

Ozzie

Subfreezing air filled my lungs and stung my face as I chased after the figure fleeing Claire's house. It was a man not quite my height, but he had some speed.

I urged my legs to go faster.

Rounding the intersection, I left the sidewalk and cut through the front yards of the corner lots, closing the gap.

The man glanced back, but there were too many shadows for me to see his face.

"State police! Stop!"

My shout only spurred the man to run faster.

Grinding out a quick growl of frustration, I wondered sometimes why I bothered wasting my breath.

We turned another corner onto a dead-end street. Beyond the last house, wilderness stretched. This area of Parker's Landing was little more than a thin strip of houses before it melded into the forest.

I eeked the last bit of speed out of my legs, but it wasn't enough. The man disappeared into the trees fifteen yards ahead of me. I dashed in after him, but the dense foliage stopped me after only twenty feet or so. In the dark and in the heavy bush, I'd never find him. Not without help.

But I'd have to go back to Claire's to get it. My phone was still in my truck.

Staring into the darkness, I listened, hoping to hear him crashing through the brush. But not so much as a twig snapped. Either he was hunkered down, waiting for me to leave, or he knew the woods well and could move with much more ease than me.

It really could be either. Some people who lived around here spent more time outside than in.

Frustration clawing at me, I backed out of the woods and jogged back to Claire's. By the time I reached her house, a cruiser sat out front, it's red and blue lights bouncing off the house and lighting up the street.

A quick peek in the car's windows revealed it to be empty. I headed toward Claire's front door. The officer must be inside with her.

The knob turned easily under my hand as I let myself in. Officer Rich Kreiger and Claire stood in the living room, Pebbles clutched to Claire's chest. She barked when she saw me and squirmed in her owner's arms.

I wasn't sure if that meant she was happy to see me or wanted to bite my fingers off. She hadn't been too pleased when I scooped her out of my yard earlier—or when I halted her escape the other morning—but she'd settled down and been rather friendly in the truck on the way over here.

"You lost him, didn't you?" Claire's shoulders slumped.

I nodded. "He ran into the forest off Crane Road."

"Why didn't you call?" Kreiger spoke up. "I could have headed there and helped establish a perimeter."

"I left my phone in my truck." A grimace stole over my face. You'd think I was a rookie, pulling a move like that. But I hadn't been anticipating a foot chase.

"I'll call it in. See if Juneau can lend us their dog."

I waved him off. "I wouldn't bother. By the time the K-9 unit gets here, the guy will be long gone. He probably already is. Get some other officers here, though. We can retrace his path and make sure he didn't ditch anything."

Kreiger's head bobbed once. "On it." He stepped out of the room to radio dispatch.

"You doing okay?" I quirked an eyebrow at Claire once Kreiger left.

Her mouth flattened, but she nodded. "Yeah. Did you see who it was?"

"No. It was too dark, and he had a hood up. All I could tell was that it was a man a little smaller than me. Do you know why someone would want to break into your house?"

The small frown wrinkling her forehead deepened. "I've been wondering the same thing, but I can't think of a reason. I don't really have any major real estate transactions in the works right now. At least, nothing that someone would risk breaking into my house to get a look at the contracts for."

"What contracts are you working at the moment?"

"A couple of houses, and my friend, Mina, is in the process of buying the space attached to her coffeeshop so she can expand her business. That's it."

"What about a rival? Are any of those contracts lucrative enough someone would want to steal them from you?"

"Maybe just Mina's, but the only real estate agent in town who would do that is Miranda Bennett, and she's representing the seller. She's privy to all the same information I am, so she'd have no need to break in to get the contract." She waved a hand, dismissively. "If this were about real estate, my office would be the far more likely target."

"Possibly. Do you bring work home a lot?"

Claire lifted a shoulder, then scratched at Pebbles's head. "Here and there. I try to get everything done at the office so my evenings are for me." She met my gaze. "There's a reason I sell real estate here and not in some major market. I'm not a workaholic. I like my free time."

"Okay." I chewed on the corner of my mouth and glanced toward the stairs. "Have you been upstairs yet?"

"No. Officer Kreiger said we should wait for you. He didn't want us to disturb any evidence until you had a chance to process the scene."

"Good. I need to run out to my truck and get my crime scene kit. Hang tight."

At her nod, I turned and jogged outside, past Kreiger, who still talked to dispatch, coordinating resources. They probably had to call in backup from Juneau or from another state office. Parker's Landing wasn't big enough to have more than two officers on duty at any given time. Although I didn't count toward that total, since I was a special detachment.

Reaching my truck, I opened the back door and took out the small duffel I kept stored on the floorboard. It contained a digital camera, fingerprint powder and cards, some evidence markers, and evidence bags in assorted sizes. I'd carried something similar in North Carolina but rarely used it. There, most cases I worked for the state bureau of investigation had an actual forensic unit dispatched to process crime scenes. Up here, though, those were reserved for the biggest cases. Parker's Landing didn't have a forensic team. We had to borrow Juneau's or the state's for major cases. Everything else, the police units processed.

I closed the truck door and glanced up as I backed away from the vehicle. A shiver of unease skittered down my spine as I stared into the flickering shadows. I could feel eyes watching.

I didn't want to believe the guy would be brazen enough to come back, but the boldness of his break-in told me it wasn't beyond the realm of possibility for the man to be sitting in the shadows, watching us.

But why?

What did Claire have that he wanted? Was it connected to the Hammond case? Or was it something else entirely?

Giving the neighborhood one last sweeping look, I went back inside Claire's white two-story house. Kreiger was in the living room with Claire again, but they weren't talking now. She had her face pressed against Pebbles's head as she stared at the wall opposite the fireplace, lost in thought. Kreiger alternated watching her and the window. He glanced my way as I approached.

"Backup units are on their way," he said.

"Good. Keep an eye out. I'm going to take Ms. Holmes upstairs." My gaze flicked to her. She blinked at the sound of her name, but didn't move.

"Claire?" I tipped my head toward the staircase.

"Oh. Right." Feet now in motion, she moved away from Kreiger.

"Don't touch anything," I cautioned as we ascended the steps.

"Not a problem." She clutched Pebbles to her chest.

Once on the second floor, I led her to the front bedroom that doubled as an office-slash-library. An oversize, velvety-soft, gray chair dominated the far corner by the window. A gray and cream throw sat haphazardly over the arm, as though she'd tossed it aside to get up after snuggling in with a good book.

Closer to us, an oak desk and gray leather executive's chair took up space in front of a wall of bookcases, all of which were stuffed full. Small potted plants dotted the shelves, some of them cascading gently over the edge. On the floor, a pale pink and yellow, delicate floral rug covered part of the beige carpet. It was a rather cozy space.

Only the sheer cream curtains fluttering in the ice-cold breeze coming through the window ruined the atmosphere.

"He dove through that window when I came up the stairs." I nodded toward it. "Is there anything in here with any value?"

Her midnight blue gaze ran over the room, a small frown

dipping between her brows. "Not really. My laptop is still in my bag downstairs. I keep some records in the desk drawer, but anything truly important is locked in the filing cabinet in the closet." She pointed to the closed door on the far side of the room.

I set my evidence kit on the floor and opened it, taking out a pair of black nitrile gloves. After putting them on, I picked up the fingerprint powder and a fluffy brush, then crossed to the closet and dusted the doorknob.

Leaning in, I squinted at what the powder revealed. "There are a couple of prints here, but they're probably yours." I glanced at her over my shoulder. "We need to fingerprint you before I leave."

Mouth flat, she nodded.

Lifting the prints, I stowed the cards in the kit, then opened the closet. Her filing cabinet sat against the back wall amidst a suitcase and a plastic tote, seemingly untouched.

Once again, I dusted for prints, then tried the drawers. They were all locked.

"I don't think he got into these." I peered at the lock. "They don't look tampered with. Where do you keep the key?"

Her mouth twisted. "In my desk."

It was my turn to frown. That was a terrible place to put a filing cabinet key. It was the first spot anyone would look.

She huffed. "Don't give me that look. I know it's dumb, but this is Parker's Landing. I'm not even sure why I keep the drawers locked."

I tipped my head. She had a point. I hadn't been in town long, but as part of orienting myself to the area, I'd studied crime statistics. There really wasn't much.

Leaving the closet, I asked her to show me where she kept the key. After dusting for prints again, I opened the drawer and found it. Exactly where she said it would be.

"Let's see if you had a considerate burglar." Key in hand, I traipsed back to the closet and unlocked the filing cabinet's top drawer. Claire peered over my shoulder as I leafed through the files.

"It looks like it's all there."

Shutting the drawer, I moved to the next one, and then the next. The intruder hadn't taken any of the contents.

"Let's check your bedroom." Closing the bottom drawer with a thunk, I stood up and led her from the room after collecting my evidence kit.

Outside her door, she put a hand on my arm, gripping my sleeve.

"Oscar."

Frowning, I glanced at her. She stared at the closed door with wide, frightened eyes.

"What?"

"That door should be open."

My frown deepened. "You're sure?"

She nodded. "Contrary to my habits at my listings, I don't close the interior doors at home. Unless I'm sleeping. I know I left that door open after I changed clothes."

Her voice rang with conviction.

Pulling out my trusty fingerprint kit once more, I dusted the doorknob, then the light switch inside before flipping on the light.

Claire's gasp said it all.

The room was in complete disarray.

Clothes hung from the dresser. The bedding had been pulled off, revealing the pale pink fitted sheet covering the mattress—a mattress which was askew, exposing the box spring. All the pillows were on the floor, scattered around like they'd been flung off the bed.

"Why would they ransack this room and not my office?" She wandered a few feet into the space, eyes fixed on the mess.

I had my theories, but I didn't want to mention them to

her. No use making her more scared by telling her some people were just sick perverts. Though I wasn't sure that was the case. It felt too coincidental that the person connected to my homicide case would also be the victim of some perverse stalker.

Unless it wasn't supposed to be Marie Hammond who died.

The thought hit me like a Mack truck.

My jaw worked.

Was Claire the intended target? Did the killer think it was her in the house? Who would have a motive to harm her, though?

"Have you had any dealings with anyone who seemed… off, lately?" I tried to keep the question casual. Again, not wanting to alarm her.

She turned a confused frown on me. "What do you mean?"

I lifted a shoulder, digging into the evidence kit for the digital camera. "Just someone who seemed odd. Did anyone make you think twice about what they said or did? It could be something as simple as a comment they made in line at the store or a phone call."

Her brows twitched as she thought. "No," she finally answered. "Not that I can remember. Do you think I know who did this?" She swept a hand out at the mess.

"Maybe. Do you ever work in your bedroom?"

"All the time. I like to sit in bed with my laptop and the TV playing. It's cozy."

I turned on the camera and aimed it at the bed. "Do people know you do that?"

"Some, yes. I don't broadcast it, but people who know me have heard me talk about working in here."

A bit of the tension eased from my shoulders. I far preferred the theory that someone was looking for information on the Hammond case and not here for Claire specifically.

"Okay." I snapped a few more pictures of the room, then looked at her. "Was there anything in here, work-wise?"

Immediately, she shook her head. "I didn't bring anything home tonight. And I never leave anything in here. It always goes back to the office with me in the morning. Usually, when I work up here, it's loading pictures for a listing. Sometimes it's a contract, but usually, I'm working on a listing."

My gaze sharpened. "Listing photos, you say?"

She nodded.

"Where's your camera?"

"Lynne usually takes the pictures. She brings me an SD card or a thumb drive, and I upload from that."

"Do you have one of those for the Hammond house?"

"N—" she stopped, mid-word. The slight frown on her face opened into a surprised look. "Actually, I don't have listing photos, but I have pre-listing photos. Remember how I told you I closed all the doors when I took pictures for Lynne? So she could stage the place?"

My heartbeat quickened. "Yes. I think I need to see those pictures." There could be something there. Something someone didn't want anyone else to see.

"I don't have it, though." Her expression turned worried. "Lynne does."

CHAPTER 12

Ozzie

The keyboard clicked softly as I paged through the photos on the SD card I got from Lynne Young. Claire's stager had been more than happy to turn over the pictures when Claire asked and I explained my theory. But so far, nothing in the images jumped out at me. If there was something here, it wasn't obvious to anyone except the people involved.

I shut the laptop with a frustrated huff and looked out the window of the small plane I was on. One look at the mountains crossing below us, and I regretted that decision. The flight to Hoonah wasn't a long one, which meant another tiny plane. Maybe one day I'd get used to being on small aircraft, but that day wasn't today.

Turning away from the stomach-churning sights, I spotted Claire's blonde head a few rows in front of me. Much to my surprise, she was also on her way to Hoonah this morning. But not to investigate Marie Hammond's murder or Warren Hammond's disappearance. She said she was going to talk to a client.

I glanced out the window again.

Must be some client if she was willing to fly to another city to meet with them.

We soon descended into the airport and made a smooth touchdown, much to my relief. I hoped the weather held for my return flight.

When that would be, I didn't know. At least tomorrow. It all depended on what I found here and what I could investigate on my own. Riggs had okayed me bringing Ellis, but he'd come down with a stomach virus and was currently chained to the toilet in his bathroom.

A shudder went through me. He better keep that shit—no pun intended—to himself.

The plane taxied toward the terminal. Once we stopped and the seatbelt sign turned off, I donned my coat. Unlike a normal commercial flight, my carry-on wasn't stored overhead. All the luggage on this plane was in the cargo hold. Which meant I had to stand on the tarmac and wait for the pilot to unload it.

At least it wasn't that cold today. Or raining.

Through the window, I saw one of the airport staff behind the wheel of the jet bridge, maneuvering it toward the plane. Moments later, it parked outside the door.

Chilly air filtered into the cabin when the pilot opened the door, ushering us out with a smile.

Once on the ground, I zipped my coat. It wasn't frigid, but the bite to the air was enough to make me ready for the terminal's warmth. Like small planes, the cold was something I needed to acclimate to. It would happen. One day.

Stuffing my hands into my pockets, I gazed around, noting the planes parked near several buildings, thick, red covers covering some of their engines. It was strange standing out here. This side of the terminal was a place I'd never been outside of an airplane.

Apparently, it was routine for everyone else, including

Claire. She had her phone out, checking messages while we waited on bags.

I let my eyes travel over her tall frame, taking her moment of distraction to study her more in-depth. Long legs cloaked in cream linen pants peeked out from beneath the knee-length, camel-colored trench she wore. Black gloves adorned her slender hands. The collar of an icy blue silk shirt peeped from the vee of her coat below the colorful green and blue scarf wrapped around her neck. She looked like the consummate professional. It was quite the contrast to the woman in the bathrobe I found scurrying down the sidewalk near her house. It was still difficult to reconcile the two. Who was the real Claire Holmes? This woman or the one who lived in the frosty-blue bathrobe?

My money was on the woman in the robe.

A gust of wind whipped by, snaking down inside my coat. I tugged up the zipper and hunched my shoulders, turning away from the wind and the woman capturing my thoughts.

Seven minutes later, rolling carry-on in hand, I followed the other passengers inside. As we wove through the people waiting to board the plane we just disembarked, I caught up to Claire.

"Do you need a ride?" I had a rental waiting for me.

She glanced over, the beginnings of a kind smile in her eyes. "Actually, that would be great, if you don't mind. I was going to take a taxi to my hotel." She lowered her voice. "Don't tell anyone I said this, but the taxis here always smell faintly of day-old fish."

My nose wrinkled. "That sounds… yummy."

A low chuckle escaped her.

"Would you like to wait here or walk with me to the rental counter?" I nodded to the row of chairs under the window in the small terminal, then to the car rental counter in the corner.

"I'll come with you. No point in taking up a seat someone else might need." Her gaze traveled toward the door, where a family entered, a man a little older than Ellis helping an elderly woman inside.

My words to my brother the other day echoed through my mind.

Nice. Claire Holmes was *nice*.

The trip to the rental counter and the process to get my car only took a few minutes. Then we were back out in the blustery weather.

I glanced at the sky as we got into the sleek, black SUV I rented. The clouds had thickened since we landed. It looked like snow was on the way.

"So, where are you headed from here?" she asked as we settled into the car. "The local police station? Or the Hammonds' cabin?"

"Police station. I'm hoping by some miracle, they can spare someone to go with me to the Hammonds' place. I've hiked all my life, but the Alaskan wilderness is unfamiliar territory. Ellis was supposed to come with me, but he's sick." I pulled onto the main road and headed into town.

"If you really need a guide, let me know. I can swing an extra day here. I grew up in Alaska and spent a lot of time over this way. Hoonah's wilderness is like home."

I cast a skeptical look at her, taking in her linen pants and silk blouse once more and remembering her dash through the night after her dog in her bathrobe and slippers. "You're comfortable traipsing through the woods?"

An impish look crossed her face, bringing a smile to mine.

"Don't let the fancy clothes fool you. While I might prefer my creature comforts, that doesn't mean I can't survive in the wilderness. My dad made sure of that."

"And you just so happen to have survival gear packed into your carry-on?" I quirked an eyebrow in question.

Her smile turned sheepish. "Well, no. But I have some friends in town. I can borrow some clothing and gear." She raised an eyebrow back at me. "Did you pack survival gear?"

"I'm wearing my boots, and I have some extra layers in my bag, yes."

She snorted. "Those boots on your feet are not meant for long treks through the forest. Not the Alaskan forest, anyway. Where are you from? I'm guessing the South, somewhere, judging by your accent."

"North Carolina."

Her head bobbed. "That explains the shoes. Before you go off to the Hammonds' cabin, please get some proper footwear. Even if you can drive most of the way there, you need the right shoes. Just in case. Roads out here—" She paused, shaking her head. "Let's just say they can turn ugly real quick."

"You sound like Ellis."

"Well, if he cautioned you to respect the land, then he's right. Alaska is not a place you fuck around and find out."

That surprised a short laugh out of me. "You are a walking ball of contradictions, Ms. Holmes."

"Gotta keep you on your toes, somehow, Detective."

She certainly did that. She and her little dog.

I shifted a foot to the brake, feeling my hiking boot flex around my ankle. "So, where would one go to get proper footwear in this town?"

A wide smile slid over her face. "Turn left at that light." She pointed ahead to the traffic signal half a mile away.

"Yes, ma'am."

CHAPTER 13

Claire

I shot a glare at the ringing hotel phone from my position snuggled up on the bed in my bathrobe with my paper cup full of wine and the *I Love Lucy* reruns playing on the TV. For half a second, I debated whether to answer. No one knew my room number, so it had to be the front desk. What they could possibly want, though, I didn't know.

With a huff, I sat up and scooted toward the edge of the mattress so I could pick up the receiver.

"Hello?"

"Hi, Ms. Holmes. This is Kaitlyn at the front desk. I'm sorry to bother you. There's a man here asking for you. Oscar Quartermaine?" Her voice lowered. "He says he's a cop."

Amusement brought a slight smile to my face. I could just picture the young woman I'd met earlier giving the handsome detective the side eye as she spoke.

"You can send him up. He's a friend."

"Okay. So long as there's no trouble. We're a quiet establishment."

"I know. Everything is fine. Thank you."

"Yes, ma'am. He'll be up shortly."

I thanked her again and hung up.

Glancing down at myself, I sighed. It was becoming a bit of a habit to be around the man in my bathrobe.

Too bad it wasn't for fun reasons.

Standing, I shuffled into the bathroom. I could at least make sure none of my snack was stuck in my teeth. The sesame crackers and cheese were yummy, but the seeds liked to hide.

After a quick check—and finding nothing lurking—I stuffed my feet into my hot pink slippers, feeling the chill now that I was out of my cozy cocoon.

At the soft knock on the door, I tucked a flyaway wisp of hair behind my ear, then immediately rolled my eyes at myself. Whatever the reason he was here, it wasn't because he was interested in me. Most likely, he was here to take me up on my offer to be his wilderness guide.

Grasping the lever handle, it turned smoothly in my hand.

My brain short-circuited as I got my first look at him. He'd ditched the puffy coat in favor of the heavy vest and sweater combo he bought at the outfitter's this morning. The heathered charcoal wool sweater and dark khaki vest made him look like a lumberjack. Red tinged his cheeks from the cold, and the wind had attacked that swath of wavy dark hair on his head, leaving it mussed.

One dark eyebrow rose as his nearly black eyes took in my attire.

"I think I'm getting a sense of what your favorite outfit is." He pointed at my feet. "And the slippers have made a comeback."

"Yes, well, I'm not running through yards after Pebbles tonight." I stepped back and motioned him inside.

"Where is she, anyway? I half-expected her to catch a ride on the plane here in your purse."

I'd done that in the past. Pebbles liked exploring new places. But for this business meeting, I'd left her at home.

"She's with my friend, Mina." Who was no doubt spoiling her rotten with bits of bacon and sausage.

Turning, I offered him a polite smile. "What can I do for you, Detective?"

"It's Oscar, please. Or Oz, as Ellis calls me."

"Not Ozzie?" A spate of jealousy speared me as I thought of the faceless Piper who'd given him the nickname.

He sighed. "You caught that, huh?"

I smiled. "I did. Do you not like it?"

He lifted one shoulder. "It's not terrible. It's just not a name I grew up with, so it's strange, you know?"

I tipped my head. "I get that. But you look like an Ozzie, not an Oscar."

Lifting a hand, he ran it through his hair, further mussing the strands. I stuffed my hands into my robe pockets, so I wasn't tempted to fix it.

"You can call me whatever you want. Piper will probably be pleased her nickname has spread beyond our friend group back home."

"Who is this Piper? Your girlfriend?" I was fishing, and he probably knew it, but I didn't care. Curiosity got the best of me.

"No. She's just a friend. It's a long story, but we met a little over a year ago on a case. I was assigned to her protection detail."

My eyes rounded. "Protection detail?"

"Yeah. She was a witness to some drug theft that involved a Colombian cartel. It was a whole"—he circled a hand in the air—"thing."

"Sounds like it."

"Anyway, I'm not here to talk about my past life. Are you still willing to go with me to the Hammonds' cabin? I'll keep you at a safe distance. I just need you to get me close, and to be another set of eyes and ears. I spoke to the Hoonah police chief today. It's only him and one other officer, so he can't spare anyone. My fellow staties will take a week or more to get someone here. I thought about hiring a guide, but I wasn't given the budget for that. The chief here gave me permission to use their equipment, though. ATVs, camping gear, that sort of thing. I know it's a lot to ask, but—"

I waved a hand, cutting him off. "It's fine. I volunteered."

"Are you sure? What about your meeting?"

"I had it earlier, and everything is squared away."

"That was quick."

I lifted a shoulder. "There wasn't much to it. Just a normal closing." Well, sort of. I didn't normally fly to Hoonah for closings. A lot of times, my clients flew to Juneau to the bigger banks, and we signed papers there. But for Mrs. Avondale, I would always make an exception. She'd been a family friend since before I could walk, and traveling was hard on her now that she was in her eighties. I didn't mind coming to her to close on the hunting land she transferred to her grandson.

"So, do you have everything ready so we can leave first thing?" I asked.

"I think so. Chief Bartles helped me gather everything. I'm not clueless when it comes to hiking and camping, so it was just a matter of making sure we have the right cold-weather gear."

"Okay. Sounds good." We might be into the first week of March now, but the nights could be brutal yet, and the weather still liked to shift on a dime. "Are you staying here?" I pointed a finger to the floor, indicating the hotel. "Or is the chief putting you up?"

"I'm staying here. He and his family fed me dinner. They offered me a room, but I'd already booked one here." His mouth twisted and a lopsided smile formed. "I'll know not to do that in the future. His wife berated me and told me not to be so dense the next time."

I laughed. "That sounds like Christina."

"You know her?"

"She's the friend I told you about from whom I could borrow clothing." I would give her a call this evening to make the request. We could pick it up before we set out, then.

He huffed an unsurprised laugh. "Of course it is. Is there anyone you don't know?"

I shrugged. "Probably, but not many." It was true. I'd grown up in this area of the state. It was vast, but it still had a small-town feel. And I was a real estate agent. I spent a lot of time in the local communities.

Smiling, he glanced away, and his gaze lit on the TV. "You like *I Love Lucy* too?"

I turned to look at the television. "Of course. TV Land and I have a great relationship. Especially when I travel."

"Same. It seems like every other channel is some strange fishing show or cartoons. Or the Lifetime movies." He sent a horrified look my way. "Please tell me you're not one of those people who lives and breathes them."

A soft chuckle escaped. "No. I'll admit, I've watched a few, but it's not the first thing I look for. You think they're terrible?"

"Just too much drama for me. They're all doom and gloom. Where's the fun in that?"

"In the mystery."

"I get enough of that at work."

"True," I acknowledged with a quick tip of my head. "Would you like to stay and watch *I Love Lucy*?" The words were out before I even realized my brain wanted to make the request.

His gaze flicked to the bed directly in front of the TV. The only place to sit in the room, other than the small wooden desk chair, which wasn't comfortable for more than a couple of minutes.

My face heated.

"Thank you for the offer, but I should probably head to my room. Catch up on a few things before heading to bed."

"Right." I nodded once, thankful he'd declined gracefully. Lounging with him on the bed probably wouldn't have been the best idea for my sanity. He rattled it enough just standing there looking like a snack. A lumbersnack.

I stifled a laugh.

Perhaps I had too much wine.

Or maybe it was just me being awkward around a handsome man.

Or both, my inner voice countered.

I fought not to roll my eyes. Yes. It was both.

"Okay, so, um, can we meet in the lobby at around seven? Bartles and I looked up the cabin on the map. It's a couple of hours outside of town by ATV. Up in the mountains."

"That's fine. We need to stop at his house so I can get clothes from Christina, but that won't take long. I'll call her this evening so she's ready for us."

"Sounds good." He turned, heading for the door. "Thank you, Claire. I know this is—unusual, but this whole case is odd."

"I agree. I'm hoping we find Warren Hammond out there. Alive and just scared." A shiver went through me as I thought of the alternatives. Ozzie was right to want company on this trip. It could turn dangerous in a heartbeat if Warren wasn't innocent in Marie's death.

Nerves skated down my spine. I made a mental note to ask Christina to include a rifle in the things I borrowed.

"Me too." He grasped the door handle, letting himself out. "I'll see you in the morning. Thank you, again."

"You're welcome." I moved closer, taking hold of the door's edge.

He stood in the doorway, staring down at me.

My knees turned to jelly as I looked up. It wasn't often I

had to do that with men. Most were nearly at eye level thanks to my five-ten height.

There was something to be said for feeling smaller. Like he'd protect me.

Not that I needed protection.

But it was nice to know he could.

Inwardly, I rolled my eyes. Definitely too much wine.

"Get some sleep, yeah?" He lifted a hand, his fingers gravitating to the flyaway hair framing my face before they dipped and he lightly skimmed the collar of my robe.

My gaze met his, and something arced between us. A jolt of awareness electrified my limbs and made my skin tingle.

He balled his hand and lowered it, stepping back. "Goodnight, Claire."

Taking a shaky breath, I clutched the door with both hands. "Goodnight, Ozzie."

The amused smile twisting his lips was the last thing I saw before he turned away.

I closed the door with a soft snick, then leaned my head against it, groaning quietly. "What was that?"

Pushing away, I turned and moved deeper into the room. My eyes landed on the paper cup and half-empty wine bottle.

With determined strides, I crossed to the nightstand and lifted both, taking them into the bathroom.

"Definitely too much wine," I muttered, dumping the rest down the drain.

CHAPTER 14

Ozzie

Heavy boots on the Bartles's wooden floor drew my attention away from the window. Turning, my gut clenched as I took in the vision before me.

There was no other way to describe it.

This was the real Claire Holmes.

Not the woman in the professional clothes and all the makeup, nor the woman in the icy-blue bathrobe and hot-pink fuzzy slippers.

It was this woman in insulated grayish-blue bibs, heavy boots, mauve wool sweater, and her blonde hair twisted into a messy bun on her head, face scrubbed free of makeup.

She was beautiful.

Her friend, and the chief's wife, Christina walked alongside her. She met my gaze. A knowing smile spread over her face and into her dark eyes.

I cleared my throat and looked away. "All set?"

Claire smiled. "Yep." She moved to the kitchen table and picked up the coat to match her bibs that was draped over a chair, and swung it around to thread her arms into the sleeves. With a quick rasp, she zipped it, then grabbed the hat and gloves on the table.

I zipped up my own coat and pulled a stocking cap on low over my ears. It wasn't terribly cold—it was March now, after all—but once we got going, it would feel much colder with the wind in our faces.

The back door opened and Chief Bartles clomped inside. "The ATVs are gassed up and ready. Claire, I strapped Christina's rifle to yours. It's loaded and there's more ammo in the pack on the back."

I wanted to protest arming a civilian but held my tongue. That rifle wasn't to ward off humans.

Bartles's gaze turned to me. "Quartermaine, I don't think I need to tell you to watch yourselves, do I?"

"No, sir."

He gave a sharp nod. "I don't like that Claire's going with you, but out here, sometimes what's frowned upon is a necessity. Bring our girl back the way you took her out, please."

"I will." And I would, even if I had to step in front of a bear to save her.

Claire tugged on her hat. "It's not me you should be worried about, Tom. You know I grew up hiking the bush with my dad. I could hunt before I could read. He"—she hooked a thumb toward me—"grew up in the *Appalachians*." She wrinkled her nose like it was a dirty word. "Are they even mountains?"

"Hey." I scowled at her. "Lay off my mountains."

"You mean your hills?"

I just raised an eyebrow and shook my head. "Can we go?"

Her musical chuckle filled the small kitchen. "Fine." She turned to our hostess. "Christina, thank you again for the clothes. I'll try not to get them too dirty."

The woman waved a hand. "They wash. You two stay safe." She looked at her husband. "You gave him the satellite phone, right?"

Tom nodded. "Hopefully, they won't need it."

I hoped so too. Because if I had to call in reinforcements, it meant all hell had broken loose. "We'll see you hopefully later this afternoon, Chief. Thanks again for the gear." I took a step toward the back door, ushering Claire in the same direction.

We made our escape and settled onto our ATVs. Tom had brought them here from the department's storage facility. His house was closer to the Hammonds' cabin and near the forest. It just made sense to leave from here.

Donning our helmets and firing up our four-wheelers, we pulled away from the Bartles's house, Claire in front. We both had a GPS device, but had decided it would be best if she took the lead. While I was no stranger to rough terrain, the land here was much different to what I was used to in North Carolina.

At first, we kept a quick clip, sticking to the road that led east, away from town.

But the Hammonds' cabin wasn't on a road. It was well off into the bush.

After half an hour, she turned off the road and plunged into the wilderness.

Immediately, our speed slowed. Deadfall timber and boulders littered the forest floor, impeding our progress.

Steadily, though, we maneuvered through the bush and up the mountain. When, finally, the pin on the map was within five minutes of our location, I signaled Claire to stop.

She killed the engine on her ATV and removed her helmet. "Are you sure you want me to stay back this far? It's half a mile away still."

"Yes." I cut the engine on my own machine and got off, removing my helmet. "I'll hike in. You have your radio?"

She unzipped a pack on the back of her four-wheeler and produced the handheld radio Chief Bartles gave each of us.

I removed the one from my pack, along with a box of ammunition and my rifle. Normally, I carried a 9mm handgun, but it was impossible to holster with the heavy clothing.

The rifle was more practical, anyway. It had more stopping power against a grizzly than my nine.

"Don't forget the satellite phone." She pointed at my pack.

"You keep it. I might not be in a position to use it. Do you know the morse code for S.O.S.?"

"Yes."

"Good. Hopefully, it won't come to that, but just in case…"

She gave me a tight smile. "Yeah. Just in case," she said, her voice soft and thin. Those deep, midnight eyes darted away.

I slung the rifle across my chest and turned it so it lay over my back, business end facing the ground, then stepped toward her. "Claire. Hey, look at me."

The wariness in her pretty eyes pulled at my heart. She'd been fierce and in control through all of this so far. Even when she was worried about her damn dog, I hadn't seen this… stress or deep worry on her face.

I took her hand. "Everything will be fine. Even if Warren is there and armed, I know what I'm doing. He won't be the first criminal with a weapon I've faced."

"Maybe not, but out here, help is a long way away. Even with the sat phone and the ability to call in a helicopter, it's probably an hour to the nearest hospital." The worry in her eyes turned to sternness, and she jabbed me in the chest with her free hand. "Don't get shot. Or stabbed."

I offered her my sunniest smile, hoping to set her at ease. "I'll be fine. Keep the grizzlies off my back, okay?"

She rolled her eyes and pulled her hand away, the worry finally fading from her eyes. "Oh, go away."

But it was still there in her voice.

Sobering, I took her hand again. "I promise I will be fine, okay?"

She gave a jerky nod, meeting my gaze, then looked away. "You better be."

Giving her fingers one last squeeze, knowing there was nothing I could say to completely assuage her fears, I snatched the GPS device from my ATV, noting my current coordinates, and left her with the vehicles.

It didn't take long to lose sight of her. Even with the bare lower branches of the pines, there were just so many, it obscured her and the vehicles from view.

The first stirrings of apprehension slithered through my gut, making the hair on the back of my neck stand on end. Someone—or something—could sneak up on me out here, and I wouldn't see them coming until the last moment.

Hopefully, I'd hear a bear or a moose long before I saw them.

Luckily, I saw neither.

Not quite ten minutes later, I stopped on the edge of the clearing that housed the cabin and studied the small, log-frame building.

The windows were dark, but that didn't necessarily mean no one was home. It was daylight.

But the bigger clue it was empty was the lack of smoke drifting from the chimney. I didn't even smell remnants of it. The cabin was too crude to have a furnace, even if it had a generator. There was also no propane tank in sight.

After watching the windows for several minutes, and still seeing no signs of life, I pulled my rifle around. I left the safety on but kept it at chest level. Cautiously, I approached the cabin door.

Standing to the side, I rapped my knuckles on the door. "Warren Hammond! It's the police. Open up."

I waited about fifteen seconds, then tried again. After the third time and still no answer, I tried the doorknob. It turned freely under my hand.

Heart thumping, I pushed the door inward. It creaked on its hinges as it opened.

"Hammond, I'm coming in." Raising my rifle, I rounded the doorjamb and stepped over the threshold.

Blinking to make my eyes adjust to the dim interior, I scanned the tiny one-room cabin, noting the twin bed along the left wall, the couch in front of a small table in the middle, and the two-person table jammed into the corner to my right at the edge of the minuscule kitchen space. The woodstove stuck out in the middle of the wall to my right.

I walked over and held a hand out, feeling for heat. When I felt nothing, I removed my glove and laid my hand on top. It was stone cold.

Opening the door on the front, I peered inside. It was clear of ash. Taking a quick glance around, I noted the absence of wood inside the cabin. Even the floor was swept clean. It was like someone winterized the place and hadn't been back since.

"Damn." I rubbed my forehead, perturbed by the lack of progress in this case. Every time I turned around, I hit another dead end. No one had been here in months.

After rummaging through the cupboards and checking under the bed and mattress for *anything* that might offer a clue, I left empty-handed and with just as many questions as before.

CHAPTER 15

Claire

Straddling the ATV, I watched the forest where Ozzie disappeared close to thirty minutes ago. I knew it would take some time for him to reach the cabin, search, and then walk back—even more if he found someone or something—but my anxiety ratcheted up with every passing minute.

Had he found Warren? Alive? Was he in a stand-off right now with the man? Or the person who killed Marie and possibly Warren?

Had he run across a moose?

With a huff, I looked away, scanning the rest of the woods. Ozzie might have been joking about keeping the grizzlies off his back, but having one stumble across us was a possibility. Most of them were still hibernating, but there were always some that didn't follow the rules. Honestly, though, I was more concerned about moose. They could be just as nasty as the bears. Especially if it was a mama with a baby.

Movement in the distance caught my eye. I stilled, hoping if it were a moose or a hungry, fresh-from-hibernation grizzly, that it would walk on by without paying me any heed.

But it only took a moment for me to recognize Ozzie. The

deep, rusty red hat on his head stood out against the pale bark of the bald pines.

The air left my lungs on a relieved breath. He was safe.

But he was also alone.

"Nothing?" I asked as he approached.

He shook his head, removing his rifle as he reached his ATV. "Not a damn thing. The place was winterized and doesn't look like it's been touched in months."

I wrinkled my nose. That's not what I'd wanted to hear. "So now what? Do you have any other leads on Warren?"

"Nothing concrete. An assumption he left the area." Unzipping the scabbard secured to the ATV, he stowed the rifle.

I could see the frustration that clawed at him. It was in the stiff line of his shoulders and the set to his jaw.

He pulled off his hat and ran a hand through his hair. "Do you know of any other properties they owned?"

"Not that they disclosed. The credit check I ran only showed the mortgage on their house."

"There's no mortgage on the cabin?" He hooked a thumb toward the trees.

"No. Warren said he paid cash for the land."

Ozzie hummed, staring off into the distance. "Did either of them mention a place they liked to go? For, like, vacation, or to visit family or friends?"

I pulled the corner of my lip between my teeth, thinking. "Not really, no. Marie mentioned once that Warren had a brother, when I asked about why they were moving to Massachusetts. I asked if it was to be closer to family. She said hers was out that way, in Virginia, but that Warren's only family, his brother, lived out of the country."

"Really? What country?"

"I don't know. Why?"

"Because maybe that's where Warren went." He turned, swinging a leg over his ATV. Settling onto the machine, he picked up his helmet. "Come on. Let's get back so I can do some digging into Warren Hammond's family."

Not about to argue—I wanted answers too—I donned my helmet and hopped onto my four-wheeler.

This time, he led the way.

So, I let my mind wander.

I thought about the Hammonds and poor Marie. Why would someone want to kill her? She was a schoolteacher. Did her husband do it? Did she cheat on him? Or he on her? In any case, that didn't warrant murder. Few things did.

But if he didn't do it, who else would want her dead? Was it a break-in gone wrong? Did the burglar expect the house to be empty, and she surprised them?

Except nothing was missing. Not that I could tell, anyway. Ozzie wasn't being very forthcoming with the details.

Not that I could blame him. I wasn't a detective. Just someone with a vested interest, since I knew the victim and found her body.

A quick shudder went through me. Last night was the first night I hadn't had a nightmare about finding her. I wasn't sure tonight would be the same. Not with our excursion drudging up all the memories.

I rolled my shoulders, trying to shrug off my maudlin thoughts. I just needed to replace those memories with something pleasant.

My gaze traveled over Ozzie's broad back as he rode in front of me.

Maybe if I held on to the image of his sunny smile when I fell asleep it would banish the bad dreams.

The man had a potent smile. It made my insides mushy. Which perplexed me a little. His brother had the same smile, but I didn't get the same feeling with Ellis.

Movement registered in my peripheral vision. I looked over in time to see the long, expansive brown face of a moose coming directly at me.

A quick shriek flew from my lips, and I yanked on the ATV's handlebars, hoping to avoid a collision with the animal.

But I turned too hard, and the machine tipped.

As I toppled over, hooves pounded the earth inches from my face.

CHAPTER 16

Ozzie

The change in pitch of Claire's ATV engine was my only clue something was amiss before I heard the crunching scrape of metal and plastic over the rocky ground.

I let off the throttle and glanced back.

It took several moments and a few rapid blinks for my brain to believe what it saw. Running away from Claire's overturned ATV was a moose with one antler.

Her four-wheeler's front tires spun lazily and the engine sputtered.

"Claire!" I braked and spun around, riding back to check on her.

Riding around the other side, I found her lying on the ground, helmet beside her, kicking at the seat of the ATV with her right leg, the left one pinned beneath the machine.

I cut my engine and hopped off. "Shit! Are you all right? What happened?"

"That moose came out of nowhere. I swerved to avoid him and tipped over. Can you set this thing up so I can get my leg free?" She pushed at the seat again with a wince.

"Yeah." Tipping my head, I studied the way it fell. It wouldn't be so simple as picking it up and putting it on its wheels. It wasn't like a bike. The ATV weighed probably five hundred pounds or more.

After shutting it off, I moved to the rear of the machine and grasped the cargo frame with both hands. My hope was that I could lift it high enough she could slide her leg out.

Instead, she let out a sharp cry of pain and waved me off. "That's not going to work. Lifting like that just puts pressure on my ankle. There's rope in my pack. Rig it to your ATV and use it to pull mine upright."

Angles and attachment points ran through my mind as I dug out the rope. The line probably needed to be attached low so it would roll up onto its wheels instead of just sliding over the ground.

"You doing okay?" I asked as I made a loop with the rope and attached it to the machine's frame at the front and rear. "There's some pain medicine in the first aid kit."

"You'll have it off me before it can take effect. I'm fine."

She said that, but I could see the pinch to her features. I just hoped the pain didn't mean something was broken.

Once I had the rope tied to her ATV, I repositioned mine and attached the line to the back.

"Put this on." I walked over and picked up her helmet, handing it to her. "Just in case a piece breaks off and flies back at you."

She took it and slipped it over her head.

I headed for my four-wheeler, glancing back as I reached the machine. "You ready?"

Giving me a thumbs up, she flipped down the helmet's visor.

Slowly, I throttled up my ATV, taking the slack out of the rope. The angles looked right, so I gave it more gas. It slid forward a few inches, but then the tires bit into the ground and it began to tip upright.

Keeping steady pressure on the line, I gave the ATV more gas and slowly tipped her four-wheeler onto its tires.

Claire scooted away from the machine but stayed on the ground.

I shut off my ATV and removed my helmet, returning to her side to crouch next to her. "How's it feel?"

"Sore." She tugged off her helmet, letting it fall to the ground beside her as she winced.

"Can you move it?"

She bent her knee, then flexed her ankle. A hiss escaped from between her teeth. "I think it's okay. Just sore."

I tipped my head and arched an eyebrow. "That didn't sound like it felt okay."

"It's not crunchy feeling. It just hurts." She held up a hand. "Help me up."

Standing, I reached down, grasping her upper arm and her hand. With a little hop, she made it to her feet.

"Take it easy. If it hurts, don't put weight on it." I steadied her with a hand around her waist.

Tentatively, she put her foot down. A slight grimace covered her face, but she didn't cry out or pull it up again.

"I think it's okay." She shifted, putting more weight on it. "Just sore." Pulling back a bit, she took a step. Her grimace deepened, but she took another.

"Okay?"

"Yeah. I think so. It'll probably turn pretty colors and be painful for a few days, but I think I'm all right." She turned toward her ATV. "Let's see if this thing is okay."

I helped her to the machine, and she sat down on it, starting it up. It sputtered to life, hiccupping a bit before settling into a steady rhythm.

"It sounds all right," I said.

Her head bobbed. "Yep. Can you hand me my helmet?" She pointed to it.

I scooped it up and passed it to her. "You sure you're okay?"

"I'm fine. Let's get back so I can ice my leg."

She was going to get more than ice. I planned to haul her into the emergency room for an x-ray. "You sure you can ride alone? We can leave it here and you can ride with me."

"That just creates more work. I'll be fine. We don't have that far to go."

"It's an hour yet, Claire. We aren't even back to the road."

"But we almost are. Now stop yapping and drive." She waved a hand in the general direction we needed to go.

Scowling, I started my ATV. "You lead, so I don't go too fast for you."

I didn't have to tell her twice. She shifted her four-wheeler into gear and took off.

She didn't stop once on the way back. Nor did she slow down. Once we hit the road, she sped up. I couldn't decide if that was a good or bad thing. In any case, I was cursing her stubbornness. She didn't need to be putting pressure on that leg until we knew how bad the injury was. I doubted Chief Bartles would mind coming back out with me tomorrow—or even later today—to pick up the machine.

When we reached the Bartles's backyard fifty minutes later, I pulled up alongside Claire and was at her side before she could stand on her own. The bone-jarring ride likely hadn't helped her pain level. I didn't want her to fall when she tried to stand.

She shut off her four-wheeler and swung her legs over, holding onto my forearms as she stood. When she took a step forward, her leg buckled.

"Let's not be superwoman." I scooped her into my arms and turned toward the house.

"Ozzie! Put me down. I can walk."

"Maybe. But should you?" I trudged across the muddy ground.

She huffed and speared me with a glare. "You're going to freak Christina and Tom out."

"Don't care. It'll get them on my side so we can convince you to go to the hospital."

"I'm fine."

"No, you're not. You need an x-ray."

The back door swung open. "What on earth happened?" Christina called from the doorway.

"A moose tried to take her out," I replied at the same time Claire said she was fine.

"A moose?" Christina's eyebrows winged upward. "Did it kick you?"

"No. We were coming back and it ran out of the trees. I didn't see it until it was on me, and I had to swerve. My ATV tipped and pinned my leg. I'm *fine*." Claire turned her icy glare on me again, but I ignored her. "Someone's just being overly cautious."

"You still can't walk without pain. You need an x-ray." I walked up the two steps into the house.

"Take her into the living room." Christina gestured to the doorway leading out of the kitchen.

"Are you sure?" I paused by the table and glanced at my feet. "My boots are muddy."

"Yes. I have a mop. It's fine."

Maneuvering through the tight space, I went into the living room and deposited Claire on the sofa, then crouched in front of her.

"We need to check out this leg." I touched her boot. "Do you want to take it off yourself or are you okay with me doing it?"

"It might be easier if you do it. Just go slow."

I looked at her through my lashes. The tight pinch to her mouth told me it hurt. "Singing, is it?"

She gave a short, choppy nod. "Yeah."

"I'll be careful." I slid my hand beneath her pant leg, finding the top of the boot. Pulling on the laces, I loosened it, then gently slid it off her foot. Her fingers dug into the couch cushion, but she didn't cry out or stop me.

Her sock came next, and I winced as I got my first look at her ankle and lower calf. "Ouch." It was several shades of purple.

"Oh, Claire. I think Detective Quartermaine is right. You need an x-ray. That looks—" Christina stopped and shook her head.

Claire wrinkled her nose and sighed. "Dammit. Stupid moose."

"Hey, at least it didn't attack you when you went down," I said. "It could have been worse."

Lips pressed together firmly, she nodded.

I glanced up at Christina. "Are we okay to leave the ATVs and the gear behind your house while I take her to get checked out?"

She nodded. "I'll bring your packs in and call Tom to let him know what happened. He'll probably bring the trailer over and pick up the four-wheelers. I can sort the gear and take out what's yours."

"We can do it when we get back," Claire said.

Christina waved a hand. "Nonsense. It won't take long." She made a shooing motion. "Go get that looked at. And send him to your hotel to get your things." She nodded to me. "You can stay here tonight."

Claire sighed and shook her head. "Thank you, but that's not necessary. I'm all spread out and—"

"Then give me your room key and I'll do it." Christina held out a hand, her tone brooking no argument.

I smothered a smile.

"How about we wait and see what the doctor says?" Claire countered. "If I can walk on it, I'll be fine at the hotel."

Christina crossed her arms and shook her head. She looked at me. "Work on her while you're gone."

I chuckled. "I'll do my best." Though if her friend couldn't convince her, I doubted I could.

Burying a hand in the inner pocket of my coat, I produced my car keys and held them out to Christina. "Unlock my car?"

She took them, leaving me free to scoop Claire off the couch.

This close and the rush of adrenaline and worry missing, the light vanilla scent of her soap filled my nose, along with something much more potent. My scalp prickled with an awareness that only grew as her warm curves settled against my chest.

Teeth clenched, I warned my body to behave as I followed Christina out of the house.

This was ridiculous. Claire was injured. I was merely helping her. My brain knew that, but my body didn't get the memo.

It needed to.

Because at the end of the day, I didn't take advantage of women.

And Claire was still a witness.

CHAPTER 17

Claire

The elevator dinged, and I maneuvered through the doors ahead of Ozzie, crutches creaking as I went. Much to my dismay, he'd been right to haul me in for an x-ray. The test revealed a fracture to the bottom of my fibula.

My foot was already hot inside the black boot the doctor stuck me in.

Agitation spurred me on, making me clumsy, and I caught the tip of one crutch on the gap in the floor. Stumbling forward, I landed hard on my booted foot. Pain rocketed up my leg, turning my muscles to mush, and I sagged, the ground rushing up to meet me.

A strong arm snatched my waist, and hauled me back, keeping me from crashing to the floor.

"Whoa. You okay?"

Ozzie's warm, firm chest at my back wasn't helping my equilibrium. I looked like something a rat dragged through the sewer; my hair was a tangled mess, tendrils plastered to my face from sweat. Splotches dotted my makeup-free skin from a combination of anger, pain meds, and the cold.

And I smelled too. Like dirt and body odor. I wanted a shower, some food, and some sleep. In that order.

"I'm fine." I straightened, getting my crutches under me again, and limped my way toward my hotel room. My leg was on fire now, thanks to my little misstep, but I hoped once I got off of it, it would settle back to the dull roar the pain meds had reduced it to earlier.

"You should have taken Christina up on her offer. No elevators at her house."

Maybe not, but I didn't want to be fussed over. I loved Christina. She was wonderful. But she and her daughters would have smothered me with attention. I really just wanted to lie in bed and be left alone.

So, I trudged forward to my room and shoved the keycard into the slot and pushed the door open.

"Thanks for walking me back. I'll be good—"

"I'm not leaving," Ozzie interrupted. "Not yet, anyway."

A deep scowl formed on my face as I stared at him. "Detective—"

Again, he interrupted me, stepping into my personal space.

"One day, I'll get you to stop calling me 'Detective.'"

I blew a long breath through my nose and closed my eyes, hanging my head. "Oscar, I'm tired."

"I know."

The compassion in his voice brought my gaze back to his. It shimmered in his dark eyes and in the soft, kind smile toying with his lush lips.

"Do you think you can handle a shower on your own?"

"Yes." Even if I didn't, there was no way I was inviting him in to help me. I would want so much more than his assistance undressing and dressing if he came into the bathroom with me.

Just the thought of what his hands would feel like removing my clothes sent coils of heat snaking through my belly.

That was not an option, even if I weren't nursing a broken

leg. He hadn't made a single pass at me, and I was not about to put myself on the line like that. More than likely, he'd reject me, and I did not want to suffer that embarrassment.

I turned away, limping over to my suitcase to get some clean underwear and my pajamas.

"Give me your keycard. I'll go get you some dinner while you shower."

"I can call the front desk. I'm sure someone would run across the street to the diner and get me a burger." I glanced over to see him holding out a hand.

"Yep, but I can, too, and you don't have to tip me. Besides, I'm hungry as well." He rubbed his fingers together. "Keycard, Claire."

I held his gaze with a glower for a moment longer before finally relinquishing. He wasn't giving up, and I was too tired and hungry to fight. I passed him the card.

"Thank you." Smiling, he turned and headed for the door. "Leave the bathroom door unlocked." He glanced back. "Just in case."

Then he was gone.

"Just in case," I mocked as the door closed.

Rolling my eyes, I chucked one crutch onto the bed, then shuffled to the bathroom, clothes clutched in my free hand. The doctor said I could bear weight on my leg, but to use the crutches to help take off some of the pressure. It was easier with one. When I got home, I'd have to look into getting a cane.

Steam filled the bathroom as I turned the water on as hot as it would go. I pulled a deep breath into my lungs and tried to center my mind. I was being petty and ungrateful. He was just trying to help. And being squirrely wouldn't change my situation. I needed to accept it and move on. The boot was my friend for several weeks.

Except for the next few minutes.

I sat down on the edge of the tub and unfastened the

Velcro straps, toeing it off with my other foot. Cooler air hit my sweaty flesh. With a grimace, I wiggled my toes.

That wasn't too terrible. It sure did look pretty, though. The outside of my ankle was a mottled purple with red around the edges and a decent amount of swelling.

"Stupid moose," I mumbled under my breath.

It could be worse, though. The hoof that crashed to the ground near my head could have hit its mark and bashed my face.

Removing my clothes, I spun around and eased into the tub, using the grab bars to stand. It was a delicate balancing act, but I managed to wash my hair and body without falling over or sending the shooting pain through my leg again.

Once I was squeaky clean and my skin lobster red, I stayed an extra minute, then shut the water off. Using the bars once again to lower myself to the edge of the tub, I climbed out and pulled a towel from the bar to dry off. Once my skin was dry, I used the towel to squeeze excess water out of my long hair. From my perch on the side of the bathtub, I wiggled into my underwear, then pulled the loose t-shirt I slept in over my head.

Making sure my right leg was firmly planted on the tile floor, I stood and grabbed my boot and my crutch, slowly limping back to the bedroom. Ozzie sat in the desk chair, getting up when he saw me hobbling out.

"You're supposed to wear that and use both crutches." He pointed to the boot in my hand.

"Yeah, well, I'm still damp and this thing gets sweaty even when I'm dry." I wished I had the other crutch, though. Walking without the boot hurt more than I thought it would.

Eyes on the bed—my goal—I didn't realize Ozzie's intentions until his arms were around my waist and my feet left the ground.

Startled, my gaze connected with his. This close, I could see the lighter brown flecks in his dark eyes.

His steps faltered a few feet from the bed, and he stopped, but didn't put me down.

My mushy insides returned. The hands I'd laid on his shoulders to steady myself drifted toward his neck, my fingers inching into the nearly black hair at the back of his head.

His lips parted on a quick intake of breath.

Mine tingled, wanting to taste him.

If he didn't put me down in the next couple of seconds, that was going to happen.

Naturally, I didn't say anything.

What woman would when in the arms of a man like Ozzie?

I pushed my hands deeper into the silky strands of his hair.

His jaw worked. "Claire."

"Hmm?"

"This is… it's not a good idea."

"Probably not." But that didn't stop me from bringing my hands forward to frame his face. My earlier admonition to myself floated through my mind, but I pushed it away. This didn't count. He wanted to kiss me as much as I wanted to kiss him. I could see it in his eyes. No embarrassment happening here.

Beard stubble rasped beneath my fingers. I leaned in, pausing so close our breaths mingled.

With a pained groan, he closed the gap.

Lightning flashed behind my eyes at the first touch of his mouth on mine. It pierced through me in an instant, leaving me humming from the ends of my hair to the tips of my toes.

He pulled back. Those lovely dark eyes had turned midnight black.

For several heated seconds, he just stared. I could see the debate going on in his mind. The same one warred within me.

Was this wise?

I didn't know much about police investigations, but it had to mean something that I was involved in his case. It was probably a no-no for us to get involved.

At least I wasn't a direct witness to Marie's murder. That would definitely be frowned upon.

So, I pushed my misgivings aside and reveled in the fact that the man who looked like he should be on a billboard, modeling the latest underwear fashions, found *me* attractive.

With a slow, provocative smile, I threaded my fingers into his hair again and gripped the strands, leaning in for another taste of his delectable lips.

It was the catalyst he needed.

The arms banded around my waist shifted, one going beneath my butt to hold me up, and the other snaking up my back to grip my neck.

He deepened our kiss, diving into my mouth for a taste.

Not about to be outdone, I responded in kind, tasting the coffee he had at the hospital while we waited. It paired perfectly with the taste of *him*.

Heat built in my belly, flooding my limbs. Need pulsed throughout my body.

In the back of my mind, my sanity screamed at me. That some of what I was feeling was from the painkillers. I wasn't normally this... uninhibited. Making the first move wasn't my thing. Ever. Even if I could tell a man was interested.

But if I got results like this, I needed to try it more often.

Ozzie nipped at my bottom lip, sparking an electric jolt that went straight to my core.

A soft whimper escaped me. Oh, I wanted more.

The sane part of my brain broke through the lust fog again, yelling, "What are you doing? We don't do this sort of thing! You barely know this man."

Doubt filtered in. My rational side was right. Casual relationships weren't my thing.

Even if the man looked like sin and could kiss like he had a Ph.D. in it.

I wrenched my mouth away, breathing heavily. "I think"— I swallowed hard, then continued—"we need to slow things down."

Chest heaving, he nodded. With a couple of long strides, he moved to the bed and lowered me to the mattress to sit, then let go.

"I'm sorry. I don't know what got into me." Ozzie shoved a hand into his hair, smoothing the strands I'd mussed.

"Don't apologize. I didn't say I didn't like it. Just that we need to take it down a notch."

"You're part of my investigation. I can't—"

"I'm not a witness. Not really. I didn't see her murdered. Just found her."

"Well, someone thinks you did."

I frowned at the reminder of the break-in at my house the other day. "We don't know that for sure."

"Why else would someone break into your house? I don't believe in coincidences, Claire." Some of the need left his expression, replaced by the hard-edged cop.

"Well, I do. Until you can prove that's why someone broke in, I'll consider all possibilities." Not wanting to argue or give him more time to think of reasons why we shouldn't get involved, I changed the subject. "You said you were going to get me food, yes?"

For several seconds, he just gave me a hard stare. Then he blinked and blew out a breath. When his eyes opened, the edginess was gone and the more affable Ozzie had returned.

"Yeah." He gestured to the white sack on the desk. "A burger and fries, as requested."

Immediately, my mouth watered. Vinnie's had the best burgers.

Ozzie crossed to the desk and took out a wrapped burger and a paper packet of fries. Bringing them to me, he set them on the nightstand, then went back for napkins and a can of soda.

"Thank you." I sent him a sunny smile.

He nodded. "You're welcome." Returning to the desk, he picked up the bag and the other can of soda. "I think it's best if I eat in my room. If you need something, call me."

My smile dimmed. Dammit. I didn't want him to leave. But judging by the set of his shoulders, I knew I'd never convince him to stay. "I will."

"I'll see you in the morning. Have a good night."

"Goodnight." I raised a hand in farewell, but he didn't see it, already on his way to the door. In a blink he was gone.

I sighed, looking around the now empty room. With him gone, it was suddenly quiet.

Really quiet.

My fingers gripped the bedspread beneath me as loneliness took hold. I could really use another presence in the room to banish the heavy silence.

Swallowing hard, I flopped back on the bed.

I wished Pebbles were here.

CHAPTER 18

Ozzie

Dammit. Why did she always have to look so good?

I clenched my teeth as Claire answered the door. Her blonde hair fanned around her pretty face, which only had minimal makeup highlighting her features. An oversize sage-green sweater that hung to mid-thigh hinted at the curves I'd felt up-close-and-personal last night. Hiding them only made me want to strip the sweater off of her so I could see and feel them again.

It hadn't escaped my notice she hadn't worn a bra beneath her sleepshirt last night. I don't know what possessed me to pick her up like that. It would have been just as easy to take the boot from her and pass her the other crutch.

But no. Crippled Claire turned me into a caveman.

My gaze traveled south, taking in the cream leggings and the orthotic boot on her foot. It ruined her outfit, but it also didn't matter. Her beauty and confidence still shined through.

"Hi." A sunny smile lit her face.

I scowled, holding on to my anger at myself for being unable to resist her charms. Riggs would ream me out for getting involved with her. I just thanked my lucky stars she hadn't actually witnessed anything. It would jeopardize any case I built once I had a suspect. "You ready to go?"

Her smile dimmed, a touch of confusion entering her eyes.

Guilt hollowed my stomach. It wasn't her fault I couldn't keep my hands to myself.

"Yeah. Can you get my suitcase?" She looked back, then shifted to the side so I could enter.

The door snicked shut as I walked into the room, my carry-on rolling behind me. Her crutches creaked as she followed.

I picked up her small case from where it rested on the luggage rack and raised the handle, turning it so it was back-to-back with mine.

She shrugged into her coat and picked up her purse, slinging the long strap over her head so the bag rested against her chest.

I frowned and held out a hand. "Give me that. It looks heavy."

"It's fine. Let's go." She shuffled forward.

Another scowl darkened my face. I didn't like that she matched my energy now.

Raking a hand through my hair and tipping my head up, I huffed a quick breath before looking at her. "I think we need to clear the air."

"You obviously regret it, so there's nothing to clear. Let's go." She shuffled toward the door again, but I stepped into her path.

"Excuse me, Detective."

My molars ground together. "We're back to that, huh?"

She just raised an eyebrow.

"Look, can we just agree the timing sucks? Maybe in the future—"

Faster than I thought she could move with a bum leg and crutches, she stepped around me. "I'm not pining away for you, so don't count on the future."

"Claire—"

"We're going to be late." She reached the door and pulled it open, her crutch clattering against the panel as she attempted to maneuver through.

Tipping my face skyward and growling softly in frustration, I hurried over, grabbing the door's edge to hold it for her.

"Thank you." Head held high, she swung through.

At the elevator, she stabbed the button with her index finger.

I folded my hands over the top of the suitcase handles, staring at the light above the elevator.

My eyes flicked toward her. She, too, stared at the indicator, her expression blank.

How did I make this right? How did I make her understand where I was coming from?

I *did* like her. She had to know that. The kiss we shared made that fairly obvious. But why couldn't she understand my reservations?

The elevator dinged and the doors slid open. I waited for her to enter, then got on. She pushed the button for the first floor.

As the doors slid shut, I glanced at her again. She still had that carefully blank expression on her face.

It hit me then that maybe she wasn't upset I didn't want to move forward right now. Maybe she was hurt that I essentially promised her more and then took that away.

"I'm sorry if I led you on. That was not my intention. I never wanted to hurt you."

She looked at me, that carefully-crafted mask still in place. "I didn't say you did."

The first bite of anger took hold. Why was she being so obstinate? "Then what is it?" I asked, my tone sharp. "Yesterday, I thought we were on the road to being friends. Then things got a little heated, and I made it clear I can't pursue a relationship with you. Now you act like I'm a pariah or something. Clearly, you're angry at me."

"It's not that." Her eyes flashed fire and color popped on her cheeks. "I'm not angry at you. I'm angry at myself. Because I heard you, and I know the timing is wrong, but that doesn't change the fact that I wish the elevator would get stuck so *maybe* the embers that erupted last night could catch fire again." Chest heaving and the low burn of need in her eyes, she stared at me.

The elevator dinged and the doors rumbled open.

Letting out a frustrated, screechy growl, she whirled toward the opening on her crutches and hurried out.

My mind glitched, like a lagging internet connection.

What?

The doors began to slide closed.

Cursing under my breath, I shoved my carry-on forward, making the doors reverse direction.

She was pissed because she wanted me? And didn't want to want me?

My ego sat up and purred.

And rightfully so. I'd dated beautiful women. Successful ones too. But there was something about Claire Holmes that was just… classy. And wholesome. Sure, she was beautiful and successful, but she was also kind and funny. There was no artifice about her, and it seemed like she truly cared about people.

I'd never met anyone like her.

Frustration tamped down my ego. Why did I have to meet her now, like this? Why couldn't our first encounter over Pebbles and the fact we were neighbors be the sole reason for our acquaintance? The complications involving my case were a setback neither of us wanted.

But there was nothing I could do.

Gritting my teeth, I stepped off the elevator and followed her to the front desk. This case needed to be over.

CHAPTER 19

Claire

I was so ready for this day to end. My leg throbbed. So did my head. I probably could have alleviated the leg pain if I'd bothered to use both of my crutches today, but they got in my way, so I continued to only use one. Coupled with a restless night thanks to the way Ozzie and I parted ways at the airport and the hunger gnawing at my stomach, I was *cranky*.

Leaning forward, I peered through the windshield, like that would make the road I needed magically appear.

Where was it?

Lifting my foot off the gas, I glanced at my phone.

Still no bars.

I really should have left when the client did, but no. Silly me wanted to take more photos of the view.

Now it was dark, I couldn't see any of the landmarks I noted on the way in, and I had no phone signal to pull up a map.

Getting lost in the bush was not on my to-do list this evening.

My headlights illuminated an intersection.

"Oh! Yay!" I came to a stop, then put the car in park and turned on the overhead light, reaching into the backseat for the paper map I kept in the car. There weren't many cross-roads in the area. I might be able to figure out where I was.

Studying the map, I traced the faint lines indicating dirt roads and found the house I was at earlier. From there, I tried to figure out where I went wrong.

"Ha!" I stabbed the map with my index finger. "There it is. I knew I missed a turn." Laying it on the passenger seat, I put the car in gear and did a U-turn in the intersection. I remembered now where the turn was. It was overgrown and easy to miss in the dark.

Pausing a couple of times to look at the map again, I finally made it back to the area near the road I missed. With my foot barely on the gas, I crawled forward, brights on, eyes glued to the trees on my left.

After five minutes at a snail's pace, I started to wonder if I'd missed it again.

How, I didn't know. I'd scarcely blinked.

My lights glinted off something in the trees. I slowed further and squinted into the dark.

"What is that?"

I braked, peering into the heavy evergreen branches.

It looked like a car. But there was no road there.

Shifting into park, I got out and hobbled around the back of my vehicle to get the flashlight from my emergency kit in the cargo well.

The light came on with a click. I swept the forest with the beam, looking for any large animals, then, cognizant of my booted foot, I took my crutch from the backseat before I stepped off the edge of the road and into the woods.

It was slow-going, and the throb through my lower leg intensified, but I kept moving.

Just past the first line of trees, my light bounced off a silver BMW X5 about fifty feet away. "Whoa. How did that get here?" Slowly picking my way forward, I passed the flashlight beam over the area around it as I neared. Behind the car, tire tracks ran through the undergrowth and disappeared into the darkness. Someone must have driven in from another road.

But why was it here?

I walked around it, looking for signs of life. It was a nice vehicle. Only a couple of years old, if that. Scratches marred the paint from its drive through the bush, but it otherwise looked okay. Footprints led away from the driver's door. They went toward the road where I left my car.

Aiming the light at the windows, I peered inside.

It was spotless. Like it had just come off the dealership lot.

Was it stolen? That could be why it was out here. The thieves had taken it for a joyride, then ditched it.

Another thought struck me.

Could it be Warren Hammond's car? I didn't know what he drove. But I knew he and his vehicle were missing, and that he had expensive taste.

I chewed on the corner of my mouth, eyeing the area with new eyes. If this was Warren's car, did that mean he was nearby?

Immediately, I dashed that thought. Judging by the tire tracks, the car hadn't moved in days, and there weren't any buildings close by he could be holed up in. Only the cabin and hunting property I was just contracted to sell were nearby, and there was no sign someone had been hiding out there when the man showed me the property. The owner had a couple of small hunting stands set up in the woods, too, but they were little more than boards nailed to a frame to keep out the wind while a hunter waited. Completely unsuitable for someone to live in.

Scanning the ground around the car, I noted some areas where the snow and foliage beneath were trampled. Some of it right outside the driver's door. Beyond that, it was hard to tell. Whoever left the car here could have walked in the tire tracks back to the road.

I backed away from the vehicle. I needed to find a phone signal and call Oscar.

My brain shouted at me to hurry. That this was creepy, and I needed to get to safety, but I forced myself to take careful steps and use the crutch for balance. Walking in this boot wasn't easy.

Finally, leaving the woods, I glanced back, and a thought struck me. How would I find this spot again? I couldn't put a pin in the map on my phone, because I didn't have a signal.

The branches waving in the wind gave me an idea. Clicking off the flashlight, I opened the driver's door and tossed it onto the seat, then opened the rear passenger door and leaned inside to rummage in my giant tote bag. The scarf I wore to town on Saturday was still in it. I took it off before finishing my errands. It made me too hot.

My fingers touched soft, cool fabric. "Found you." Grinning to myself, I pulled it out, then made my way to the tree line and picked a branch that stuck out away from the others.

"Oh, I'm glad Dad taught me how to tie good knots," I mumbled.

With the scarf secure, I returned to my car and climbed in. Shifting into gear, I glanced at the clock, making a mental note of the time. I'd stay at a steady speed until I found the road, then note the time again as an added way to mark where the vehicle was.

I drove another two minutes down the road, then spotted the road cut.

"Thank goodness!" Turning, I picked up speed, keeping an eye on the signal bars mirrored on my infotainment screen from my phone.

When two appeared, I braked, throwing the car into park.

"Please work," I whispered as I dialed Ozzie's number.

With each soft trill, I drummed my fingers faster on the steering wheel.

On the fourth ring, his deep baritone came through the car's speakers.

"Detective Quartermaine."

I could hear the distraction in his voice.

"Ozzie, it's Claire."

"Claire? Is everything all right?" The distracted tone quickly disappeared. "You sound upset."

"Not upset. Just… weirded out. I found something I think you should see. If I give you directions, can you meet me?"

"Right now?"

"Yes."

"Um…"

I heard papers rustling.

"Sure. What's going on?"

"What kind of car does Warren Hammond drive?"

His sharp intake of breath was loud in the confines of the car. "You found a car? Where?"

"In the woods. Near the property I'm getting ready to list. It's a silver BMW X5."

"Of all the…" He stopped and drew in a breath. "Warren drives the same car. Did you touch it?"

"No. Just looked in the windows. It's empty." Thank goodness common sense kicked in when I was in the woods. Having my fingerprints on the vehicle wouldn't be a good thing. I found Marie's body and now Warren's car. What were the odds?

"Good. Keep it that way. Give me those directions you mentioned."

"I'll text you a pin to my location. I think you should have enough signal to get you this far. I had to drive a bit to call you."

"Okay. Stay put. I'll be there as quickly as I can."

The line clicked, and the infotainment screen returned to the main screen.

I picked up my phone and dropped a pin in my location, then texted it to him.

A gust of wind blasted the side of my car. I glanced through the windshield at the dark sky. Nothing much was visible thanks to the heavy cloud cover. Another storm system was on the way, and the heaviness of promised snow hung in the air. Even my headlights had a hard time cutting through the darkness.

Normally, I wasn't one to be afraid in the bush at night. But this evening was different. The specter of what that car could mean loomed over everything.

Was someone lurking in the woods?

Watching?

Waiting?

A shiver ran down my spine. The car locks had disengaged when I parked, so I stabbed the button to lock them again.

My theories were far-fetched, but not out of the realm of possibility.

It was better to be safe than sorry.

CHAPTER 20

Ozzie

Jaw cracking with a wide yawn, I blinked the moisture from my eyes as I turned onto a dirt road from the highway. The last two days had been busy. After delving into Warren Hammond's brother, Darren, I'd worked on some of my other active cases, prepped for court for one of them, and caught another for a stolen car. Last night, I thought I would sleep like the dead, but Claire invaded my dreams, and we'd acted out that elevator scenario. Multiple times.

When my alarm went off this morning, I jerked awake, still aroused and exhausted.

The arousal part had improved as I dove into work, but the exhaustion hadn't. I'd been an hour, tops, away from going home and crashing when she called.

Now, I was not only lengthening my day—probably considerably—I was most likely guaranteeing another restless night by having fresh memories of Claire front and center in my mind.

Maybe I should just say screw it and take her up on her offer.

Minus the elevator.

I inhaled a breath and let it out on a groan. Would Riggs believe we were seeing each other before the murder?

Immediately, I slapped down that idea. Lying to the boss was never a good plan, especially in my profession. Besides, Riggs already knew from the conversations we had about this case that I didn't know Claire beforehand.

Another yawn overtook me. I ran a hand through my hair and over my face. Solving the problem wouldn't happen tonight. I was too tired.

Eight minutes later, my headlights washed over Claire's Land Rover. I pulled up behind her and put the truck in park, leaving it running, then got out.

She met me outside her driver's door.

"Thanks for coming." She huddled into her coat against the wind that had picked up in the last hour or so and offered me a strained smile.

It was enough to kick my heart rate into overdrive as memories of my dreams sparked.

I willed them back into their box. "Of course. You want to lead the way? Or we can take my truck." I tipped my head toward the vehicle.

"Just follow me. I don't want to leave my car here."

With a nod, I took a step back toward my pickup. "Sounds good. How far is it?"

"Ten minutes or so."

A frown pulled at the corners of my mouth. She'd been out here alone and that far out with no cell signal? "Okay. Don't lose me."

"I won't." She opened her car door.

Taking that as my cue, I turned and jogged the few feet back to the truck, climbing inside. Her brake lights lit up, then she put the SUV in gear.

Less than a minute into the drive, my phone lost signal. I had a radio, but I wasn't sure it would work out here. To the south, the faint glow that was Juneau lit up the sky over the mountaintops. If there was no transmitter on the summit, I wouldn't be able to quickly call for help unless there was a ranger or a state trooper on this side of it. This truly was the sticks.

Claire's brake lights glowed, then her blinker lit up, and she turned onto another dirt road, this one barely wide enough for a single vehicle. The forest closed around us, blocking out most of the starlight. It was like driving into a blackhole.

Several minutes later, she braked again, making another turn. When she crawled along at just under twenty miles an hour, I knew we had to be close.

I saw the fabric flapping in the wind at the same time Claire braked again. She rolled to a stop and parked. I pulled in behind her.

"Here we go," I muttered. Shutting off the engine, I went around the vehicle to the passenger side and opened the rear door. The patrol truck had a storage compartment built into the backseat. Grabbing a flashlight and my evidence kit, I closed the door and walked toward Claire.

"It's back there." She raised the black flashlight in her hand and pointed. The beam bounced off the pine boughs and the colorful fabric waving like a windsock. It took me a moment, but I recognized it as the scarf she'd worn Saturday when I ran into her at The Cozy Cup.

"That was genius." I motioned to the scarf.

"Thanks. I knew I'd never find it again if I didn't mark it. I don't know how I found it in the first place. Probably because I was looking for that road we turned off of a couple minutes ago. I saw the shine in my headlights and thought it was unusual. There's nothing out here but a cabin and a few ramshackle hunting blinds." A gust of wind hit, and she raised her shoulders, shielding her ears.

Gooseflesh erupted on my neck and down my arms inside my coat. "Let's go take a look before this weather system fully arrives. I don't want to get caught out in the snow."

"Me, either." She opened the rear door and removed her crutch, then stepped off the road.

I snagged her coat sleeve. "You sure you should be walking through there?" I gestured to the boot on her foot.

She glanced down, then shrugged. "It already aches. The car isn't that far in. I'll be fine."

Lips clamped together tightly, I narrowed my eyes. "How about you wait in your car?"

"Uh-uh. It's too creepy." She waved a hand. "I'm not one who normally gets the willies in the woods, but tonight?" She shook her head. "There's just something about all this that's just... It's weird." With her light, she shooed me toward the trees. "Let's go. We're wasting time and the storm's only getting closer."

I didn't like it, but I understood her reasoning. I could also see by the set to her jaw and the look in her eyes she wouldn't stay behind unless I handcuffed her in the back of my truck.

"Fine." I swept out a hand, indicating she should lead the way.

Without a word, she hobbled down the embankment and entered the forest.

Just a few feet in, I saw the car. Most of it was hidden by the trees, but the badge on the front grille was unmistakable.

"Stay here." I held up a hand to Claire as we got close.

She halted, reaching behind her head to raise her hood. "It came in from another direction. There are tire tracks behind it. I walked all the way around it."

Nodding, I moved forward, watching my step. Small branches and pine needles crunched under my boots. A few feet from the car, I stopped, shining my light over the ground. Claire's lopsided fresh prints stood out, but there were some older ones, mostly near the driver's door. The ground cover wasn't quite as springy there as elsewhere.

I tucked my light under my arm and took the digital camera from my evidence kit. Making sure the flash was on, I snapped a few pictures.

It certainly looked like the right car. Taking careful steps and photographing as I went, I reached the back.

The license plate matched. I still needed to look at the VIN to confirm it, but I'd put money on this being Hammond's vehicle.

Continuing around the other side, nothing else stood out except the tire tracks disappearing into the darkness. I took a peek through the SUV's windows, and saw it was empty, as Claire said.

It was also extremely clean. There were even vacuum tracks in the carpet in the passenger footwell. Either Hammond was a complete neat-freak, or someone had thoroughly cleaned the car before dumping it in the woods.

My question was whether that someone was Warren.

After snapping a picture of the VIN, I walked back to Claire.

"All done?" She peered at me from beneath her hood. In the light from my flashlight, I could see the redness on the end of her nose.

"For now. I want to double-check the VIN, then I need to see if I can get a message to the station on the radio."

"It's Warren's car, isn't it?" She fell into step beside me as I started toward the road.

"I think so. The license plate matches. Unless someone put his plate on the exact same car, it's his."

"And you still don't know where he is? Did you find his brother?"

"Not exactly. I found his name and social media pages. From what I can tell, he lives in Indonesia."

"Indonesia? What?" Incredulity laced her tone.

"Yeah. Surprised me too. He owns an import-export business. I haven't been able to contact him yet, though. He has little info about his company on his social media pages, and I have, so far, struck out searching state databases for business holdings in his name. A judge granted me a warrant late yesterday so I could submit a request to the IRS for any information on his company. I was also granted one to get access to Warren Hammond's passport usage from Customs and Border Protection. But I haven't heard back from either agency yet." Hopefully, it wouldn't take weeks for them to run their searches.

Every day I spent investigating was another day Hammond's trail ran cold. Even if I could track him to a specific city, if he went off the grid, I would have to rely on witnesses to help me locate him, and memories faded with time. The sooner I could pin down where he went—if he'd indeed left the area—the better.

We broke through the trees, reaching the road. I jogged ahead of her to my truck and opened the passenger door. "Get in."

Claire walked up, but stopped short of climbing in. An eyebrow winged upward as she eyed the bottom of the doorframe, then lifted her booted foot. "Not sure that's going to work."

"It's not that much higher than your car." I backed away, reaching for the rear passenger door. "Hang on." Opening the door, I tossed my evidence kit and flashlight onto the backseat, then returned to her side. Reaching into the cab, I plucked the manila folder with my case notes off the seat and put it on the dash. "Okay. Let me help you in." I held out a hand.

She tucked a gloved hand into mine and pushed off the ground with her good leg. Slipping my other hand under her elbow, I guided her in.

"Thank you." She swung her legs in, and I took her crutch and closed the door.

After retrieving the camera from the backseat and stowing

the crutch, I joined her up front.

"Dig into that folder and find the page with Hammond's vehicle information, would you?" I gestured to the folder on the dash, then started the truck, getting the heater going again, before picking up the radio mic.

"Sure." She poked the button above our heads to turn on the cab lights, then grabbed the folder. The soft rustle of papers filled the confined space.

I turned up the volume on my radio, then checked the frequency and said a prayer dispatch could hear me as I pressed the transmission button. "PL-two-twelve to dispatch, over." I lifted my thumb and waited.

Static erupted, then Hailey Branson's voice filled the car. "PL-two-twelve, go ahead."

Relief flooded my veins. Things just got much simpler. I pressed the transmission button again. "Dispatch, PL-two-twelve. I'm on-scene of a ten-twenty-eight. Silver BMW X5. Requesting a tow truck to my location. And let Chief Riggs know. I have limited cell reception out here."

"PL-two-twelve, Dispatch, copy. Contacting A-1 Wrecking to dispatch to your location and contacting Chief Riggs. All correct? Over."

"Dispatch, PL-two-twelve, all correct, over."

"PL-two-twelve, Dispatch. We'll contact you when resources are en route, out."

I hung up the mic and looked at Claire. "Did you find the vehicle information?"

She pointed to the open folder.

"Great." I turned on the camera. "Let's see if we have a match." I pulled up the stored photos and found the one I took of the VIN. "I'm going to read it off. You ready?"

"Yep."

I read off the combination of letters and numbers, then glanced up, meeting her gaze.

"It's a match," she said.

"That's what I figured." Switching the camera off, I stretched an arm between the seats and slipped it back into the evidence collection case. "I'm not sure what good it'll do to have it, though. It looked clean. Too clean." I chewed on the corner of my mouth, staring through the windshield at the darkened forest as my mind turned. "Who owns the property you were out here to list?" I glanced at her.

"Robert McGuffey."

"What do you know about him? Is he a long-time resident? Did he say why he was selling?"

"He's elderly, and his health took a turn. He decided to move in with his son in Seattle. Are you thinking Warren knows him?"

"Maybe." I drummed my fingers on the steering wheel. From the sound of it, though, I doubted the two were acquainted. "Has he been out of town a lot? You said his health was poor."

Claire nodded. "I actually met with his son tonight and talked to Robert via FaceTime. He's in Seattle, recovering from heart surgery."

"Do people know his house is vacant? That no one's out here?"

She lifted a shoulder. "Probably, some, yes. But there are so many places to dump a car up here, it's not even funny. Why would he pick a place where someone *might* find it sooner rather than later?"

That was a damn good question.

"Unless he wanted it to be found."

I frowned in question. "What do you mean?"

"Maybe he needed to ditch it, but wanted it found. It could be Warren isn't the killer, and he hid the car to throw off the real murderer."

"But why hide it?" I asked. "And clean it? If he wanted the killer to think he left town, why not just abandon it at the airport, or even just leave it in his driveway and call a taxi to the airport? And there would be no reason to detail it before dumping it."

She shrugged one shoulder. "Who's to say he didn't detail it before Marie died? That's entirely possible. You saw their house. It was neat as a pin. And it always looks like that. If anything, it was sparse. Lynne was going to add furniture because they didn't have enough. Normally, she has to take pieces out and then add some décor to give it a cohesive look."

I thought about the Hammonds' house. Claire wasn't wrong. It was exceptionally clean and well-organized. I'd chalked that up to the fact they were selling it, though.

"You're sure it was always like that?"

"Yes. From what I saw, anyway. I asked Marie about it too. She said they didn't like clutter. And since they didn't have children, two of the bedrooms weren't needed, which is why they were empty. There was an office downstairs where Warren worked sometimes. Marie only brought grading home and could do that on the couch or at the dining table. The third spare bedroom was their gym."

The more I learned about the Hammonds—Warren, specifically—the more I wondered what they'd been up to. Their daily habits and the way they lived were just… strange. From their spartan house to the secrets they kept from each other and the people in their lives, it all screamed they had bigger things to hide.

Tomorrow, I needed to put the screws to the IRS and Customs. The answer to what skeletons lurked in the Hammonds' closet was likely in that information.

"They never mentioned anyone who might have been a friend? Someone who might check on their house while they're away? Bring in their mail? Or maybe just be someone they talked to on a regular basis?"

She glanced away for a moment, her forehead furrowing,

then shook her head. "No. I don't think either of them mentioned anyone except their family."

Mouth pressed flat, I drummed my fingers on the steering wheel and looked outside again. "Okay." Blowing out a breath, I turned back to her.

In the harsh overhead light, the pinch to her face created deep shadows under her eyes. I touched her arm. "You doing okay? How's the leg?"

"It's fine." She glanced down, briefly.

For half a second, I thought about calling her out on the blatant lie. She'd already admitted it hurt, and her face said it hurt more than a little. But that wouldn't do anything except make her put up her guard and drive a wedge between us.

Though the latter might not be a bad thing. It would help me keep my hands to myself. Because right now, all I wanted to do was haul her into my arms and make her forget her leg hurt.

She looked up again, her gaze locking with mine. Need unfurled in my stomach and heated my blood.

I clenched the steering wheel until my knuckles hurt, trying to hold on just as tightly to my control.

Swallowing hard, I broke the stare. "You should head home. Get it propped up. I don't need anything else from you here."

As soon as the words left my mouth, I regretted them. They did not come out the way I intended.

Her little harrumph said it all. She slapped the folder onto the dash and reached for the door before I could explain myself.

I scrambled out of the truck, running around to the other side before she could get out. It was a decent drop to the ground, and I'd parked close to the edge of the road. I didn't want her to fall and reinjure herself.

"Let me help you out." I reached for her arm, but she smacked my hands away.

"I can get out of a truck, Detective."

Even in just the glow from the interior light and my head-lights, I could see the fire flashing in her blue eyes. "This is going to be a thing with us, isn't it? I make you mad, and you resort to my title?" I pushed past her waving arms and wrapped my hands around her waist, lifting her out of the truck.

"Since I'm nothing more than a person connected to your case, I think it's… fitting." Her voice trailed away, the last word coming out quiet and hesitant as her body made contact with mine.

I knew how she felt. Words were stuck in my throat too.

Through the heavy layer of her coat, warmth seeped into my hands. Her breath washed over my face, the sweet scent like a drug that went straight to my head.

All the reasons why this was a bad idea blew away with the wind, and I did what I promised myself I wouldn't do again until this case was resolved.

I kissed her.

CHAPTER 21
Claire

Y*es!*

My inner voice fist pumped and eagerly kissed him back.

It won't last, my rational side countered.

I opened the soundproof vault in my mind and shoved Ms. Rationality inside, slamming the door. I didn't care if this lasted or not. It was happening now.

Ozzie backed up, pressing me against the doorframe. He slid one knee between my thighs, letting me rest on it so his hands were free to glide up my neck and into my hair. The press of his long fingers to my scalp sent a wave of tingles racing over my skin. I clutched at the lapels of his jacket and held on.

For long moments, we devoured each other, lost in the sensations overwhelming everything else. I didn't feel the snow flurries that had started to fall, melting on my face, nor the icy wind whipping around us.

But Ms. Rationality battled her way out of her box. Curling her fingers over the edge of the door and poking her head through, she screamed at me. *You're on the side of a road in the bush, waiting on a tow truck to come get a potential murderer's car! Have you lost your mind?*

Indeed, I had.

I wanted to say I didn't care. That the feel of our bodies pressed together, the glide of his lips over mine was all that mattered.

Except, how did this end? In the backseat of my car?

We weren't teenagers.

My rational mind made it a little further through the door, one leg on the other side now. *End this now. Before he does. He'll just come up with more excuses not to see you.*

Ugh, she was right.

I wrenched my mouth away and laid my head on Ozzie's shoulder, breathing hard. His fingers clenched, then unclenched in my hair.

"I—" My voice cracked, so I swallowed and tried again, lifting my head. "I should probably go." It was then I noticed the snow drifting down around us. "Before this gets any worse." I pointed at the sky, thankful for the innocent excuse. I didn't want to draw attention to the case and remind him of his reasons for resisting a relationship in the first place.

He cleared his throat. "Yeah. Probably." Taking a step back, he let me slowly slide down his thigh to the ground.

Oh my…

The hot zing that went through me from the friction almost made me say screw it and pull his head back down for another kiss. But my rational side screamed, "Resist!" and finally clawed her way all the way through the door to stand front and center with her hands on her hips.

I scowled and tried to weakly push her back to the vault, but she didn't budge. My inner hussy had lost this particular battle.

Pushing away from the car, I took a step, but my knees were still jelly, and I stumbled.

"Careful." Ozzie grabbed my arm, supporting me under my elbow. "Here. Let me help you back to your car." He shuffled me away from the truck far enough to get my crutch from the back seat, then helped me across the uneven ground toward my SUV.

I wanted to protest. To argue that I was fine. But face-planting on the cold, wet ground wasn't on the list today, so I gritted my teeth and let him help me to my driver's door. This time, I let my rational side take control. Having his help meant I got out of here more quickly.

Away from temptation.

I couldn't leave without knowing I'd see him again, though. So, I slapped a hand over Ms. Rationality's mouth as I asked, "Can you meet me for coffee Saturday morning? Around nine."

Indecision lit in his dark eyes.

Not about to let him think about it long enough to say no, I took my crutch from him and opened my door, sliding it in between the front seats to the second row.

"Claire…"

"The Cozy Cup," I said over my shoulder. "Coffee's on me." I turned and sat, swinging my legs inside, then reached for the door handle as I aimed a sunny smile his way. Before he could protest again, I pulled the door shut and started the engine. Buckling up, I tossed him a quick wave and put the car in gear. He stepped back, and I performed a quick three-point turn.

A quick glance in the rearview mirror as I drove away showed him standing on the berm. His headlights silhouetted his tall frame as he watched me leave.

That funny, heated, giddy feeling sprang to life in my belly again. The side of me that wanted to act like a teenager and jump his bones in my backseat begged me to turn around.

But I let the adult in me win this time and kept driving.

It would happen. But when, where, and what it would mean I didn't know.

Maybe I'd get a better idea about it Saturday.

If he showed up.

I rolled my eyes. Getting stood up was a distinct possibility. He'd wanted to say no. I could see it in his eyes. His mind was already telling him it was a bad idea because I was part of his case.

His body had other ideas, though.

I shifted in my seat as the heated feeling spread south.

So did mine.

CHAPTER 22

Claire

My fingers drummed a steady tattoo on the wooden table as I stared out the front window of The Cozy Cup.

Ozzie was late.

Not that I was surprised.

Though I was a little surprised he hadn't called or texted to tell me he wasn't coming. He struck me as more considerate than that.

Maybe he wasn't who I thought he was. Maybe it was a good thing he hadn't shown up.

"You going to sit here all morning or are you going to take the coffee to him?"

I glanced up at the sound of Mina's voice. She held a to-go cup in her hand.

"What?" I frowned.

She held out the cup. "Coffee. For your detective." With a quick tip of her head, she motioned to the door. "Go. He either stood you up or he forgot." I told her who I was here to meet when I arrived half an hour ago.

"Either way," Mina continued, "you can't let that slide. If he forgot—because, hello, murder investigation—then he could probably use some decent coffee and a break. If he stood you up, it wouldn't hurt for him to know that's not cool. Maybe he'll grovel at your feet and offer to take you to dinner." She shrugged one shoulder, a naughty smile forming on her face.

I chuckled and took the coffee. "I doubt that will happen, but it will at least let him know I'm not a pushover."

Mina laughed. "I think he knows that already."

Grinning, I stood. "Probably." I slung my purse over my shoulder, then picked up my coffee. "Thanks, Mina. I needed the kick in the pants."

She cocked out a hip, resting a hand on it as she smiled. "I know. Someone has to make sure you two don't screw this up."

Huffing a short laugh, I headed for the door—crutch-free now. My leg still ached, but it was bearable, and I was tired of only having one hand free. "Like you're one to talk. How's Ivan?" Mina's last relationship with Ivan Milanovich ended with a soft fizzle several months ago. They both led busy lives, and Mina said they didn't have enough chemistry to want to make time for each other.

Mina narrowed her eyes at me, but there was no malice in her expression. Only amusement. "I'm content being single."

"Who says I'm not?" I tossed her a look as I put my shoulder into the door.

"Me. The pinch to your expression as you spent the last half an hour staring out the window, waiting on Oscar, spoke volumes," she retorted.

I scowled, unaware I'd been so transparent. "I need to work on my poker face."

Mina chuckled. "You do that." She flapped a hand in farewell as I stepped out the door. "Call me later with all the details."

With a wave of my own, I hurried off to my car. Hopefully, the details would be good ones.

It was a quick drive to the Parker's Landing police station. I could only hope he was there. It was Saturday. If not, I might go full stalker mode and try to find his house. I knew he lived in my neighborhood, but not which house. Though I could make an educated guess. There were only a couple that had been up for sale recently. Sometimes, being a real estate agent came in handy.

Turning into the visitor section of the department's lot, I breathed a sigh of relief as I spotted Oscar's truck—both his personal one and the patrol truck he'd driven to meet me Thursday night—in the employee lot beyond the automated barrier. He was here.

I parked near the sidewalk and got out. Salt crunched under my feet as I limped up the concrete path to the door. Someone had shoveled it and laid down salt.

Tucking one coffee cup between my arm and my chest, I tugged on the door and let myself in. The same officer who'd been there the last time I came in looked up.

"Good morning, Ms. Holmes. How can I help you?"

"Is Detective Quartermaine here?"

"He is. I take it he's not expecting you?"

"Not exactly."

The man smiled and picked up the phone. "Let me see if he's free."

I nodded. "Thank you."

After a short pause, the officer spoke into the receiver. "Detective, Claire Holmes is here to see you." A moment later, he pulled the phone away from his ear to look at it with a frown. His brown eyes met mine. "He hung up."

Before I could say anything, a door down the hall opened and Ozzie stepped out, a deep scowl on his handsome face.

Uh-oh. Maybe I really had been stood up.

He crooked a finger.

I glanced at the officer and gave him a wary smile. "Thank you."

The man raised an eyebrow, looking at Ozzie's dark expression, then at me. "Good luck, ma'am."

Filling my lungs, I raised my chin. Ozzie would not intimidate me.

With determined strides, even if they were uneven, I walked toward him. My two different boots made soft thuds on the tile floor, and I wished I'd worn a low heel on my good foot. The sound would add an air of confidence.

Stopping a little over a foot away, I held out the coffee. "Good morning."

His dark eyes held mine for several heartbeats before he reached out and took the drink. With a quick tip of his head, he motioned me into his office.

Not missing a beat, I walked in, head held high. He followed me in and closed the door as I turned to look at him.

Dark gaze fixed on me, he moved around the desk to his chair. "Why are you here, Claire?"

"We had a date, remember?" I knew I was pushing it, calling it a date. Especially when he hadn't even agreed to meet me. He hadn't disagreed, either, though.

One perfect black eyebrow shot up. "A date, huh?"

I walked around and perched on the corner of his desk. "That's probably what it should be, don't you think? After Thursday evening?"

He sat back with a sigh and pinched the bridge of his nose. "Claire, I don't really have time to discuss this. I have—"

"A murder to solve." I waved a hand as I cut him off. "I know. And I'm not asking you to forget about your case. Just take a break."

He lifted the coffee and took a sip. "Seems I don't have a choice."

I rolled my eyes. "Stop with the passive-aggressive stuff. If you don't want me here, just say so." My heart lodged in my throat, but I was proud of myself. The words had come out with confidence.

Ozzie blew out a quick breath and sat up. "It's not that." He ran a hand through his hair. "Dammit, Claire. It's… complicated."

"It's really not, Ozzie," I said quietly. "I think I've made it pretty clear how I feel. What I want. The whole reason I asked to meet you for coffee this morning was so we could discuss whether to move forward with this." I wagged a finger between us.

"I realize that. It's just not that simple. I…" He trailed off, looking away for several moments, deep in thought. When his gaze met mine again, the guard he'd thrown up when I arrived was down.

"You know I'm attracted to you. I can't deny that, and I don't want to. But until this case is solved, we can't do anything about it."

I raised my cup, taking a drink to hide the disappointment flattening my mouth.

"It's probably best if we don't see each other unless it's for official purposes," he continued.

"And what if you never solve this case?" Because the way things were looking, that was a distinct possibility. He didn't have many leads that I knew of.

"We'll cross that bridge if we get to it."

I hummed, not liking that answer.

Suddenly, he rose, looming over me.

I gripped the desk with my free hand and stared at him with wide eyes.

"Trust me, Claire. This isn't easy for me, either. I've done little but dream every night about what it would be like to finish what we started. But I can't jeopardize my investigation or my career."

He was so close, I could see those gold flecks in his eyes again.

"Think of it this way; I have some powerful motivation to close this case."

A smile toyed with my lips. "I guess so."

His gaze dropped to my mouth. Fire leaped to life in his eyes.

An answering burn ignited in my belly. I understood where he was coming from. It didn't mean I liked it, but I understood it. To me, it wasn't a big deal. I was a minor player in his investigation. But apparently, it was a bigger issue than I thought.

So, I vowed not to push it.

Because, like it or not, if I wanted a relationship with this man and not just a quick roll between the sheets, I had to respect his boundaries.

Even if my body was currently attempting to shove my rational side into the vault again.

Staving off the urge to wrap my arms around his neck and haul him in for a fierce kiss took every degree of willpower I had, though, and kept me rooted to my spot on his desk.

He seemed to be in the same boat. Fire still blazed in his eyes.

"You should get back to work," I said, barely above a whisper.

"I should." He leaned closer, his voice low.

I swallowed, my eyes dropping to his mouth. I thought we weren't doing this. Why were we doing this? "I should go."

"You should."

His warm breath puffed against my lips. It was enough to send prickles over my scalp and racing down my spine. My eyelids fluttered closed.

The warm, firm press of his mouth to mine sent the prickles everywhere. I let go of the desk to clutch the hair at the nape of his neck.

It was a brief kiss, but it packed a punch. After just a couple of seconds, he lifted his head. I opened my eyes to stare into his as my lungs fought for air. He'd sent it all scattering to the wind.

Slowly, he eased back and offered me a hand, helping me off the desk.

"Go home, Claire. Let me do my job." The words were harsh, but his tone wasn't. It pleaded with me to be patient.

I pressed my lips together, tasting him there, and nodded. "Work fast, Detective."

Forcing my legs to function, I spun and hurried out of his office as fast as my broken leg would let me. Another vow echoed through my mind. One to avoid him as much as possible until this case was over. I wasn't sure I could handle walking away again.

CHAPTER 23

Ozzie

The bitter scent of the department's burnt coffee wrinkled my nose as I lifted the black mug with my old unit's logo on it. Stifling a yawn, I couldn't help but wish it was filled with the same brew Claire brought me earlier today. That was long gone, though.

At least this stuff was hot. Cold, burnt coffee was the worst.

"Why are you drinking that swill?"

I turned slightly to see Chief Riggs as he walked into the breakroom, empty coffee mug dangling from his fingers. His face scrunched with disgust as he walked over to the pot and picked up the carafe, dumping the remnants down the drain.

"It was already made, and I needed the jolt."

"Bad enough you can't wait for a new pot to brew?" He raised an eyebrow as he unloaded the old filter and grounds, tossing them into the trash.

Considering I only slept a couple of hours both Thursday and Friday night, and the sleep I did get was fitful and packed with dreams of Claire, no. Waiting wasn't an option if I didn't want to drop where I stood.

In answer, I grunted and took another sip of the dreadful coffee. "Did you see the report on Hammond's car?"

Riggs nodded. "Blood on the driver's seat, but not Marie's."

"Yeah. I went back to the evidence we collected from their house and took their toothbrushes to the lab. Hopefully, one will be a match. Though I'm not sure it'll tell us much except Warren was bleeding. It wasn't enough to indicate he was mortally wounded." The car had been thoroughly cleaned, but the blood had soaked through the seams in the leather and into the padding below.

"No. But maybe he cut himself with the knife he used to stab his wife."

"Or he was stabbed, too, but was able to react and get away before the killer could deliver a fatal blow." I wasn't convinced Warren was innocent, but what Claire said Thursday night stuck with me. Why would he hide his car where it was likely to be found? There were so many places he could have taken it where it would stay hidden for decades.

One of the chief's eyebrows quirked. "True."

The yawn I suppressed earlier threatened again. I tried to hold it back but couldn't this time. The coffee—good or bad—wasn't helping. I needed a nap. That wouldn't happen anytime soon, so I raised my mug and took another drink.

Riggs chuckled, setting his cup on the counter before opening the cupboard to take out the large tub of coffee. "Let me guess. Your lack of sleep has something to do with Claire Holmes?"

Startled, I lowered my mug and frowned. "How did you know?" My eyes widened as I realized how that sounded and what he probably thought. "Nothing's going on. I've been clear with her that nothing can happen."

Opening the coffee canister, Riggs replaced the filter and dumped several scoops into the machine. It was the kind that hooked up to a direct water supply, so he flipped the lid shut and hit start, then turned to me, crossing his arms as he pierced me with a candid look. "Other than finding Mrs. Hammond's body and Mr. Hammond's car, she hasn't actually witnessed anything, correct?"

I frowned, unsure what he was getting at. "No."

"That's what I thought. I double-checked her alibi. She's not a suspect. Not unless she's some master criminal, adept at hiring assassins and hiding her tracks."

My frown deepened, a low-level anger flaring to life in my chest. "You double-checked her alibi? Don't you trust me to do my job?"

Riggs shrugged. "You're new. And I didn't vet you before you showed up; the state did. I know you have a stellar reputation with your previous department. They wouldn't have hired you otherwise. But it's still a new environment. New people and places. New procedures. I wanted to make sure you've settled in all right. So, I confirmed some of the details on the case."

I crossed my arms and glared at my boss. "And have I passed muster?" If he said no, I would be on the phone to my superiors in Anchorage, requesting a transfer to a different detachment as soon as one opened. Working for someone who didn't trust me and didn't think me capable wasn't something I would tolerate.

The chief's lips flattened, and he shot me a "don't be dumb" look. "It never hurts to have extra eyes on a case. And because I've independently confirmed she has an alibi, I can tell you to turn any further formal interaction with her over to me, leaving you free to take her to Parker's Landing's finest dinner establishment tonight."

Confusion replaced some of the anger in my frown. Coffee sputtered from the machine as I stared at him in silence for a long moment. Finally, I found my voice. "What?"

"This case could drag on." He picked up his coffee mug

and turned on the faucet, rinsing it out. "We don't exactly live in a bustling metropolis where the opportunities to meet people are around every corner. She didn't witness anything and will never have to testify. From here on out, tell her to come to me if she uncovers anything about the Hammonds. Though I doubt she will. Not unless Warren Hammond contacts her."

My thoughts went to the other elements of the case that seemingly involved Claire. "What about the break-in at her house? Someone thinks she knows something." That meant she was more than just a minor player.

Riggs shrugged. "Maybe. Or maybe someone's obsessed with her. In that case, I think it would be better if you stuck close, don't you?"

I narrowed my eyes and studied him. "You don't think the break-in was related to the Hammond case?"

"It's coincidental, I know, but sometimes that's all it is. I think it would behoove you to consider all the possibilities. Claire's a beautiful woman, and she spends a lot of time out in the community alone." He dried off his cup, then lifted the carafe, pausing the brew cycle, and filled the mug.

My brows dipped and creases formed on my forehead as I considered what he said. Had I dismissed the break-in, chalking it up as part of my case, too quickly? Could there be someone out there obsessed with Claire, as Chief Riggs said? He was right; I was new here. I didn't know the people or the community. I didn't have my ear to the ground the way I should. Not yet.

The glass carafe clacked on the hot plate as Riggs replaced it. "Think about it. But in any case, all communication about this case with Claire needs to go through me from now on. Whether you're dating or not, she's compromised your objectivity."

My fierce frown returned.

He held up a hand. "I'm not saying that's a bad thing. For

one, it tells me you're human. You're a stellar detective, Oscar, and your record had me wondering what kind of man I was getting. I'm glad to see you have some faults. Though I'm not sure falling for someone like Claire Holmes is a fault." He smiled.

"I haven't fallen for her." My frown let up, but only slightly.

Riggs sipped his coffee, studying me over the rim of the mug for several seconds before he pushed away from the counter. I could tell he didn't believe me. I wasn't sure I believed myself.

"Go home, Detective. Make sure you foster a life outside of this place, yeah?"

I turned, my gaze tracking my boss as he walked toward the door. "What about you? You're still here at this hour on a Saturday. Are you trying to tell me not to turn into you?"

Riggs stopped at the door and smiled broadly, his gray eyes warm. "No. I'm not a workaholic. I just came in to check on things after spending this morning and afternoon with my kids. I've got another hour before dinner at the real, finest dining establishment in Parker's Landing—my wife's kitchen —is ready." With a wink, he pushed through the door and disappeared.

I took another sip of the bitter coffee in my mug as I stared after him. Grimacing, I walked over to the sink and dumped it.

After rinsing the mug, I set it down, then braced my hands on the counter's edge and stared at the wall, considering the chief's words.

He had a point. Claire wouldn't have to testify. She didn't see anything. Only found the body and the car. Others could corroborate her whereabouts for Marie's time of death— though the jury was still out on the car. We didn't know how long it had been in the woods.

But her prints weren't on or in it. Nor had the techs found

any long blonde hairs. She didn't strike me as the type who would know how to scrub any traces of herself from a crime scene. Or as a psychopath. Because it would be that kind of person who would hide a car, then "find" it so they could insert themselves into the investigation.

Besides, she had no motive for the murder.

I really didn't know who did, if not Warren.

Closing my eyes, I ran a hand over my face. My brain was running in circles. And now I got to add in the problem of what to do about Claire.

Riggs had virtually given me his blessing. My reason for keeping her at arm's length was gone.

The one I stated, anyway.

Was I ready for the kind of commitment a woman like Claire required? I was only thirty-one. I had friends who hadn't married until they were nearly forty. I'd always assumed that would be me. My career had come first for over a decade. Relationships had ended because I couldn't ignore work calls. Would Claire understand that sometimes I *had* to go? Up here, especially, it wasn't like there was someone who could fill in for me at the drop of a hat. There wasn't another unit that could take up the slack if I didn't answer.

I straightened and scooped my mug off the counter. Playing "what if" wouldn't answer any of my questions. The only way to know was to ask. And to live it.

Pushing through the breakroom door, I headed for Riggs's office and poked my head inside after a quick knock. "Hey. Other than your wife's kitchen, what's the finest dining establishment in Parker's Landing?"

CHAPTER 24
Claire

Headlights swept through the front window, drawing my attention away from the movie playing on TV. Pebbles stood up from her spot on the blanket in my lap and barked.

I scratched her head. "It's probably just someone turning around. Relax."

But she spun in a circle, barked again, and launched herself off my lap, making a beeline for the front door.

Pausing my movie—I couldn't hear it over her—I put an arm over the back of the couch to turn and watch her while I waited for her to realize it was nothing.

The doorbell pealed.

Okay. Maybe it wasn't nothing.

Frowning, I pushed the blue throw off my lap and got up. Wary of all the craziness lately, I peeked out the front window first.

Ozzie's truck sat in my driveway.

Eyes growing wide, I straightened and looked at the door. What was he doing here?

Pebbles barked again, her little tail wiggling. She spun in a circle, then looked at me and barked.

"I'm coming, crazy girl. Hang on."

One hot pink slipper slapping softly on the floor, I nudged her back as I reached the door. She darted around my foot, nose pressed to the crack.

With a huff I scooped her off the ground. "You're not escaping. Not this time." Throwing the locks, I turned the handle and opened the door.

My heart tripped at the cautious smile on Ozzie's handsome face.

He held up a white plastic bag with the words "Thank You" printed on it in red. "I brought dinner. Can I come in?"

Dinner? After we agreed it was best to keep things on a professional level?

I cocked my head. "Why?"

He lowered the bag. "I talked to Chief Riggs. Or I should say, he talked to me. It was… enlightening."

A spark of hope lit in my chest. "Really?"

"Really." A slow, sexy smile spread over his face. "So, are you gonna let me in?"

My feet moved back without my permission, leaving enough space for him to enter. I guess I was.

"Thanks." He stopped in front of me, just inches separating us.

I tipped my head back so I could see his face. A quick shiver of excitement raced through my veins, leaving me buzzing with anticipation. Once again, I marveled at how good it felt to have a man be so much taller than me. With his boots on, he topped out at close to six-foot-four. I was in my slippers and felt every inch of the six-inch height difference.

It was glorious.

"I hope you're hungry."

He meant the food, but the heat in his eyes as he stood so close added another meaning. One my body caught onto without missing a beat.

"What did you bring?" I forced myself to ask, instead of

hopping up with my good foot to wrap my legs around him and fuse our mouths together. But I set Pebbles on the floor, so I'd be ready to do just that if the opportunity presented itself.

"Crab legs. From Kellerman's." His brow wrinkled. "You're not allergic to shellfish, are you? That would be unfortunate, living up here."

A smile crossed my face, the concern he showed only endearing him to me more. "No. I like crab legs." I swayed closer, unable to stop myself. If he didn't kiss me soon—even just as a hello—I'd do it for him.

"I'm glad." He shifted nearer, his head lowering. "Do you think they'll keep?"

The meaning of his whispered words registered a moment before his lips landed on mine.

With a soft thump and a rustle, the bag hit the floor. My feet left the wooden planks as Ozzie banded strong arms around my hips and lifted me against him.

All rationality fled. Even that part of me who protested so much just the other day knew this was an amazing idea.

But she had one last thing to say before she retreated, and that was to put away the food.

I wrenched my mouth away. "Grab that bag."

The cutest look of confusion crossed his face before he remembered the food he'd brought. It did my ego good to know I could make a man forget everything with just a kiss.

"Right." He lowered me to the floor, sliding me down his tall frame.

My thoughts scattered with the friction. That needed to happen when we were naked.

Leaning to the side, he shooed Pebbles away from the bag and hooked the handles, then straightened. "Lead the way."

Swallowing hard, I tamped down the urge to forget all about preserving our dinner and spun around. I drew in a breath through my nose and told my body to cool it. It would get what it wanted, but it needed to have a little patience.

Ozzie followed me into the kitchen. So did Pebbles, her tiny claws tapping softly on the wooden floor. Silently, I opened the refrigerator door. He set the bag inside.

The door handle was barely out of my hand as I closed it when he scooped me up again.

"Where were we?" His mouth hovered millimeters from mine, his warm breath puffing over my face.

In answer, I kissed him.

He backed me into the counter, his hands roving down my sides and back up, caressing me through my sweater, which just wouldn't do. I needed his hands on my skin.

Grasping the hem of my top, I pulled it up and over my head, only breaking our kiss for an instant. Those long, strong fingers wrapped around my ribcage as I dropped my shirt to the floor.

Pebbles barked, but I ignored her. She'd get tired of being ignored and go settle on her bed, eventually.

My hands went to Ozzie's chest. I tugged the zipper down on his coat and pushed it off his shoulders. It landed in a heap behind him as I spread my fingers over the soft green and black flannel covering his muscular torso.

Starting at his neck, I pushed buttons through their holes, somehow maintaining the dexterity in my hands as his mouth and wicked tongue tantalized me.

His shirt followed his coat to the floor.

But I still wasn't at bare skin. He wore a plain, gray t-shirt underneath.

I tunneled my hands beneath the fabric, glorying in the contact. Smooth skin, dusted with crisp hair met my fingers. Muscles jumped beneath my touch.

A soft groan left him. He pulled back and yanked his shirt over his head.

Rather than kiss me again, though, he hooked his fingers in the waistband of my leggings and peeled them down my legs. My underwear tried to go with them, so I helped them out and pushed them down. They dropped on top of the gathered fabric around my calves and the top of my orthotic boot.

Crouched in front of me, Ozzie splayed his hands over my hipbones. His thumbs ghosted over the apex of my thighs.

A wave of heat washed over me from head to toe. My head fell back as I let out a mewling cry. How did that feel so good? He'd barely touched me.

The pressure increased as he dipped his thumbs into the vee. Moisture flooded my core, and my breath came out on a short pant.

A warm puff of air was my only warning before his tongue darted out to taste me.

"Oh!" With fumbling hands, I gripped the counter as my knees sagged. I tried to spread my feet to give him better access, but my leggings held my ankles together, effectively trapping me where I was.

I eased back and lifted my good leg, trying to free myself.

Ozzie pressed closer, still teasing my center with his mouth. One hand slipped over the inside of my thigh and down my leg. He grabbed a handful of material and pulled, freeing my foot.

But that didn't mean he gave me control of it. Instead, he lifted my leg, putting it over his shoulder. With his mouth still laving attention on my lady bits, the hand that freed my foot traveled back up my leg to slide over my belly and grasp my breast. When he swirled his hand over my nipple and then gave it a quick pinch, my body erupted.

With a sharp cry, I flew apart, sagging against the cool countertop behind me.

While the echoes of pleasure still moved through me, he

stood, leaning over me. "We're not making it to the bedroom. Not until later."

Two fingers took over for that wicked, wicked mouth, robbing me of breath.

"Much, much later," he said, his voice low and gravely as he buried his face in the crook of my neck.

I gripped his shoulders. "That's fine." Dear *Lord*, was that high-pitched squeak my voice?

The fingers swirling over my center delved inside my channel and any ability I had to speak fled along with the rest of the air in my lungs.

My eyelids slid shut, and I just let myself feel. Those long fingers continued to create a lovely friction, driving me wild with a slow, steady pace.

It was both torture and the best thing I'd ever felt in my life. No one had ever come close to making me feel the way Ozzie did. And certainly not before we'd ever even done the deed.

Vaguely, the quiet rasp of a zipper and the rustling of denim made it through the fog of lust clouding my mind. Silken steel replaced his fingers, just teasing at my entrance.

Yes!

Another wave of moisture flooded my core, anticipating what was to come.

His wallet landed next to my arm. I opened my eyes, bringing my hands up to clutch the sides of his head. I was glad he could still think straight. If I'd been in charge, I'd already be riding him, damn the consequences.

With deft fingers, he plucked the condom from inside. A moment and a wrapper crinkle later, he wrapped his hands around my waist and lifted me onto the edge of the counter.

One hand came up and gripped my chin, bringing my eyes to his.

How eyes that were nearly black could burn, I didn't

know. But Ozzie's did exactly that. The little flecks of gold shone bright with an inner fire.

With a slow roll of his hips, our eyes still locked together, he fused our bodies.

CHAPTER 25

Ozzie

I really thought we'd eat before anything happened.

But I couldn't complain about eating cold crab in my boxer-briefs while sitting on our pile of clothes on Claire's kitchen floor.

This was hands down the best date I'd ever had.

And not just because of the sex.

There was a comfort level with her I'd never experienced before. None of my previous girlfriends were ever comfortable being this uninhibited and content before or after lovemaking. Outwardly, Claire fit the type of woman I went for.

Professional and career minded. Friendly. Smart.

Blonde.

But underneath the veneer of makeup and clothes was a woman who did everything with her soul. It ruled her actions and emotions, making her more… *real* than any other woman I'd ever met.

Honestly, I shouldn't be surprised by our current circumstances. The Claire who had hopped on an ATV and led me to a potentially dangerous encounter with a likely murderer was most definitely the kind of woman to have sex in a kitchen and then eat crab while sitting on the floor in little more than her underwear.

My gaze traveled over the slice of her collarbone exposed by the gaping neckline of my flannel shirt.

She'd slipped it on, along with her underwear, not long ago. With our bodies sated and limp, we'd spent a decent bit of time cuddled together on the floor before her grumbling stomach forced us to take action.

I'd watched—hungry for more than just crab—as she got up, divesting herself of her boot long enough to take off her leggings and then pull up her panties and put on my shirt. Once she was put together, she grabbed a roll of paper towels and the bag of crab from the fridge.

I hadn't bothered with my pants or my t-shirt. Our love-making left me warm, so I'd covered up out of decency, using the rest of my clothes and hers to keep us off the kitchen tile.

The boxer-briefs also kept me a little safer from Pebbles and her tiny claws. The dog had left at some point while Claire and I made love, but once we pulled out the food, she'd come running back. All it had taken was for her to scramble onto my abdomen, eager to get to her mistress, for me to pick up my underwear and slide them on.

Now she nibbled on pieces of crab Claire tore off and put on a napkin for her.

I wiped my fingers on some toweling, then wadded it up and stuffed it into the empty bag. "I'm full. That was good." Even cold, the crab was juicy and full of flavor. Riggs was right. I doubted any place could top it.

Claire sucked the last piece of meat out of her crab leg and set the shell in the to-go box, humming her agreement.

Once again, the skin exposed at her neck caught my attention. I leaned in and nuzzled the spot with my nose. She smelled so good. Like flowers and her own heady scent mixed in. "What do you think we should do the rest of the evening?"

Her low chuckle brought an answering smile to my mouth. She knew what I was thinking. I'd bet everything I owned it was the same thing she was.

Sucking butter off her fingers, she tipped her head, giving me better access.

"Maybe we'll make it to the bedroom this time," I said against her skin.

Her soft, low chuckle sent a zing through my veins. "My back would thank you."

"So would my knees." Easing away, I met her gaze with a broad smile. Shifting, I moved to get up. "Come on." I offered her a hand.

As we rose, the musical trill of a phone filtered in from the living room.

"That's my cell." Claire frowned, looking toward the sound.

"Ignore it." I gathered her close, not wanting anything to intrude on our evening. The world could wait.

I planted my lips along her jaw, working my way down the long line of her neck.

The phone quit ringing.

She relaxed into me.

The trill started again, and she stiffened, pushing at my shoulders.

With a sigh, I let her go. Back-to-back calls likely meant it was important.

"I'll try to be quick." With an apologetic look, she hurried out of the kitchen as fast as her booted foot would let her. The ringing stopped, but I didn't hear her answer. A moment later, my phone rang from the cargo pocket of my pants.

A shiver of trepidation skated over my nerve endings. What were the odds?

It took me a moment to find the right pocket, but I got to the phone before it quit ringing.

"Chief Riggs" appeared on the screen when I lifted it.

Now I was even more concerned.

I slid my thumb over the screen. "Quartermaine."

"Are you with Claire?" His voice held no censure, just concern.

"Yes." My forehead wrinkled. "Why?"

"Her real estate office is on fire."

The breath stalled in my lungs.

"I'm standing outside it now. When the call came through dispatch, the fire was flagged as suspicious, so they called me. One of her employees, Savannah Smith, is the one who called it in. She saw someone driving away, she said."

"Ozzie!"

Claire's voice carried through from the living room. The offbeat slap-thump of her feet on the hard floor soon followed. A couple seconds later, she appeared in the kitchen doorway, phone to her ear.

"We'll be right there," I told Riggs, then hung up. "Is that Savannah?" I nodded to the phone in her hand.

"Yes."

"Tell her we're on our way." I set my phone on the counter, then shook out my pants. Standing on one foot, I shoved my other one into the pant leg.

She relayed the message, then ended the call.

Her phone hit the countertop with a clatter as she hurried around to pick up her own clothes from the floor.

My shirt came sailing over her head as she whipped it off.

Mouth going slack, my brain hiccupped, and I could do nothing but stare for several beats.

The flannel smacked me in the chest, spurring me back into motion. Setting the shirt down, I turned away, removing the tempting sight from my field of vision. I needed a clear head so I could think.

If the fire at her office was indeed suspicious, it made me wonder why someone would torch it. What did she have there—or what did someone think she had there—that would warrant that kind of action?

"Did the Hammonds give you any documents pertaining to their property?" I glanced back.

Static made her blonde hair stick out as she poked her head through the neck of her sweater. "Only the standard stuff. Why?"

I slipped into my t-shirt, then picked up my flannel from the counter. "Just trying to puzzle out why someone would want to burn down your office."

She stilled. "What did you say?"

I frowned at her, pausing in the process of shrugging into my flannel. "What do you mean? You said you were talking to Savannah."

"I was. She said the office was on fire, not that someone did it on purpose!"

"Riggs said she told dispatch she saw someone fleeing the scene."

Her blue eyes went wide. "Oh my God," she breathed. She sank to the floor and tore at the Velcro strips holding her boot in place. It needed to come off so she could put her leggings on.

I buttoned up my shirt and squatted to help her.

Pebbles ran around us, barking. I couldn't blame her. She sensed something was wrong.

Together, Claire and I got her leggings on and the boot refastened.

Rising, I held out a hand, helping her to her feet, then grabbed my coat from the floor.

"We can take my truck," I said as she plucked her coat off the hook by the garage door. "I'm parked behind your garage, so I'd have to move, anyway."

"Okay." She shoved her arms into the coat sleeves, then bent down to scoop up a still barking Pebbles. "Let's go."

I frowned. "You want to take the dog?"

She turned a determined look on me. "Someone's lured her out of the yard, broken into my house, and now burned my office down. Yes."

When she put it like that… listing things off really made it hit home that whether this was about Marie Hammond's death or not, someone had it out for Claire.

"All right." I put a hand on her back and ushered her toward the front door.

Running as best she could, Claire led the way outside to the truck. The lights flashed as I unlocked it. In less than thirty seconds, we were pulling away from the house.

Pebbles stood on Claire's lap, front paws on the dash, her little tail wagging furiously. If it weren't for the seriousness of the situation weighing on me, I'd laugh at her antics. The tiny dog had grown on me. It helped that she tolerated me now. Ever since I rescued her from the cold, she'd decided I wasn't as bad as she first thought.

After several minutes and a few rolling stops, we made it to Claire's office. The fire was out, but smoke still billowed from the structure. We hadn't missed the flames by much.

Parking behind a firetruck, I got out and hurried around to help Claire down. Once she had both feet firmly on the ground and Pebbles tucked under her arm, I glanced around, looking for Riggs. He stood near the second fire engine, deep in conversation with one of the firefighters.

I took Claire's free hand, pointing with my other. "Riggs."

She nodded, and we headed that way.

On the way, we passed an ambulance. Claire came to an abrupt halt.

I glanced back with a frown. She stared at the window. "Claire?"

Disentangling our hands, she walked up to it and opened the back door. "Savannah?"

"Claire!" a woman on the stretcher cried out. Almost

immediately, she started hacking behind the oxygen mask on her face.

The paramedic with her adjusted the mask, then turned a disapproving frown on us. A touch of it smoothed out as recognition dawned on his face. "Claire, now's not the best time."

"Stuff it, Jedidiah. She's my friend." Claire stepped into the ambulance. Pebbles barked and wagged her tail, recognizing Savannah.

I moved in behind Claire and introduced myself. "I'm Detective Quartermaine." My gaze went to Savannah's soot-streaked face. "Are you all right?"

She coughed again but nodded.

"Smoke inhalation," the paramedic said, still frowning. He pushed a button on the monitor by Savannah's head, and the cuff on her arm began to inflate. "She really shouldn't talk much."

Savannah rolled her head to the side to look at him, then turned back to us. "Black—" she coughed, waving a hand. "Black SUV. A woman."

My brows knit together. "A woman? You're sure?" I had chased a man away from Claire's house after the break-in.

At least, I was pretty sure it was a man.

My frown deepened as I thought about the foot chase into the woods. The person had been tall and wearing men's clothes. It had looked like a man, but I hadn't actually seen his face. I supposed it was possible it was a woman hiding under the hoodie and jeans.

But that just didn't feel right. I'd been so sure it was a guy.

"Did you recognize her?" I asked.

Savannah shook her head. "Only saw… hair," she said between slight coughs.

"Hair? Long hair?" I asked.

Again, she nodded. "Brown."

"What were you doing here?" Claire asked. "It's Saturday. And it's late."

"Showing. I had… paperwork, and I needed the home… info." Her soft coughs punctuated her words until she finally broke into another round of deep hacking.

"That's enough questions for now." Jedidiah wrote down the blood pressure reading on the monitor and speared us with a look that clearly said we should leave.

I nodded to him, recognizing Savannah's rough shape. "Are you taking her to Juneau?"

The man nodded.

"All right, thanks." I took Claire's hand, tugging her back to the ground. "Let's go talk to Riggs."

She spared me a quick look as we stepped out, then turned to Savannah. "I'll call your parents. If you need anything else, please don't hesitate to contact me."

Savannah offered her a weak smile. "Thanks," she rasped.

Claire gave a final wave as I shut the ambulance door.

Her face crumpled as the panel shut, and she sniffed, blotting at her eyes with her sleeve. "She looked terrible."

I agreed. "She's in good hands. Come on." I squeezed her hand and took a step away from the ambulance.

This time, she followed me.

"Riggs!"

The chief looked up as I called his name. He motioned us over.

I helped Claire navigate the firehoses littering the ground on our way to him.

"We saw Savannah Smith just now." I tipped my head toward the ambulance. "She said she saw a dark-haired woman get into a black SUV."

"That's what she told me too." Riggs turned to Claire. "Ms. Holmes, do you have any surveillance cameras? Perhaps some that back up to a cloud server?"

"I have a Ring camera on the back door. It's hard to hear when the delivery guys knock, so that was my solution."

I glanced at the building. The rear of it faced the street behind. She had entrances to her parking lot on the side and the rear, since it was on the corner. Most of the parking was on the side or on the street in front.

"Did Savannah tell you where she saw the car?" I asked Riggs.

"No. I got about as much as you did. She couldn't talk much without coughing. Maybe once she's been treated for her smoke inhalation, she'll be able to talk better, and we can get a few more details."

Propping my hands on my hips as I continued to study the area, I made a soft, non-committal grunt, then looked at Claire. "Can you access the Ring footage from your phone?"

"Yes." She shifted Pebbles, then held her out to me. "Here. Hold her for a minute."

I took the little dog, cuddling her to my chest. She licked my chin.

Claire dug into her bag for her phone and came up with it a few seconds later. After a couple of clicks, she had the app open and the footage pulled up.

"May I?" Riggs held out a hand.

"Of course. You'll know better than me what's suspicious." She passed him the phone, then shuffled closer so she could see the screen.

I did the same on his other side.

"Bateman?" Riggs glanced over his shoulder at the fireman supervising the fire scene.

"Yeah?"

"What time did the fire start?"

"Call came in at twenty-sixteen."

Riggs's head bobbed, and he returned his attention to Claire's phone, rewinding to about eight o'clock.

Fast-forwarding in increments, we watched until a hooded figure appeared.

"Is that a gas can?" Claire pointed at the screen. The person held a rectangular object with a spout in their left hand.

"Looks like it," Riggs said. "Might be diesel or kerosene, though. Can't tell the can color."

Silently, we watched the figure pour a liquid from the can along the back wall of the building, then disappear out of view. For several minutes, there was nothing else, then smoke drifted into the picture. Moments later, flames erupted.

Banging and a woman's screams came from inside the building.

Claire gasped and covered her mouth.

The back door rattled, and the screams and bangs were closer now, but soon faded. Moments later, glass shattered.

"That's Ms. Smith climbing through the front window. She smashed it with a chair from the reception area. She managed to tell me she couldn't find the door locks in all the smoke and that the front door was too hot for her to open. That's when she saw the car driving away too—when she came through the window to get out."

"God." Claire closed her eyes, distress etched into every line of her face.

I gave a soft head shake. Savannah Smith was lucky to be alive.

"Do we think the perpetrator knew she was in the building?"

"I'd say it's a distinct possibility." Riggs paused the video. "Her car is in the lot. She had the lights on inside."

"Maybe—" Claire spoke up, but paused, swallowing hard. "Maybe they thought it was me there. People know I own the business because my name is on it, but they might not know what kind of car I drive. Or that I have other realtors on my team. We live in a small town, but it's not that small. It could be they saw the car and thought I was working late."

Riggs and I shared a glance. I could tell he thought the same thing: she could be on to something.

"Ms. Holmes, can I send this footage to myself?" Riggs pointed at the phone.

"Of course."

"Great. Once I do that, Quartermaine, I want you to take her home. You are officially off the Hammond murder and—"

"What?" My spine straightened and my eyebrows slammed down. "Why? You—"

Riggs held up a hand. "Whoa, whoa, whoa. Hold on. You didn't let me finish."

Fuming, I clamped my teeth together and motioned for him to continue.

"Ms. Holmes is obviously a target. If what happened tonight is a case of mistaken identity, she needs full-time protection. You are the obvious choice since the two of you have a relationship. I'm assuming, anyway." He raised an eyebrow.

I nodded an affirmative.

"You can stay with her, keep an eye out, and I'll take over the murder, and now arson, investigation. Because you can't touch that scene"—he jabbed a finger at the smoldering building—"with a ten-foot pole. Any judge worth their salt would be all over us for conflict of interest."

I looked away, chewing on the inside of my cheek as I considered his words.

Claire moaned. "But why is someone targeting me? I don't know anything!"

"It doesn't matter," Riggs said. "Someone thinks you do. Was everything about the Hammonds' real estate transactions in your office?"

"Yes."

"You're sure?" I asked. "You don't have any notes at home or pictures?"

"No—wait." A small frown wrinkled her forehead, then her eyes rounded. "The staging photos."

"Staging photos?" It was Riggs's turn to frown.

A light bulb went off in my head, but before I could speak, Claire continued.

She nodded. "The house needed staging. Normally, Lynne meets me, and we go through the house together. She makes notes and comes up with a plan. Sometimes she takes pictures, but most of the time it's just notes. For their house, she couldn't meet me, so I took a bunch of pictures and gave them to her so she could figure out what furniture and décor she needed. The Hammonds were adamant the house go on the market as quickly as possible. It was the fastest solution."

I shared a look with Riggs. "I looked through them earlier this week. I didn't see anything out of the ordinary, but I can check them again." Someone thought she had information. Whatever the killer was looking for could be in those images. She took them Friday. Mrs. Hammond died Monday morning.

He nodded. "Send them to me too. The more eyes, the better."

"I will. I think there's something else we need to consider, though." I shifted, my gaze scanning the still smoldering ruins of Claire's office.

Riggs sent me a curious frown. "What's that?"

"Who knew she took pictures?" I wagged a finger at her.

Understanding lit the chief's face. "That's a good point. Who did you tell about that, Ms. Holmes?"

"Oh, gosh." She tipped her head back, thinking. "My staff knew. Lynne's staff. The Hammonds. My friend, Mina, because I tell her everything." She turned her attention to me again. "Some of my competitors might wonder if I took pictures, but they wouldn't know for sure. That's about it.

You." She lifted a hand gesturing to me. "We talked about it the day I found Marie. On the porch? And you've seen the photos."

I nodded, remembering when she first mentioned them, and turned to Riggs. "That narrows things down some."

"Possibly. It gives us a place to start, at least. And some different theories. But someone still could have seen her there Friday but not known who she was until after the murder, then just assumed she took pictures. Or we could be entirely off base and there's something else they think she has."

That was true, but it didn't feel likely. I wouldn't discount the idea—that would be idiotic. But I couldn't chase down a ghost. I could, however, chase down Claire and Lynne's employees.

"If your theory is correct, though"—Riggs waved a finger—"we can take Warren off the suspect list."

"Why?" Claire asked. "Wouldn't it put him higher on the list? He's one of the few people who knows I took pictures."

I knew what Riggs was thinking, so I answered. "He knew what you were doing *before* you took the pictures. If there was something in the house he didn't want you to see or didn't want to get inadvertently photographed, he'd have removed it before you showed up."

"Oh." A crease formed between her eyebrows, then smoothed out. "That makes sense."

"But he's not off the list. Not until we can prove there's something in those pictures that someone would want to kill over." I looked at Riggs as I spoke.

He nodded once. "We'll go over them with a fine-toothed comb."

CHAPTER 26

Ozzie

Metal scraped metal as I inserted the key into the Hammonds' front door. Dropping it back into its evidence bag, I pocketed the plastic bag, then removed the crime scene tape from the door and pushed it open. From my other pocket, I produced a pair of paper booties and stepped onto the disposable pad just inside the door and slipped them over my shoes.

Reaching for the light switch, I flipped it up and light flooded the room.

I squinted against the glare and resisted the urge to rub my gritty eyes. I needed several hours of uninterrupted sleep, but I needed answers more. I knew if I tried to go home or even back to Claire's to sleep, I would just lie awake and wonder what, if anything, was missing from the house. So, here I was at almost one a.m., a phone full of photographs in hand. Riggs might have pulled me off the murder case, but checking photos wasn't a conflict of interest. I could have easily gone to the station and compared Claire's listing pictures with the ones the crime scene team took, but I figured I'd see more if I went to the house and compared things. The house hadn't been touched since the pictures were taken, so I could confirm anything I found with the photos in the case file.

Relocking the door behind me—I didn't want any surprises—I took out my phone and pulled up the folder I downloaded earlier.

When Claire sent me them earlier in the week, she kept them in the order she took them, which started with the outside of the house. I bypassed those—it was too dark to see anything amiss outside—and found the first few of the interior. I would just follow her path through the house.

Zooming in and out, I went through the living room, kitchen, and the couple other rooms downstairs, as well as the garage. Nothing looked different. Not that I expected it to. Whatever it was, I figured it was in Warren's home office or the bedroom. Someplace out of sight of anyone who just happened by.

Systematically, I went through the spare bedrooms. They were bare. In both the photographs and now. Just to be sure, I checked the edges of the carpet all the way around the perimeter of the rooms, but it was tight to the walls.

Warren's office and the master suite were last at the end of the upstairs hallway.

Finding the series of pictures of the office, I stepped inside. The space was neat and tidy. Everything had a home, and it all looked the same as the pictures. I checked out the books on the shelves and picked up all the little statuettes and other small décor pieces Warren had, but there were no hidden items anywhere.

That just left the master.

There had to be something there. This theory made sense. It fit with everything that had happened in the last week and a half.

With determined strides, I left the office and walked the few feet to the master bedroom. Flipping on the light, I took a quick initial stock of the room. A sharp metallic smell filled the air, courtesy of the blood stain on the wooden subfloor. Forensics had removed the carpet and padding beneath Marie's body, both to check for the presence of someone else's blood and for trace evidence.

With a picture of what the room currently looked like fresh in my mind, I took a look at the images Claire captured.

Nothing struck me as different.

I zoomed in on the dresser, looking at the handful of items on top, then both nightstands.

Absolutely nothing.

Clenching my teeth and trying not to swear a blue streak, I entered the walk-in closet. Piece by piece, I went through the clothes and paid particular attention to the safe.

Everything matched Claire's pictures.

Now, only the master bath remained. I held on to the sliver of hope I still had left, but it was dangling by a frayed rope.

Walking in, I ran a quick glance over the room. The counters were clean. Only the soap dispensers beside each sink and a small vase with a single-stem fake flower between them decorated the space. A set of pristine gray towels hung from the towel bar by the shower. They matched the gray bathmat. In the corner, stood a wicker hamper with the lid closed.

The last thread of the rope snapped, letting my hope flutter away.

This should be easy to compare.

I scrolled to the images of the bathroom, noting the same barren counters, the same gray towels and bathmat, and the same hamper, the lid—

Wait…

My heart leapt into my throat. The lid in the picture was closed, but there was something on top.

Gaze darting to the hamper, then back to the image on my phone, I zoomed in.

It looked like a sweatshirt.

Gray in color, it sat in a heap atop the hamper lid.

I zoomed in further. There was something on it; a logo of some sort. It looked a bit like the state flag, but I couldn't tell for sure. There wasn't enough of it visible.

Something niggled in the back of my mind.

It looked familiar. Not just because it looked like the state flag. I'd seen it before, but I couldn't remember where.

Lowering the phone, I looked at the hamper again.

It definitely wasn't there.

Maybe it was inside? Claire could have moved it. Or the forensics team, though I doubted that. They'd have made a note of it and I didn't recall seeing anything about them moving clothing.

But I still walked over to the hamper and lifted the lid to look inside.

It was empty.

I let the lid fall back into place.

So, where was the sweatshirt? Whose was it? And what was the logo on the front?

Excitement built in my veins. Did the shirt belong to Marie Hammond's killer? Or maybe he or she used it to wipe their hands or hide the murder weapon and took it with them.

Another possibility struck me. It could belong to one of the Hammonds and Marie or Warren moved it before the murder.

I spun on my heel and retraced my steps to the bedroom and went straight into the closet. Meticulously, I went through every item of clothing again. When the closet yielded nothing, I checked the dresser.

Nothing.

That hope I lost floated back into the room.

Lashing onto it with a stronger rope, I left the master suite and rechecked all the rooms upstairs.

Not finding the shirt, I descended the steps, heading for the laundry room.

Both the washer and dryer were empty.

That hope got a little stronger.

I went through the rest of the downstairs, even checking the garage again, but there was no sign of the shirt.

Was it Warren's? Did he take it with him when he fled the house?

Had he even been here after Marie's murder? I didn't have any evidence he was at the house after he said he left for Boston.

But if it wasn't his, whose was it?

CHAPTER 27

Claire

Bleary-eyed and with Pebbles tucked under my arm, I entered the kitchen, rubbing at my eyes as I turned on the lights.

Coffee. I needed coffee.

I'd lain awake for several hours, hoping Ozzie would come back after he finished at work, even though he told me he would probably just go home so he didn't disturb my sleep.

It wasn't like I hadn't tried to go to sleep without him. The hope rattling around my brain was a giddy annoyance I hadn't been able to silence easily. Finally, around three, I'd fallen into a fitful sleep plagued with decadent dreams about Ozzie and all the wicked things we'd done just hours before.

My gaze stopped on the island in front of the fridge.

The scene from last night unfolded in my mind, heating my blood.

I drew in a deep, cleansing breath and forced myself to look away. Spending the day in a perpetual state of arousal wouldn't do me any good. While it wasn't technically a workday, I did have things to do.

Like file a claim with my insurance company. And call all my clients.

Hence the reason I was awake at seven a.m. after only sleeping for a few hours.

Thank goodness I kept online records. I would lose some days just dealing with the fallout, but business wouldn't suffer too much. I could work from home or Mina's shop.

Yawning, I set Pebbles on the floor and made my way to the coffeepot. Today, I added a pod to the single-cup brewer side of the machine and pressed start. Once I had a cup of the gods' nectar in me, I would take a quick shower then get online and start the claims process with my insurance company. I was very glad they offered that option. Eventually, I knew I would have to talk to a real person on the phone, but I wasn't ready for that. Just thinking about what happened made me tear up.

After that, I would start contacting clients. I wanted to check on Savannah too. Hopefully, the hospital didn't keep her, but she'd been coughing quite a bit, so I wasn't sure. Smoke inhalation could be nasty.

The coffeemaker sputtered, and the scent of fresh coffee filled the room.

While I waited on the coffee, I put a scoop of food in Pebbles's bowl, to which she turned up her nose and trotted toward the back door.

"You stay in the yard, you little terror." I opened the door, and she dashed out, quickly disappearing into the darkness.

Flipping on the outside light, I stayed by the window and watched. I could just see her at the edge of the light's glow, moving back and forth, looking for the perfect spot to do her business. Finally, she squatted to pee.

Mid tinkle, she barked and took off toward the gate.

Groaning, I opened the door. What was she after now? "Pebbles!"

She ignored me.

I called her name again, but she just stood at the gate, raising hell.

"Definitely looking into obedience classes, you little turd." I put one foot out the door to go get her, but the doorbell pealing stopped me.

Pebbles turned around, running full speed for the back door, still barking.

I let her in, then shut the door before following her to the front of the house.

A quick peek through the windows revealed Ozzie standing on the porch.

My heart stuttered, then launched into double time.

I glanced down at my attire, self-conscious of how I was dressed, then huffed a short laugh. He'd seen me naked. How was my bathrobe and pajamas worse?

Rolling my eyes at myself, I opened the door. "Hey." With a bright smile of welcome, I stepped back to let him in.

He stepped over the threshold, his eyes heating as he took in my robe. A touch of amusement entered his gaze when he spotted my slipper. "I might frame those if you ever decide to throw them away."

I raised the hem of my robe admiring the pink shoe on my foot. "Best nineteen-ninety-five I ever spent."

Chuckling, he moved closer, wrapping an arm around my waist before leaning down to kiss me soundly.

My blood immediately heated, wanting more, but he pulled back, letting me go. "Sorry I didn't come back last night. Things got busy."

"I figured. It was a long shot, anyway. You already said you didn't want to disturb me."

He hummed, trailing behind me when I turned to head for the kitchen. "Doesn't mean I wasn't tempted. You wearing anything under that robe?"

I glanced over my shoulder to see him staring at my butt

as I walked. A devilish smile lit my face. "Be good and you might find out."

His dark eyes met mine. Need burned in their depths. "Witch."

I let out my best cackle, then laughed for real. "Do you want some coffee?"

"Yes, if you've got enough brewed."

"I used the pod side of the machine today, but it won't take long to make another cup." Reaching the counter, I removed my mug from the tray, then put a clean one in its place and a fresh pod in the machine. In just over a minute, we took our steaming cups to the living room.

Sinking onto the couch, I cuddled up to Ozzie's side. Pebbles jumped up with us, filling in the gap between our thighs.

"So tell me about your night." I lifted my mug to blow across the surface of the steaming brew. "You said it turned busy. Does that mean you found something?"

"It's what I didn't find." He took a sip of his coffee, then set it on the end table.

"Oh?"

"I went through the house picture by picture, comparing everything. Nothing was different. Not until I reached the master bathroom."

A frown knit my eyebrows together. "The master bathroom? You found something out of place in there? How?" There hadn't been much personality to the room. The Hammonds had swept all their toiletries into drawers or taken them with them.

"Do you remember a sweatshirt sitting on top of the hamper?"

My frown deepened as I pictured the room. I'd barely been in there. Just long enough to snap a couple of pictures. But now that he mentioned it, yes. "I do. It looked out of place in the spotless bathroom. Why? Did it have a bloodstain on it or something?" I supposed it was possible the killer had gone in there to clean up after stabbing Marie and brushed up against it.

"No. It's missing."

"Missing?"

He nodded. Absently, his hand covered Pebbles's back and he stroked her fur. "I looked all over the house for it. Even checked the laundry room and the garage. No sign of it. You didn't move it, did you?"

"No. I just took pictures. If it had still been there when we staged, Lynne or one of her staff would have slid it into the hamper, but we didn't get that far that morning." That was strange that it was the only thing missing.

"I don't suppose you took a look at it? It has a logo on the front, but with the way it's lying on the hamper lid, I can't tell what it's for."

"Um..." Biting my lower lip, I closed my eyes, trying to picture it. "It was black with gold letters. And I think, maybe, I saw part of the state flag."

"Yeah. That's the same general impression I got." He blew out a breath and picked up his coffee again.

My face pulled with dismay. "I'm sorry I can't be of more help. I was really only in the bathroom for a few seconds. Just long enough to take the pictures."

"I know. It's fine. I just... I feel like I've seen it." Grimacing, he stared off into space. "I just can't place it."

I raised a hand to my face, chewing on a magenta-colored nail as I thought about the logo. "Is it a police thing? Now that I'm really thinking about it, the side I could see had that swoop to it, like a shield." I drew the shape in the air with one finger.

His frown grew fiercer. "Maybe. I'm not sure." The deep vee between his eyebrows smoothed out as he exhaled. "It'll come to me at some point. Trying to force it, though, will just make it more elusive." He turned his head, those dark eyes meeting my gaze. "Let's talk about something else."

"Okay." I was more than willing to talk about whatever he wanted. Staying right here snuggled against him was fine by me. My to-do list could wait. "What do you want to talk about?"

Fire shot to life in his midnight eyes. "How about what you have on under this robe?"

The arm over my shoulders tightened and his hand slid around the side of my neck and over my collarbone to snake beneath the lapel of my bathrobe. In moments, he reached the top swell of my breast and gooseflesh erupted on my skin.

My gooseflesh got gooseflesh when his delightful mouth pressed against the pulse point on my neck.

The coffee mug wavered in my hand.

He noticed. After setting his down, he removed it from my fingers and placed it next to his on the table. Giving Pebbles a nudge, he shooed her off the couch, then shifted me, pulling me onto his lap. Those delightful lips continued to tease the sensitive skin by my ear.

I clutched silky strands of dark hair between my fingers and let my head fall back, giving him better access.

The belt around my waist loosened. Cooler air slipped inside my robe. I wasn't naked, but I didn't sleep in much, even in the colder months. I had a mountain of blankets on my bed, so I preferred to sleep in a tank top or t-shirt and shorts or thin pants. Last night, I'd been warm thanks to memories of Ozzie, so I put on a tank top and shorts.

Ozzie hummed against my skin. "What will I find?" The sides of my robe parted, then his hand wrapped over my hip beneath the warm fabric. "Hmm… feels like satin. Shame. I was hoping for nothing."

"It comes off quick," I muttered, my voice airy.

I felt him smile against my neck. "Good." With a slow but

deliberate pace, he worked his way along my jaw until his mouth covered mine, stealing my breath.

Distant bells reached my ears.

Ozzie growled, but not in a good way.

He pulled back. "I'm going to throw that thing into the ocean."

My eyelids fluttered open. What? What was he talking about?

Half a second later, I realized the bells weren't bells, but my ringtone. For Mina.

I groaned. "It's Mina. She probably heard about the fire." I pushed him back and swung my legs off his lap. I needed to answer her. She'd never stop calling if I didn't and would in fact show up here if I failed to answer.

Fumbling with my robe, I got the pocket around and shoved my hand inside. With a quick swipe of my finger, I answered it just before it rolled to voicemail. "Mina?"

"Claire! Girl, what happened? All people can talk about this morning is the fire. Are you okay? Is Savannah? I heard she was there. No one can tell me how badly she's hurt, though. I've gotten everything from not a scratch to she got hit with a beam and is in a coma and paralyzed."

Shock rounded my eyes. People had vivid imaginations. "She's fine, as far as I know. Some smoke inhalation." I glanced at Ozzie, hoping he could confirm my words. He still frowned but nodded once. A little of the worry I'd been holding eased.

"I planned to call her in a little while," I continued. "Once it was a more decent hour."

"Sorry." Mina's wince came through in her tone. "I was worried, and this is the first moment I've had to call since we opened."

A soft smile lit my face. "It's okay. I was awake, actually."

"Are you dressed?"

"Not yet. Why?"

"Because you need to get your butt down here so we can have this conversation in person. I want to know everything, but I just had another wave of customers walk in. Put some clothes on and get over here. I'll caffeinate you." She hung up before I could say yes or no.

Offering Ozzie a small smile, I lowered the phone. "Did you hear that?"

He nodded. A wicked smirk hovered on his full lips. He plucked the phone from my fingers and dropped it onto the floor at our feet. "To get dressed you have to get *undressed* first, right?"

An answering smile slipped over my face. I leaned into him, threading my fingers into his hair. "Why, yes. I suppose that's right."

"Well, then, I guess it's a good thing her coffee is made on demand. It won't get cold while she waits."

Any reply I planned to make died in my throat as his mouth covered mine once again.

CHAPTER 28

Ozzie

The desk chair whined, creaking in protest as I leaned back and stretched. My neck and shoulders were stiff after being hunched over the computer screen for the last couple of hours.

They weren't the only parts of my body feeling it, either. I pressed my fingertips to my eyes, hoping to drum up some moisture. Between filling out reports, running searches for my other cases, and the continued search for the logo from the Hammond case, my eyes felt like I'd rubbed them with sandpaper.

Mostly, I felt like a hamster spinning in its wheel.

It had been three days since I discovered the missing sweatshirt, and I still had no clue what the logo was or where the shirt went. Forensics didn't have it. Riggs didn't remember seeing it. Neither did Turner. Lynne Young, Claire's stager, never went upstairs, so she didn't have a clue what I was talking about.

The break I thought I'd gotten with this case had officially hit a dead end.

Heels clacking on the tile floor brought my attention back to my surroundings. I glanced out the door and spotted

Riggs's assistant, Nina, walking past. She stuttered to a halt and reversed direction, poking her head in my door.

"Why are you still here?"

I frowned. "What do you mean?" Lifting my wrist, I checked my watch. "It's only just past five."

"Right, but you were here well before me this morning. And every morning for the last several days."

"Crimes don't solve themselves."

She narrowed her eyes. "Neither do detectives who can't see the forest through the trees because they're burned out."

"I'm fine." Molars clenched, I turned my attention to the computer screen and gave the mouse a shake to locate it.

She snorted. "That's a load of hogwash. Why don't you head out? Take that pretty girlfriend of yours out to dinner. She could probably use the distraction as much as you. Poor thing. What happened to her office is just terrible."

My body stirred at the mention of Claire. I'd spent every night at her place since Sunday. Work wasn't the only reason I was sleep-deprived.

I spared Nina a quick look. "She has to work late." Which was true. She and her staff had rescheduled appointments and showings, extending their hours to keep from losing too much ground. None of them got paid if the business didn't sell properties.

"So get it to go and surprise her with it when she's done."

Giving her another look through my lashes, I tried not to look too intrigued. That wasn't a bad idea. "You have an answer for everything, don't you?"

She grinned. "You're a quick study, Detective Quartermaine. Maybe put those brains to good use and lock down your girl? Claire Holmes is quite the catch." Tapping a hand on the doorframe, she quickly left.

I puffed out my cheeks and leaned forward. The chair creaked again with my weight, but I ignored it and went back to scrolling through the image search I'd run on the logo.

Was she right? Not about Claire being a catch. That I knew. Claire was classy, highly intelligent, beautiful, and successful. Of course she was a catch.

But was Nina right about the need to "woo" her?

It probably wouldn't hurt. It can't always be about sex.

I pressed my mouth into a thin line as the thought floated through my mind. That made sense. In fact, we'd probably done things the wrong way around.

I drummed my fingers on the desk, staring blankly at the computer screen. I definitely didn't want things to be a flash in the pan with Claire. When I moved here, it wasn't my intention to get into a relationship so quickly. But now that she was in my life, I didn't want her to walk away. Chemistry would only carry us so far.

Before I could second-guess myself, I shut my computer down and pushed away from the desk. I'd get another batch of crab legs, and this time we'd eat them hot.

Stepping out of the station, I stuffed my hands in my pockets, hunching my shoulders and tucking my head. The wind had a bite to it again, and the sky had that same leaden appearance from the other night when we got several inches of snow.

My phone buzzed in my pocket against my hand as I made my way across the parking lot to my truck. I hurried to my vehicle and hopped inside before taking it out to look at it. Ellis's name lit up on the screen.

"Hey," I answered.

"Hey, you up for a beer?"

I put my foot on the brake and started the car. Cold air blasted from the vents and the infotainment system picked up the call audio. "Can't. I have plans."

Ellis's snort filled the truck cab. "Let me guess—work?"

"No."

A beat of silence passed, then, "No way! You snagged the realtor, didn't you?"

My lips flattened, not liking his wording. "We're dating, yes."

"I thought she was off-limits because of your case. What happened to that? Did you solve it?"

"No, it's still ongoing and as frustrating as ever. Riggs just rearranged some aspects of it. Any formal contact about the case with her is going through him, and he made himself primary."

"And you don't mind that?" Ellis's tone held a note of disbelief.

"I would, normally, you're right, but he made a good point. We're not exactly in a bustling metropolis, so chances at love and happiness don't come along every day. I decided he was right."

"Wait, love? You barely know this woman."

"I know." I rested my wrist over the steering wheel. "And I didn't say I was there yet. But I can see myself getting to that point. Claire is amazing. Sometimes, the right one just comes along, you know?"

"Or the one you think is the right one." Bitterness filled my brother's voice. A pang of sorrow went through me. I hoped one day he could get past his ex-wife's betrayal and find someone to banish the darkness from his heart.

"Don't know if you don't try," I responded. "Anyway, I'm getting ready to go pick up dinner for us." Indecision had me shifting in my seat. Ellis had called to hang out, which meant he was in the mood for company, and I felt bad for turning him down. I'd moved here to be closer to him. Not to find myself a woman and push him aside for her. "Would you like to join us? We're having crab from Kellerman's."

Ellis laughed. "Are you serious? What woman wants her date to bring his brother?"

"She's not exactly expecting me, so..."

"Even more reason for me to stay behind. Unannounced visits have a different expectation."

It was my turn to snort. "It's not like I haven't stayed every night for the last several. I probably will tonight too. She won't mind if you come eat with us." He was starting to piss me off. Claire wasn't the kind of woman to care if I occasionally invited my brother over for dinner. If she was, well, then I needed to rethink moving forward with this relationship. Ellis was part of my life. A big part.

I started the car and made the decision for him. "I'm buying extra. Get your ass to her house in thirty minutes."

"Oz—"

I interrupted him and rattled off her address, then hung up. He might show up. He might not. If he didn't, well, I guess we'd have cold crab for lunch tomorrow.

Twenty-five minutes later, I had a sack full of crab and was on my way to Claire's.

The first flurries started to fall as I turned onto her street. Ellis's truck was nowhere to be seen. I tried not to let disappointment take hold. I wanted him and Claire to get to know each other. Any relationship I had with a woman would need to include him.

Parking in the drive, I had a thought. It could be that Ellis wasn't ready for the change.

With that in mind, I got out, snagging the bag of food. I wouldn't push him. Eventually, I had faith, he'd come around.

My truck beeped as I locked the doors. Anticipation built in my veins as I faced the house and took my first steps toward it. Warm light glowed from the front windows.

She was in there. Probably cross-legged on the couch, head bent as she typed away on her computer. Yesterday, she told me she was determined to be caught up by the end of the week. I didn't doubt she would be. The majority of her business documents were stored online, so it was mostly a matter of restoring systems and reprinting things they needed hard copies of, as well as scanning client documents, like statements that hadn't been digitized yet, that were lost in the fire.

But she also needed to take care of herself and eat. That's why I was here. To make her take a break.

The sound of an engine drew my attention away from the house. I glanced back to see a black truck slow and pull up to the curb.

Ellis.

A genuine smile lit my face.

The truck shut off and he got out.

"Couldn't pass up crab after all, huh?"

He waved a hand, coming up the drive. "Not from Kellerman's." Passing me, he continued toward the door. "Let's eat."

Chuckling, I followed him. As I raised my fist to knock, I heard Pebbles sound the alarm inside.

Ellis chuckled. "Who needs an alarm system with that around?"

I grinned. "She's effective, that's for sure." And probably why someone tried to take her out of the equation.

Thirty seconds later, the door swung inward. Pebbles barked from between Claire's feet, her little tail alternating between wagging when she looked at me and going rigid when she spotted Ellis.

Claire gave us a confused smile. "Hi. What are you two doing here?"

I raised the bag of crab. "Dinner."

"Oh." She looked over her shoulder, then back to us. "I have a lot of work—"

"You can take a break for food. The work will be there when you're done, and I promise to leave after we eat if that's what you want. Ellis wanted to go for beers, but I convinced him to come here instead. He and I can go do that after dinner."

Her mouth pulled to one side, but she soon stepped aside and let us in. "I suppose a quick break won't hurt."

"You can tell him to shove off," Ellis said as he stepped inside. "It might be good for his ego." Grinning, he cast a quick look at me.

Claire chuckled, sparing us a glance. When her back was turned, I flipped my brother the bird. His grin only widened.

"I was sorry to hear about your office. Oz said one of your employees was there and suffered some smoke inhalation. I hope she's all right."

"She's doing well. Back to limited duties. Emails and such. The doctor told her to take it easy for a week or so. Talking still irritates her throat. Makes her cough." Claire led us to the kitchen. Pebbles trotted along, her nails tapping on the wooden floor.

I set the bag on the counter, then bent to scratch her head in greeting.

Claire took several plates from the cabinet and some utensils from a drawer, and we divvied up the food. While she retrieved cans of soda from the fridge, I carried her plate and mine to the table.

"So, tell me more about yourself, Ellis," Claire said, settling into her seat. "Ozzie's mentioned some, but we actually haven't talked too much about our families."

My brother sent me a quick, sly look before he offered Claire a polite smile. "Not much to tell. I'm older and wiser—"

I snorted and picked up a crab leg. "In your dreams."

He narrowed his eyes in a mock glare. "Anyway, he's probably told you I'm in the Coast Guard. My enlistment ends in just a couple of weeks, and I've decided not to re-up. Gonna try my hand at commercial fishing."

Claire cracked open a leg and dipped it in the buttery sauce that came with the meal. "Why fishing? And why are you leaving the Coast Guard? You're only a few years away from being able to receive retirement, aren't you?"

"Yes and no. I get some retirement no matter when I separate, but it would be higher if I stayed another four years." He shook his head. "I just can't, though. It's all just become… ridiculous."

At the tweak of Claire's brows with an unspoken question, he elaborated slightly.

"Things have changed. It's not the same Coast Guard I signed up to. Plus, this fishing opportunity sort of fell into my lap. I took it as a sign."

"Fair enough," she said.

"I'm still in the market for a house too. I haven't forgotten. But it can wait until you're less stressed. My lease isn't up until September." A wicked smile formed on his face as he cracked a leg open. "I can always move in with Ozzie if necessary."

"Again, in your dreams." I would happily open my home to him, but no point in not giving him grief first.

"Oh, come on, Oz. You'd let your own brother go homeless?"

I rolled my eyes, a smile toying with my mouth. "You can put your stuff in storage. Most of the time you'll be on your boat, anyway."

Claire's mouth tipped up on one side as amusement danced in her pretty eyes. "In any case, I can probably put a list of properties together next week. We'll find you something so you don't have to rely on Ozzie to have a change of heart." She grinned at me, softening her words.

"That sounds good. I'll give you the skinny on this one, too, while we're out." He tipped his head toward me.

"Hey, no gossiping," I said.

Claire grinned, ignoring me. "That sounds good."

Maybe it wasn't such a great idea for Claire and Ellis to

become friends. I hadn't considered that they might team up against me.

The rest of our meal passed in much a similar fashion. We discussed Claire's family, talked about how the weather would start to change soon and the status of her insurance claim. I was hopeful it would move quickly, but I knew she'd still be working out of her home office and then a temporary office for quite some time.

True to our word, Ellis and I helped Claire clean up, then headed for the door so she could finish working.

She stopped me a few feet from the door with a hand on my sleeve. "You'll come back later?"

A lick of heat lit in my belly. "If you want, sure."

An answering fire ignited in her gaze. She pulled her bottom lip between her teeth, slowly letting it loose. "Oh, I definitely want."

Ellis groaned and continued toward the door. "Just kiss her already so we can go."

I chuckled. "Ignore him. He's just jealous."

With a soft giggle, she looped her arms around my neck. "I know."

The kiss was brief, but still enough to curl my toes and make me wish I hadn't invited my brother to tag along.

"I'm going to leave my truck in your driveway. Ellis can drive."

"That was not part of this deal," Ellis said.

"Your idea, you drive." I leaned down and scooped Pebbles off the floor, handing her to Claire so she wouldn't dart out when we left.

"Food was your idea. We'd have met at the bar if we didn't come here first."

"And you still would have had to drive," I countered.

He blinked. "Fair point. Okay. Let's go." He looked past me and smiled. "Claire, thank you for the lovely conversation."

"You're welcome. We'll have to do it again soon. You two are entertaining." She grinned.

Feeling lighthearted and happy, I moved toward the door. "I'll be back in a few hours. Lock up behind us?"

She nodded, coming forward. "I've got my guard dog too. Even sleep doesn't completely turn her off," she said with a chuckle.

Ellis opened the door and stepped out. "She needs a friend. One with bigger teeth."

I wholly agreed, but doubted Claire would go for it. And I would say I'd get one that would eventually—hopefully—end up living in the same house, but I didn't have time for a dog. I worked long, odd hours, so—

"Hey!"

Ellis's shout stopped my musings. I zeroed in on his tone, realizing in an instant he wasn't talking to either of us. His attention was on the side of the house, beyond my truck.

"You're on private property, pal."

Ellis moved to the side, heading for the driveway, giving me a clear view of what he saw.

In the side yard, a male figure backed toward the neighbor's drive.

I spared a quick glance at Claire. "Stay inside. Lock the door."

She backed up and shut the door without a word. As I moved away and toward Ellis and the man in the snow-covered grass, I heard the lock click.

"State police," I said, getting closer. I wasn't sure if it was the same person I chased off last week, but the falling snow made everything a bit fuzzy. "Sir, can we—"

The man took off.

Cursing, I broke into a run. So did Ellis.

"Hey! Stop!" Snow muffled my footfalls as I dashed through the grass.

Suddenly, the man turned right, running between two houses.

"Ellis! Go!" I pointed to the right as we passed the neighbor's.

Understanding my plan, he took off down the side yard. I needed eyes on him to make sure he didn't cross to the beach and hide amongst the rocks, but I didn't want him to cut back this way and lose him, either.

I ran up to the corner and turned, yelling before I passed the house, hoping I had made better time without the obstacle of fences, bushes, and random yard ornaments. "Ellis!"

"Here!" He yelled from my right.

I burst past the house, and with only seconds to react, I tackled a man to the ground. Snow sprayed up around us, landing down the collar of my coat. I ignored the chill and rolled the man to his stomach, keeping hold of one arm and bending it back so his fingers were near his shoulder blades.

Ellis reached us and dropped to his knees beside me. "You good?"

I nodded, keeping my attention on the man we caught. "Why were you lurking outside the house?"

The man groaned. "Let me up. This snow is cold."

He turned his head, and I got my first look at his face in the dim glow of the corner streetlight.

I frowned, my eyes narrowing as recognition niggled my mind.

"Warren?"

CHAPTER 29

Claire

Snow swirled outside the window. Ozzie's truck was covered, and the tracks he and Ellis left when they dashed off after the man in the side yard were rapidly disappearing.

I clutched Pebbles and wondered if I should call for help.

But Ozzie hadn't asked me to, and I didn't want to create a fuss if it was nothing. Maybe it was some teenager out walking. People did that around here.

Though they didn't usually cut between houses. Everyone around here was armed—me included—and didn't take kindly to trespassers.

I chewed on the inside of my cheek. If they weren't back in another five or ten minutes, maybe I would call. Ozzie had his phone, though. So did Ellis. Surely, one of them would call for help if they needed it.

Right?

Exhaling a breath through my nose, I stepped away from the window. They wouldn't magically appear while I stood there and wished for it. If anything, it would take longer. Like a watched pot.

I put Pebbles down and went into the kitchen. There were

dishes in the sink. I had a load of laundry that needed moved to the dryer too.

Pebbles's bark and subsequent skittering of her nails on the floor as she ran toward the front door made me jump. Hand on my chest, I followed her.

Spinning in circles by the door, the dog continued to bark. I went to the front windows and peered out. Three figures, obscured by the falling snow, came down the sidewalk.

I squinted. Two of them were large, and the other it was hard to tell. It looked like he was hunched over.

They passed under the streetlight and I recognized Ozzie's jacket.

My heart thumped. They'd caught the guy.

Hurrying to the door, I unlocked it, picked up Pebbles, and flung it open, eager to see who'd been harassing me.

The three of them turned and came up the driveway, but the man kept his head down. Ozzie and Ellis marched him straight up to the porch, where he finally lifted his head.

A sharp gasp left my lips. "Warren? You're the one who's been harassing me? Why would you burn down my office?"

His eyes widened. "What? No! That wasn't me, I swear."

"Let's discuss it inside." Ozzie put a hand in his pocket and took out his truck keys, then tossed them to Ellis before pushing Warren toward the door.

I stepped back and let them in, frowning as Ellis jogged toward Ozzie's vehicle. "What's he doing?"

"Getting my handcuffs."

"Oh." I closed the door to stop letting the cold air in, but didn't lock it.

"Do you have a first-aid kit?" Ozzie asked.

It was then I noticed the scrape on Warren's face.

"Oh. Yes." I turned and ran upstairs, retrieving several first-aid items from the cabinet in my bathroom.

When I returned to the main living space, Warren was on the couch, his hands handcuffed in front of him. Ozzie sat next to him, and Ellis stood to the side holding Pebbles. The little dog saw me and wagged her tail, then looked at Warren and growled.

Surprised that she'd let Ellis pick her up, my eyebrows rose for a quick second. It usually took her a few visits before she warmed up to new people enough to let them do more than give her a quick scratch.

Moving into the room, I sat next to Ozzie on the couch. "Here. I hope this works. I can get a washcloth if you need it." I piled the supplies in my lap and let him pick what he wanted.

He took a couple of gauze pads and the hydrogen peroxide. "This should work. I just want to clean him up enough I can put some bandages over the worst of the cuts to stop the bleeding." Tearing open the gauze, he wet it, then dabbed at Warren's face.

"You want to tell us what you were doing out there now?" Ozzie asked as he worked. "Since you decided to pretend you're mute after we caught you." Quickly, he read him his rights.

Muscles in Warren's jaw worked as he acknowledged that he understood.

But it wasn't obstinance I saw in his eyes. It was sorrow.

"Please tell us what you know Warren," I pleaded softly. "I found Marie. She didn't deserve to die like that, and I don't think you did it."

His gaze met mine, bleakness shining bright. "I didn't."

"Then who did?" Ozzie lowered his hand to look Warren in the face.

"Her lover."

I shared a look with Ellis, surprised at that. "Marie had a lover?"

Warren nodded.

"Who?" Ozzie asked.

"I don't know."

I watched Ozzie's eyebrows knit into a deep frown. "Then how do you know he did it?"

"Who else would? Marie was sweet. She didn't have any enemies." Warren pressed his lips together glancing away. "Look, I know things weren't the best between us, and I wasn't the best husband. She wasn't happy and never really wanted to move here, but I convinced her it would be the best thing for us. I was trying to save our marriage." He speared Ozzie with a look. "This wasn't the first time she cheated on me."

"Why did you stay with her, then?" I asked.

"I loved her. You met her. She's beautiful. Kind. Smart. What man wouldn't want her for his wife?"

Ozzie frowned, returning to doctoring Warren's face. "Okay. How about you start at the beginning? What did you see? And why are you here tonight?"

Warren's mouth pressed flat for a moment. "We were supposed to fly to Boston to house hunt, but Marie said last minute that she couldn't go. Something about being too far behind on grading." He rolled his eyes. "I knew that was a lie. If she had grading to do, she could have brought it along and done it on the plane. She has before. I didn't press the issue, though. This move was for her. I like it here. I may not look it, but the outdoors soothes me. It's why I have that cabin near Hoonah."

He flapped one hand dangling between his knees. "Anyway, I hoped—foolishly, perhaps—that moving her closer to her family would once again save our marriage. I think it was her escape plan, though." His brows pinched, then he winced as the movement pulled at the scrapes on his face.

"That explains why she didn't go to Boston, but why didn't you?" Ozzie put the gauze down and reached for the box of butterfly strips.

Warren's hands clenched into fists. "Because, as much as I loved her and wanted to save our marriage, I was tired of being cast aside. So, I stayed behind, determined to catch her cheating. If I had hard proof to take to a lawyer, I was hopeful I could get out of paying alimony." Fine lines appeared around his mouth as his features tightened. "Not that she ever wanted my money, anyway."

"Is that why she drove an outdated car and the two of you lived in a modest house?" I asked.

He nodded. "She wanted to save it all. For what, I don't know. She said retirement, but I made more than enough for us to live a more lavish lifestyle and still save plenty for retirement."

"That's interesting," Ozzie muttered, peeling a butterfly strip from the paper. "Several of Marie's colleagues said the opposite. That it was you who wouldn't let her spend the money."

A genuine frown formed on Warren's face? "What? No." His frown smoothed out and anger darkened his expression. "Let me guess—Grace and Kaya? Those two didn't like me."

"Probably with good reason. They said you treated your wife like garbage. Especially when you'd been drinking." Ozzie laid a butterfly strip over one of the deeper cuts on Warren's face.

A flush tinged Warren's cheeks. "I admit, I probably… imbibe a little too much scotch, and it can make me mean. But that still doesn't mean I murdered Marie."

"No. Tell me, Warren, were you drunk the night you decided to catch her cheating?"

Oh my. Could he have done it in a drunken rage and then blocked it out, I wondered.

Warren's eyes turned flinty. "It doesn't matter if I had anything to drink. I didn't kill her."

Ozzie let out a soft grunt, then took another butterfly strip off the paper backing. "Okay, so maybe you were drinking, maybe you weren't. But you're saying Marie's friends were wrong about how you treated her?"

"Yes. Things were tense between us. I suspected she was cheating—had for a while—and I wasn't handling it the best. I know I was probably just pushing her further away, but I couldn't help myself. I didn't know how to make things better. As for the money, that was all her. I don't know why she would tell her friends that I controlled the purse strings. She had access to it all and chose not to spend it."

But why would she lie about it? It was a simple enough thing to tell people you wanted to save for retirement. Why would she tell her friends he wouldn't spend any of his wealth on her? I couldn't wrap my brain around the idea. Warren seemed sincere, though. I had no reason not to believe him. His story made as much sense as Marie's—maybe more.

"So what happened after you decided to stay behind?" Ozzie asked.

"I left like I was going to the airport, but I just went into Juneau and wandered around until I thought her lover might be there. By then, it was dark. I didn't want to tip them off by pulling into the driveway, so I parked on the street several houses down and walked. I even went through the back, because the slider is quieter than the front door."

Some of the blood drained from his face, giving him a ghostly pallor. His Adam's apple bobbed.

"You found her first, didn't you?" I said softly.

He met my gaze, tears shimmering in his eyes. "Yes." The singular word came out on a rough whisper. He cleared his throat and took a deep breath before continuing. "The slider was open. Not just unlocked, but open. And the house was quiet. Dark too. At least, downstairs. I know I should have called the police as soon as I saw the open door, but part of me hoped that her lover had come in that way and just didn't get the door all the way closed." He lifted a shoulder before continuing.

"Anyway, I went inside and straight upstairs. The only light on was in the master bedroom."

"Did you hear anything?" Ozzie asked.

"No. My first thought was that they were sleeping, but who falls asleep with the light on?" He rubbed his palms on his thighs, his gaze shifting around the room. "She wasn't sleeping," he whispered.

My heart broke for him.

Clenching my fists, I swallowed around the lump in my throat and looked away, blinking several times to clear my eyes. How horrible that must have been for him.

Warren lifted a hand, swiping at his cheek. "She was still warm." Voice thick, he stared at the floor.

Lord, have mercy. I cleared my throat and changed the subject. "Warren, your car. Why was it in the woods?"

He looked up. It took him a moment to process my question. "Um, I wasn't sure if the person who killed her saw me. No one else was in the house, but I didn't want to take any chances, so I decided to disappear."

Ozzie's brows knit together. "If the house was empty, what made you think someone might have thought you saw them?"

"Because there was a car. When I got there. It passed me right before I got out of mine."

"Did it come from your house?" Ellis asked, breaking into the conversation for the first time.

Warren looked over. "I don't know. It came from that direction. I was so focused on the house I didn't pay attention to the street. It could have been parked out front. But it wasn't in the driveway, that I know."

"What kind of car?" Ozzie asked.

"A black SUV of some sort. I can't tell you what make or model."

"We found blood in your car that wasn't a match to your wife," Ozzie said. "It had soaked through the leather and penetrated the pad underneath. Where did that come from?"

"I slipped on the ice in my haste to get away from the

house. I fell into a bush." He leaned to the side and lifted the edge of his shirt, showing off the healing gash, complete with stitches, on the bottom of his ribcage below his left arm.

"After I went to the clinic in Juneau and got stitched up, I cleaned the car. I had Marie's"—he paused and swallowed hard—"blood on me, so I figured it was on the seat and steering wheel. Plus all of my blood. I just—" he stopped and shook his head.

"Why didn't you go to the police after you found your wife?" Ellis crossed his arms, a curious frown on his face.

Warren scoffed. "She was cheating on me. Her blood was on my clothes. I lied about leaving town. And I"—his eyes turned toward the floor—"might have had a drink or two." He raised his gaze. "You do the math." He turned to Ozzie. "I'm sorry I didn't come forward. I just… I just needed time to figure out what to do." With a look of sorrow, he swung to me. "And I'm sorry you had to find Marie like that. I—I wasn't sure who would find her or how, but I never thought it would be you."

I tipped my head, studying him. He seemed sincere. "Why did you come here? Are you the one who's been stalking me? And the one who burned my office down?"

"No!" He slashed his bound hands through the air, making the handcuffs rattle. "No. I admit, I've been hanging around you for the last few days, but not to do you any harm. I—I was hoping you could help me."

"You should have come to the police." A fierce frown settled on Ozzie's face. "I'm the one who can help you, not her." With a quick gesture, he pointed to me.

"No offense, but I didn't want to get locked up. I didn't murder my wife, Detective. I knew if I turned myself in, you'd spend all your time trying to find evidence that I did."

"First of all, I don't make assumptions. You might look guilty as hell for it, but you're still innocent until *proven* guilty. I would have looked at any and all evidence, whether it supported your guilt or exonerated you. I'm not in the business of pinning murders on innocent people. If you'd come forward, I could have been doing more to track down your wife's lover. Instead, I've been spinning my wheels trying to find *you*."

Sensing that Warren was about to argue, I decided to sidetrack him again. The two of them arguing about what could have been wouldn't help anything now. "Why did you think I could help?"

"Well, for one, I heard you found Marie, so I thought maybe you'd found other evidence or knew of other evidence the police found. Something that might tell me who she was seeing. You also know people and could ask questions without being out of place. You're always everywhere. And you're kind." His expression softened as he looked at me. "I know you could tell things weren't great between me and Marie, but you never said anything. You treated us with nothing but kindness and professionalism. I appreciated that."

While I was happy to know my demeanor made him comfortable, it didn't mean I was glad he felt like I was the only one he could trust. That was a lot to put on one person's shoulders and it left him straying into stalker territory. Desperate people could do desperate things. "Thank you for saying that, Warren. But while I'm glad you felt comfortable enough with me to think I could help you find Marie's killer, you really should have gone to the police. They've wasted a lot of time and resources attempting to locate you that would have been better spent looking for Marie's lover." Not to mention the physical pain I had endured by trying to help find him. But I wasn't going to heap that on him now. He was already hurting and had been chastised enough.

Warren hung his head, nodding.

"Okay, so if that's why you came here tonight, I think it's time we talk more about Marie's boyfriend." Ozzie lightly smacked his thighs. "I know you don't know who he is, but is there anything you can tell us about him? I mean, how do you know she was cheating? How did you know the first time?"

"Her friends told me the first time. They saw her out with some guy while I was away on business. This was back when we lived in St. Louis. Rather than confront her, I applied for a transfer. My boss had already been making noise about the position up here, that I should consider it. No one wanted to go, but he hinted that if someone took on the role it could lead to bigger and better things down the line." He lifted a shoulder. "It seemed like perfect timing, so I said I'd do it."

"So, you never said anything to her about her cheating?" Ellis raised an eyebrow, disbelief written all over his face.

"No. I figured she'd either own up to it and leave me so she could stay with him, or she wouldn't. When she agreed to come with me, it gave me some hope that we weren't over and that we could fix things. And for a while, things weren't bad. But then she started to distance herself again." Once more, he hung his head. "I can't say I'm not to blame for it. She came home late from work one day. It was our anniversary. I'd had a couple of drinks and was upset, and I said some things I shouldn't have. Stuff spiraled from there. She wouldn't talk to me, and it irritated me to no end when she gave me the silent treatment. I'm not proud of how I handled those instances."

"You belittled her," Ozzie said.

Warren's head bobbed. "And drank more."

"But you still loved your wife?"

"Yes."

"They have counselors for all those things, you know," Ellis quipped.

Ozzie shot a quick glare at him. "Not helpful, El." He turned back to Warren. "The current lover—what do you know?"

"Nothing. It's just a feeling. She'd say she was going out

with friends and then come home smelling of a man's cologne. Our sex life was practically non-existent, and if you knew Marie, you'd know that's not like her. When our marriage was good, we were together several times a week. The same thing happened when she had the affair in St. Louis. She stopped sleeping with me."

I fought to keep the disgust off my face. I did not need to know that.

A thoughtful frown appeared on his face. "Her friends might know more. Grace. And Kaya. They'd never say anything to me, but they might talk to you."

Ozzie tipped his head. "You think she'd tell them about the affair?"

Warren nodded. "Especially Grace. That woman was forever up in our business. Every time I went to a school function with Marie, she'd make some comment about something I said or did. Just to make it clear she still thought I was a dirtbag and didn't deserve her friend."

Considering that for a moment, Ozzie nodded. "All right. What about the things that have been happening with Claire? You said you've been watching her. Have you seen anyone hanging around?"

"Just you."

I sat forward, leaning in a bit. "You're sure? No cars that keep driving by that don't belong in the neighborhood, or people out running?"

"Running? In the weather we've had? No. And I don't recall any strange cars. Your street is pretty quiet. But I've only been watching for a few days, like I said."

"Where were you before that? Not your cabin, because we checked," Ozzie said.

"With a friend. His wife and kids were out of town visiting family, so he let me stay with him. She came back, though, so I had to leave. I've been squatting in an RV at a campground. That's when I decided to ask you for help." He nodded at me. "I couldn't really ask questions anywhere to find out who she'd been seeing, and the few times I tried to eavesdrop on her friends I almost got caught. I couldn't stay in the RV forever. When I heard you found my car, I figured you might be my best bet to solving my problem."

"Well, you're right about one thing." Ozzie crumpled the first-aid trash into one hand. "You can't stay in the RV. But I've got a nice warm place for you."

Warren's shoulders fell. "Jail. I figured that would be where you took me. I won't fight you, Detective. I just want this to be over."

"Good." Ozzie stood. "I need to make a couple phone calls. Thank you for telling me what you know."

"You believe me, don't you? I didn't kill her." Head tipped back, he stared up at Ozzie.

"I promise I'll do everything I can to bring her killer to justice."

I blinked. That didn't sound like he believed Warren's story.

"Ellis, keep an eye on him for a few minutes, would you?" Ozzie asked.

Ellis, arms still crossed, nodded once, and Ozzie walked away.

Giving Warren a quick, reassuring smile, I gathered the first-aid supplies in my lap and hopped up, following Ozzie into the kitchen. "You believe him, don't you?" I unloaded my armful of items onto the counter.

"I'm not sure." He pulled out the trashcan drawer and dropped the bandage packaging and gauze into it. "He could be spinning a yarn to take the focus off himself. Getting caught outside your house wasn't part of his plan. I'm inclined to say he didn't do it, but I can't rule him out until I get proof someone else did." Moving to the sink, he turned on the water.

"What are you going to do? Besides put him in jail."

"Talk to Marie's friends again, for one. And the friend he said he stayed with. I need to get a warrant for his medical records too. Make sure that gash is really from a branch and not a knife."

My eyes widened. I hadn't even considered that. "You think someone—maybe Marie—slashed him before he stabbed her?"

Ozzie shrugged. "It's possible." He squirted some soap in his palm and lathered his hands. "I'm glad we have him, but this isn't over. Not by a long shot. And you're still in danger. I do believe him when he says he wasn't the one who torched your office or broke in here. His surprise seemed genuine." He rinsed his hands. "I'm going to ask Ellis to stay with you, if that's okay? Now that we have Warren, if he's not the killer, whoever is might get bolder. They still haven't gotten the evidence they think you have."

While I would rather have Ozzie here than Ellis, I understood why it had to be that way. Ozzie had a job to do. "That's fine. Just catch him. I don't like thinking there's a murderer walking around. It's creepy."

Drying off his hands with the towel I kept draped over the bar on the oven door, he came around the counter. "I'll find this person, Claire."

Lifting a hand, I touched his chest. "I know."

Ozzie lowered his head and kissed me softly. I curled my fingers into his shirt, wishing he didn't need to leave. I couldn't help but hope Warren's presence sparked something. I wanted Ozzie all to myself and without the threat of danger lurking overhead.

CHAPTER 30

Ozzie

"You ready to do this?"

I glanced up at Riggs as he poked his head in my door. "Uh, yeah." Blinking to put the moisture back in my eyes, I logged out of my computer, leaving the search for the elusive sweatshirt logo up on my screen.

Pushing away from the desk, I grabbed a notepad and a pen and followed the chief down the hall to the room we used for interrogation.

"Are you sure you don't want to do the interviewing?" I asked him, stopping in front of the door.

"I'm sure. You already have a rapport. But remember what we talked about. Watch the light and excuse yourself if it comes on." He backed toward the door a few feet away. It led to the observation room.

I nodded. It was our signal that he had a question he wanted me to ask or information for me to use during questioning. It could also mean we'd strayed into territory where my feelings for Claire and our relationship could become a concern for the prosecution. I had to tread carefully.

Once Riggs entered the other room, I entered the code to unlock the door and walked in.

"When you called and asked me to come down to talk, I didn't think you'd lock me in an interrogation room."

Grace Alonso glared at me from her seat at the small table in the middle of the room.

I offered her my most disarming smile. "My apologies. It's the only room with recording equipment."

Her dark expression turned confused. "Recording equipment? For what?"

The metal chair legs grated across the floor as I pulled it out and sat down. "I just have a few more questions for you."

"That you need on the record? I don't know anything about Marie's murder, Detective."

Twirling the pen through my fingers, I paused, clicking it, then resumed the twirl as I studied her. "I think you know more than you say." I put up a hand as she opened her mouth to protest. "You may not know you do."

Her lips slammed shut.

"Tell me about Marie's boyfriend."

For the briefest of moments, her eyes widened.

Bingo.

"What boyfriend? She was married." Schooling her expression, she folded her hands in her lap and sat back.

I cocked my head slightly. "She was, but we both know she wasn't happy. And I have it on good authority she was having an affair. Tell me what you know about him."

"Nothing. She never talked about a boyfriend."

I arched a single eyebrow. "Never? You two were friends. Good friends. She never mentioned seeing anyone outside of her marriage?"

Grace shook her head. "No." Her gaze shifted away.

She was lying, but why? Marie was dead. Why would she protect her friend now?

Unless she wasn't protecting only Marie, but Marie's lover as well.

"This isn't the first time she cheated."

With a quick glimpse, she looked at me, then away again. "Oh?"

"Don't play coy, Ms. Alonso. I know you know."

Fire flashed in her eyes as she turned to me. "I don't know anything. Are you charging me with something? If not, I'd like to leave." Her chair scraped the floor with a rough screech as she stood. Purse in hand, she whipped it over her shoulder.

Looking past me, she glared at the two-way window behind me. "I know you're back there, Chief. I can't believe you'd haul me in here like this." She stormed toward the door.

I draped an arm over the back of my chair as I turned to watch her.

"Do you have no decency or give any consideration to your officers?" With a hand wrapped around the doorknob, she gave it a twist, but the door didn't budge.

What was she talking about? She wasn't on the police force.

"Would you mind unlocking the door?" She shot me a glare over her shoulder.

Not playing into her tantrum or her haste, I gathered my notepad and pen, rising from my chair without any hurry. At her side, I keyed in the code.

The lock clicked, and she yanked open the door.

"Think about our conversation, Ms. Alonso. You know how to find me if you remember anything."

Nose in the air, she huffed and flounced out.

Crossing my arms, still clutching my notepad and pen, I leaned against the door and watched her leave.

The door behind me opened, and I heard Riggs's footfalls as he came closer.

"What was she talking about? The officer thing?" I glanced at him.

Riggs's forehead wrinkled with a confused frown. "What?

Wait, you didn't know?"

"Know what?"

"Her brother is one of us. Turner. Alonso is her married name."

Taken aback, I blinked, staring at him for a moment. "No one mentioned that, no." I guess no one could ever accuse Riggs of bias. He'd treated Grace no differently than any other person in her situation.

But I planned to exploit the connection. Perhaps her brother could shed light on what she knew or convince her to tell me.

I pushed away from the doorframe. "Is he here?"

"He's on patrol."

Damn. I didn't have long before Kaya Strand showed up for her interview, but I could have asked him a couple of questions. I also really didn't want to give Grace the chance to tell her brother what happened.

Riggs's hand landed on my shoulder, and I looked over.

"Don't let her connection to Turner hold you back. She knows something. Make sure they both know she could be charged as an accessory if we discover she's protecting the killer."

"Oh, I will." There were few things that bothered me more than favoritism. I was glad Riggs didn't cotton to it, either.

CHAPTER 31

Ozzie

Kaya Strand was much more relaxed than her colleague.

"Hello, Detective." She offered me a polite smile as I walked into the room.

I returned it with a genuine one of my own. "Ms. Strand. Thank you for coming in. Sorry about the accommodations. I wanted to record our interview." I motioned to the camera in the corner of the ceiling as I sat down.

"That's okay. This is serious business, so I don't blame you." She folded her arms on the table and leaned forward. "I have to say, though, I'm surprised you called me in. I'm not sure what else I can tell you."

I decided to cut straight to the chase. "Marie was having an affair. What can you tell me about it?"

She blinked, surprise in her dark eyes, then sat back. "An affair?" Her forehead creased with a frown. "You're sure?"

"Yes."

The lines on her forehead cleared as she puffed out her cheeks and blew out a breath. "Wow. I mean, I guess I'm not surprised. Warren's a jerk."

"Do you have any idea who it could be?"

She frowned again. "How do you know she was having an affair if you don't know who with?"

"Evidence." Riggs and I had decided to keep Warren's presence under wraps for now. He was tucked safely into a county jail cell in Juneau until he was charged with whatever the prosecutor saw fit for his failure to report Marie's murder and arrangements could be made to put him in protective custody after he was granted bail.

Her look told me she knew I was withholding information, but she didn't press the issue.

"Marie wasn't a flirt." Her expression turned thoughtful. "But there were a couple of our fellow male teachers she seemed to… like? More than others, I mean."

"Okay." I clicked my pen, poised to write down names. "Who?"

"The top one would probably be Kevin Cottrell. He's the gym teacher. She was friendly with the middle school math teacher too. Lawrence Iverson."

Having learned my lesson with Grace and Gabe Turner, the name clicked in my head. "Is he related to Grant Iverson?" The name wasn't uncommon, but I wasn't taking any chances. If one of our forensic technicians was involved, I wanted to know.

Kaya lifted a shoulder. "Not sure."

"What makes you think either man could be her boyfriend?"

Again, she shrugged. "She talked to them more than any of the other male teachers. They're both fairly good looking too." She wrinkled her nose. "And Kevin gives me the creeps a bit. He's just"—she flipped a hand—"odd. Like, he's married, but I've seen him checking out some of the other teachers."

Nodding, I made a quick note next to his name. "What about Iverson?"

"They just spend a lot of time talking. Before and after

meetings, at whole-school functions, sometimes even after school I'd see them together."

That was interesting. Kaya might think Cottrell was the more likely candidate because he appeared to be a woman-izer, but my gut said Marie was looking for a companion. Not just a quick lay. Iverson fit that bill much better than the gym teacher. "Is Iverson a nice guy?"

Kaya tipped her head back and forth. "Yeah. I don't know him that well. We're a small school, but we're still split up by elementary, middle, and high. I really only speak to him when we have a staff meeting or an assembly for everyone."

"All right. Is there anyone else? It doesn't have to be from school. Has she ever mentioned someone? A male friend? Or have you ever seen her somewhere talking to a man?"

"I don't—" She paused, then tipped her head and stared just over my shoulder, thinking. "There was a guy." Her gaze met mine. "A few months ago. It was just before Christmas. I remember because I was out buying gifts for my family. It was at Parker Supply."

I nodded, encouraging her to continue. Parker Supply was one of the main stores in town. They sold a bit of everything.

"I was browsing the clothing, when I saw her near the underwear with a man. She had a lacy bra in her hands. When I said hello, she spun toward me. At the time, I thought I just surprised her, but thinking about it now, it could have been guilt on her face."

I knew to take that with a grain of salt. People sometimes invented memories and feelings based on current circum-stances. "Describe the man she was with."

"I didn't see him. Not his face, anyway. There was a pillar between us and a rack of coats. But he had dark hair. I saw that much as he walked away."

Pressing my lips together, slightly frustrated, I wrote that down. I knew exactly where she meant in the store. Parker Supply was in a large cabin-style building with several log beams holding up the second story and the roof. It was also chocked full of goods. The owners crammed as much into the space as they could, which meant lots of racks, often with other displays stacked on top and small walkways throughout the store. I hated going in there. It was a damn maze.

"Okay. There's nothing else about him that stuck out to you?"

She shook her head.

"Can you estimate his height?"

"Average?" She shrugged.

"Did he remind you of anyone you'd seen before?"

Her brow furrowed. "Maybe? But this is a small town, Detective. Even with our close proximity to Juneau, everyone knows everyone here. So, it could be someone I know, but I just can't tell you who because I didn't see his face."

My head bobbed even as my heart sank. That made sense. "Okay. Do you happen to remember the date you were at Parker Supply?" They had cameras, so perhaps I would get lucky and they'd let me see the footage. If they kept it that long. December was a while ago.

"Actually, yes. December eighteenth. I went right after school, and that was our last day. Marie must have had the same idea."

I jotted the date in my notes. "One more question." I glanced up at her. "Did Grace Alonso ever say anything about Marie?"

Kaya frowned. "What do you mean?"

"Was she ever derogatory toward her? Or on the flip side, overprotective?"

"Like, defensive?"

"Yes."

The woman cocked her head. "Maybe? They were closer friends than Marie and I were, so they stuck up for each other when administration tried to heap extra work on us." Her expression darkened. "A lot of times, they managed to shove it off on someone else. I did more than my fair share of *extras*."

Her tone opened a new thread in my line of theories. "Did anyone in particular take offense to the two of them teaming up to avoid extra duties?"

Kaya lifted a hand and let it flutter back to her lap. "Probably. It bothered me, and I was their friend, so it probably bothered others as well. But I don't know who. I try to stay out of all the gossip." She wrinkled her nose. "It's distasteful. I was one of those kids on the receiving end of rumors in school, so I don't participate in any of it now."

I agreed, even though I'd never been the butt of school rumors. "Not a bad idea. All right, is there anything else you can think of that might be useful to the investigation? Anyone who might have felt wronged by Marie or had a reason to be angry?"

Kaya looked away briefly, chewing on her bottom lip, her eyes searching. "Nothing's coming to mind. But I'll keep thinking."

I pushed back from the table with a smile. "That would be great." Standing, I took a business card from my pocket and held it out to her. "If you think of anything, please call."

She rose with a nod and accepted the card. "I will, thank you."

Once more, I unhurriedly gathered my notepad and pen, meeting Ms. Strand at the door. "I appreciate you coming in." Keying in the code, I let us out.

"It's no problem." She adjusted her bag strap on her shoulder. The smile on her face faded and a more somber look drew the corners of her mouth down. "I hope you find who did this. No matter what she did or to whom she did it, she didn't deserve to die." With a final serious look, she walked away.

Like Grace, I watched her leave, waiting on Riggs to exit the observation room.

"Much different to the last interview, don't you think?" I asked, eyes still on Kaya's retreating form.

"Yeah. Let's go get that footage from Parker's, and see if we can ID the guy. It might be nothing, but I don't like that he walked away without even saying hello to Ms. Strand. Not when Marie was showing him lingerie beforehand."

"You read my mind." Tucking my notepad under my arm, I stepped out of the doorway and shut the interrogation room door. "Do you think you could get Krieger or Garnett to conduct some surveillance on Grace? Without letting Turner know?"

Riggs's mouth pulled. "Maybe, but I don't want to put them in that position." A crooked smile lifted one side of his face. "I know how to keep my mouth shut, though." He clapped me on the shoulder. "Don't worry about Grace. I'll handle it."

I smiled, liking the chief even more. He wasn't afraid to pitch in when needed. "Sounds good."

"Meet me outside in two?" Riggs arched an eyebrow with a questioning look.

With a nod, I headed for my office to get my gun.

"Oscar!"

I paused, glancing over at Nina, Riggs's administrative assistant as I passed her desk.

"I put some mail on your desk."

"Okay, thank you." Lifting a hand, I acknowledged her, then continued to my office.

When I rounded my desk to sit down, I saw the pile. Brushing it aside, I set my notepad down, then unlocked my desk drawer to get my gun. I'd look at it later. Right now, I had some video footage to track down.

CHAPTER 32

Claire

"Ah!" My fingers jumped on the keyboard, adding letters I didn't want as Pebbles jumped up from her spot next to me, barking like a wild woman. Pigtail on top of her head bobbing, she ran for the front door.

Ellis laid his book down and got up from the chair. "Were you expecting someone?"

Willing my heart to stop racing, I shook my head. That dog would be the death of me one day. "No." But that didn't mean anything. Tamara had stopped by earlier without calling first. I figured that would be the norm until I could find a temporary office space.

It was a little late for unexpected work visitors, though.

I shut my laptop and set it on the coffee table, following Ellis to the door.

He peeked out the window. "It's your coffeeshop friend."

"Mina?" I moved closer to peer outside.

Sure enough, Mina was headed up the sidewalk from her car in the driveway, grocery sacks in hand.

I walked around Ellis and unlocked the door, opening it as Mina reached the porch. "What are you doing here?"

"Cooking you dinner." With a wide smile, Mina breezed

into the house. Her smile dipped a bit, confusion sparking in her eyes when she saw Ellis. "You're the wrong brother. Why are you here and not the other one?" She looked at me. "Where's the cop?"

"At work. Ellis is keeping me company." I closed the door and relocked it.

The last traces of Mina's smile disappeared. "What? No. That's a load of bullcrap. What's going on? Why do you need a babysitter?"

"He's not a babysitter." He was simply… looking out for me.

I suppressed an eyeroll. That sounded lame even to my own ears.

"I'm kind of a babysitter." Ellis flashed a playful grin.

The eyeroll couldn't stay hidden this time. "Whatever." I turned to Mina. "Why are you cooking me dinner?" I wasn't upset about it, but it was unusual. She rarely showed up unannounced for a meal. We always made plans ahead of time—even if it was for a half an hour later—when we wanted to hang out.

"You've been MIA lately. I know things have been crazy with the fire and all, but I need the tea." She eyed Ellis again. "Apparently, there's a lot of it." Not waiting for an invitation, she set off toward the kitchen.

Ellis intercepted her, taking the grocery bags and carrying them for her. He peered inside as he set them down. "What is all this?"

"Elk stew." Mina shooed him out of the way. "I slow-roasted the meat earlier this week."

My mouth watered. I would never complain about Mina showing up with homecooked food. She should have started with a café or diner instead of the coffeeshop. I understood why she did; competing with Kellerman's was not an easy task. But her food would have spoken for itself. I couldn't wait to see what she did when she expanded.

I moved to a cabinet by the stove and removed my stockpot. "This will be one of your menu items when you expand, right?"

She lifted a shoulder as she shrugged out of her coat. "Maybe. I'm not sure what all I want to put on the menu. I need to finalize the sale and renovate before I think about that."

"Well, I will always vote for elk stew." No one made better.

After washing her hands, Mina grabbed a knife and set about chopping the vegetables she pulled from the grocery bags. "Tell me why you're here." She aimed the tip of the knife at Ellis, then chopped the end off a carrot.

"Because Oz asked me to be."

Mina rolled her eyes, then looked at me. "He thinks he's funny. He's not."

I chuckled. "He's not wrong, though. With everything going on, Ozzie didn't want me to be alone at night. Ellis is here until Ozzie comes back."

A slow, knowing smile spread over Mina's face. "We'll come back to that part about the nighttime in a second. But first"—she turned to Ellis—"don't you have a job? I've seen you in uniform in my shop. Did you take time off from the Coast Guard?"

"I'm separating from the service. Other than going in for paperwork and a few training sessions for my successor, I'm done. I had nearly a month of leave saved, so I decided to split it and use some so I could take it easy at the end. The rest will get paid out in my final paycheck."

"Makes sense." She beheaded another carrot, then slid both across the granite counter toward me. "Peel those, would you?"

I opened a drawer and took out the peeler, then picked up the first carrot.

"What would you like me to do?" Ellis asked.

"Scram." Mina smiled, softening her words. "No offense, but I came to interrogate Claire."

Ellis chuckled and held up his hands, backing up. "No offense taken. Claire, I wish you luck."

I sent him a wry grin. "Gee, thanks."

"Holler if you want more help. I'll be over there." He pointed toward the living room, then walked away.

Mina cast a couple of quick looks his way as she peeled an onion. "He's just as cute as his brother."

"And very single," I hinted.

She let out an inelegant snort. "I do not need a boyfriend at this time. I barely have time for my cat."

"I'm just saying. Ellis is single."

Mina waved her knife, then sliced into the onion. "Forget him. Tell me about his brother. The one here *at night*." She waggled her eyebrows.

My cheeks heated. "There's not much to say. He's been sleeping here."

She hummed. "In your bed, by the looks of it." She gestured to my face.

The blush staining my skin deepened. I cleared my throat. "Yes."

"Ha!" She grinned. "Good. I'm guessing he's no slouch, either."

"No." The rest of my body heated, remembering how I woke up this morning. He'd slipped into bed sometime during the night and I hadn't realized it. Near the time my alarm was set to go off, what I thought was a delicious dream had turned out to be oh so very real. I'd awakened to his wandering hands driving me to the brink of heaven.

"I'm glad. You deserve a man who makes you happy. It's been a long time since you dated anyone seriously. Or at all."

"I could say the same about you." I picked up the second carrot.

"True. It'll happen eventually. I'm not worried." She

picked up the cutting board with the sliced onion and scraped it into the stockpot. "And that is not an invitation for you to 'make it happen'." She aimed a pointed look at me.

I offered her an innocent smile. "But he's so cute."

Mina laughed. "Maybe so, but he's not really my type." She cast a quick look toward the living room as she picked up a batch of parsley and washed it. "Nor is he looking for a relationship."

As much as I would love to see my best friend with Ozzie's brother, so we could be one big, happy "family," I knew Ellis wasn't the type of man for her. Mina preferred quieter, more introverted men. Someone more like Ozzie, actually. Despite her sunny disposition, Mina was an introvert at heart.

And I agreed with her that Ellis wasn't in the market for a commitment. I had a feeling he'd been badly burned once and hadn't yet fully healed.

"Fine. I'll behave."

"You will, or there will be no stew for you." To emphasize her point, she chopped the ends off the parsley stems. "So, tell me more about things with you and the handsome detective. And I don't mean the bedroom stuff." She waved her knife. "I mean the relationship stuff. Are you guys seriously serious?"

I let out a loud sigh as I took another butcher knife from the block and slid out a cutting board from the small stack behind it. "I think so. But we haven't really talked about it too much. It's been a whirlwind of feelings this past week. All I know is, I really like him. Pebbles adores him. Actually, that's mutual. He didn't seem to at first. I think it was more of that caution cops and postmen get around dogs, you know? Where they're not sure if the animal's bite is as big as its bark?"

Mina nodded.

"But after just a couple of meetings, he was carrying her around like a stuffed animal. She's his best buddy now." My face contorted with false anger. "Sometimes even more than me." I smiled.

"Check his pockets for treats."

A laugh bubbled free. "For sure." Sobering some, I thought about her question and the emotions that had been tumbling around in my brain and my heart for the last several days. "I know it's early, but he could be the one." The words felt strange to say, but also right. Ozzie had made an impression. He wasn't the gruff, standoffish man I first met who'd told me to keep my dog on a leash. Instead, I'd discovered he had a kind heart and just wanted to make the world a better place.

I looked down, concentrating on chopping the carrots. "You know, I wasn't looking for love, either." I lifted my head. "But if it's meant to find you, it will."

Mina shoved a bag of potatoes toward me. "Well, even if that's the case, it needs to wait until *after* I open the café portion of my business. I don't have time for love."

CHAPTER 33

Ozzie

The scents of old wood, new clothing, and gun powder greeted me as I stepped inside Parker Supply. I held the door for Chief Riggs, then offered Kent Morrison, the owner, a friendly smile when he greeted us.

"What can I do for you boys?" The old man, hands hooked under his bright red suspenders, came out from behind the glass counter that housed an array of knives and other hunting and fishing equipment.

My smile widened. He reminded me of Santa Claus. In more than just appearance. The man never met a stranger from what I could tell. From what others had said, he also put a lot of time and money into the community, working to make it a better place. Especially for the local youth.

"We were wondering if we could take a look at your surveillance footage," Riggs said.

The smile on Mr. Morrison's face dimmed and his bushy white eyebrows drew together. "My surveillance footage? What happened?"

"It's in connection to Marie Hammond's murder. We're hoping you caught someone we're looking for on camera," I said.

His frown only deepened. "Here? She was murdered at home, though, right? That's what the local gossip says, anyway."

"That's correct." Riggs nodded once. "But we have a lead that might help us identify a person of interest. On December eighteenth, this individual was here, and he was talking to Mrs. Hammond. Do you keep footage back that far?"

Mr. Morrison's expression opened. He nodded. "I do. I know the wheels of justice turn at a slower pace up here, so I keep twelve months of footage. Pay a pretty penny for it, but it's worth it." He motioned us forward. "Let's go up to the office."

Turning, he looked out at the store. "Kim! I'll be in the office!"

From the distant corner a female voice replied, "Okay!"

I glanced that direction, but didn't see anyone through the maze of racks and shelves. It was no wonder he had surveillance. It couldn't be easy to catch thieves in a place like this.

The old man led us upstairs and unlocked a door, waving us inside. He rounded the desk and sat in the creaky leather seat, then woke up the computer monitor. "December eighteenth, you said?"

"Yes," Riggs answered.

Morrison's arthritic hands poked at the keyboard. "Do you have a ballpark on the time? That's a lot of video to go through."

"Late afternoon," I said. "Between three and five." Kaya said after school, but she didn't say after dinner.

Finding the timestamp, Mr. Morrison left it paused, then got up from his chair. "You can do your thing." He waved me into the seat.

I glanced at Riggs, who nodded, so I sat down.

"She said lingerie." Riggs leaned in beside me and pointed at the screen.

The video footage was broken into sections by camera, so I clicked on the camera covering that part of the store, then hit fast-forward.

At the three-twenty-two mark, I spotted Marie. "Got her." Slowing the video down, I let it play. She walked into the lingerie section and lightly touched a few things, but her gaze was focused elsewhere. She kept glancing through the racks.

It took another minute before a dark-haired man appeared. I paused and zoomed in, but the video distorted too much to see his face and as he got closer to the camera, he tipped his head down, then turned away.

"Follow him." Riggs motioned to the screen. "Maybe we'll catch a better view as he exits the store."

I hit play again, watching their encounter. They talked for several seconds before Marie picked up a bra and held it to her chest.

"They're definitely flirting," I muttered.

Riggs nodded. "Yep."

Several minutes after the encounter started, Kaya entered the scene. The man's demeanor shifted immediately. His posture stiffened, and he quickly turned and walked away.

I pulled up a different camera angle, but he kept his face turned away.

The next camera was the same.

Finally, he reached the door. That one was mounted right over the exit, so there was no avoiding it, except to look down. Which he did.

My jaw worked. It bothered me that this guy seemed to know where all the cameras were. Why was he avoiding them? Had he stolen from the store before? Or was he wanted for something else?

"Back it up." Riggs leaned closer.

I rewound it, then let it play at half-speed. Just as the man walked into view, his head was up. It was too far away to make out his features. I zoomed in. The footage pixelated, but not as much as it did near the lingerie section.

I tipped my head. "Does he look familiar to you?"

Frowning, Riggs studied the screen. "Yes. Make a copy of that and email it to yourself and to me. We'll get forensics to enhance it."

"Yep." I was already working on it. The video was grainy and no one's face was terribly clear until they were practically right in front of the camera.

But he still looked familiar.

"I know who that is, but I'll be damned if I can put a name to him." Riggs pushed upright. "It's too blurry. There's something about the way he carries himself, though."

I agreed. I'd seen him before too. More than once for him to make such an impression. I just didn't know where.

After copying the video to an email, I sent it off, then got up. "Thank you, Mr. Morrison."

"Anytime, boys. Anytime." Blue eyes sparkling with a pleasant smile, he led us out of the office.

Riggs and I piled into my patrol truck outside.

"I have some photography software on my personal computer," I said. "I'm going to play around with it tonight, if you don't mind. I'll still get it over to forensics." I liked to hike and take pictures, so I bought a photo editing program years ago. I might get results faster than our forensics unit.

"Not at all. I want to catch this son of a bitch."

We made the quick drive back to the station, then immediately went our separate ways when Nina ambushed her boss the moment we stepped inside. The online reports system was down.

I hid my grin as I headed for my office. It was no skin off my back to leave my daily reports unfinished. It would make my morning tomorrow a little more hectic, but it left me free sooner to play around with the video footage.

Sitting down at my desk, I downloaded the video from my

email, then sent it to forensics and my personal email so I could work on it at home.

My phone buzzed in my pocket. I fished it out and glanced at the screen.

Ellis.

Frowning, and hoping everything was all right, I answered. "Hello?"

"Hey. This is your friendly reminder you need to eat. Claire's friend Mina is here cooking up a storm. You should take a break."

My stomach growled at the mention of food. It would have to wait, though. "Tell them to save me a plate. I'm not quite finished yet."

Ellis sighed. "Oz…"

"I won't be too late. There's just something I need to do first. I'm close, El. I can see the end of this case." I drummed my fingers on my desk, eager to head home. The man in the video was the key to all of this. I could feel it in my gut.

"Fine. But don't count on seconds. Mina's making elk stew, and it smells delicious." Without saying goodbye, he hung up.

That did sound good, and my stomach made sure I knew it.

Food would have to wait. At least for a little bit. That nagging feeling I knew who was in the footage wouldn't go away. I needed answers more than I needed food.

"Oh, Detective, I'm glad I caught you."

I looked up to see Nina in the doorway. "Hi. What's up?"

She walked in and held out a full-color flyer. "I forgot to put this in your mail stack. The deadline is in a few days."

Accepting the paper, I glanced at it, reading over the information. "A law enforcement competition?"

Smiling, she nodded. "We enter one or two people each year."

"I'll look into it, thank you." And I would, but I doubted I would enter. Not this year. I was still settling in.

"You're welcome. Have a nice evening." With a little wave, she left.

I set the paper on top of the pile of mail I already had going, then turned to my computer, closing windows, so I could shut it down.

My hand froze on the mouse as the zoomed-in photo of the sweatshirt from the crime scene came up on the screen.

Wait...

My chair protested as I leaned forward, bringing my face closer to the monitor. Was that—?

I glanced at the flyer Nina just brought.

It couldn't be.

Lifting the paper from the stack, I held it up to the screen.

The colors for the competition logo and the text placement matched.

Marie's lover was a cop?

Oh, man.

My heart thudded.

This could be bad. We were a small department. Everyone was privy to this case, because everyone had been working it. Murders were an all-hands-on-deck kind of thing here.

Shit...

I speared my fingers through my hair and sat back, chair protesting again.

Who could I trust?

The chair screeched again as I quickly sat up. With several quick clicks, I closed out the rest of the windows on my computer and shut it down. Trading my patrol truck keys for my personal truck, I hurried out of the building.

More than ever, I needed to figure out who the man was in the video.

CHAPTER 34

Claire

Steam rose from the spoonful of stew as I lifted it to my mouth. Gently blowing on it, I decided I didn't care if it was hot. A burned mouth was a small price to pay for Mina's cooking.

Flavors burst over my tongue as my lips closed over the spoon. The heat bordered on uncomfortable, but didn't burn. "Mina, this is delicious."

She smiled from across the table. "Thanks."

I dipped my spoon into my bowl for another bite but paused when the doorbell rang.

"This is small-town Alaska." Ellis frowned. "How do you have so many visitors in the same day?"

I shrugged and scooted back.

"I'll get it." He waved me back down as he stood. "Eat."

"Ellis, it's my house. Whoever it is won't know who you are." I stood up, anyway, and trailed after him.

He didn't answer and kept walking.

I rolled my eyes. He and Ozzie were so different, but also so much alike.

Flipping on the outside light, he glanced through the side window, then turned to me with a frown. "It's a cop."

"What?" My eyebrows dipped. "Answer it." I pointed to the door.

He unlocked the door and swung it open. "Officer. Hello. What can we do for you?"

I glanced around Ellis, my frown deepening. "Officer Turner?"

The polite smile on his face wavered, and he frowned as his gaze traveled between me and Ellis. "Ms. Holmes, I'm sorry to bother you. I didn't know you had company."

"That's okay. Is everything all right?" A horrible thought struck me. "Is Ozzie okay?"

"Oh, he's fine as far as I know. I was looking for him, actually. I got a call from Chief Riggs that he wanted to talk to me, but he's not at the station, and I can't reach him on his phone."

"Try his house," Ellis said. "I'm his brother. I just talked to him. He said he had a lead on his case, so I'm surprised he's not at the station. If he's not at home, he's probably out chasing down something. You might want to try dispatch then."

Nodding as he backed up, Officer Turner nodded. "I'll do that, thank you." He lifted a hand. "Sorry to bother you."

I smiled. "Not a problem. Have a good night."

"You too." Turning, he walked back toward his car.

Ellis stepped back to close the door, and I moved to the side, a small frown replacing my smile.

"What?" he asked as he saw my face.

I blinked and looked at him. "That was weird."

"Why?"

"Because no one except Chief Riggs really knows we're dating. Why would he come here?" I tipped a finger toward the door.

Ellis's eyes narrowed slightly. "You're sure he didn't know?"

"I mean, it's possible, but it would probably just be

rumors. Would you show up at the home of someone you didn't really know looking for their supposed significant other when you haven't even exhausted all the other places you could look for them?"

"Well, when you put it that way, no." A scowl darkened his face. He dug into his pocket and produced his phone.

Mina walked up. "What's going on?"

"Weird things," I answered. "Ellis is calling Ozzie."

"Should I go unlock your gun safe?"

"Not yet," Ellis said just as the call connected. He touched the speakerphone icon.

"I know, I know. Dinner. I'll be there soon." Ozzie's voice came over the line with a touch of exasperation and amusement as well as a healthy dose of distraction.

"It's not about that." Ellis met my gaze, and I could see he was taking my concerns seriously. It wasn't even that big of a deal, but it just struck me as strange.

"Okay?"

"There was an Officer Turner here a minute ago. He was looking for you."

"Oh. Riggs said he was going to ask him to come in at some point. We had a couple questions for him about something. I must have missed him."

"But why did he come *here*?" I asked.

A beat of silence passed. "That's a good point."

"Where are you?" Ellis asked. "I told him you were working a lead and to check your house and call dispatch, but that you might be out somewhere."

"I'm at home. I needed my photo-editing software. You said you sent him here?"

"Yeah. He said he tried to call you first but didn't get an answer."

"Really?" Several seconds of silence passed. "I don't see a missed call."

A moment later, he sucked in a sharp breath.

"Oz?"

My heart thumped as my gaze connected with Ellis's.

"No way," Ozzie whispered. "Son-of-a-bitch. It all makes sense now."

"What does?" I took a step forward, as though I could step through the phone and see what he did.

The sharp clatter of glass shattering on the other end made me jump.

A low grunt of surprise and a thud quickly followed.

"Oscar?" Ellis brought the phone closer to his ear.

Ozzie didn't answer. Instead, a quick series of pops and thuds filled the air.

Ellis cursed. "Those were gunshots."

"What?" With round eyes, I just stared at him. He wasn't serious. Couldn't be.

"Call Chief Riggs." He reached for the door.

"Wait!" I snagged his sleeve. "You can't go unarmed. Or alone."

Mina had already turned around and was running up the stairs.

"Where's she going?" He pointed.

"Same place we are." I tugged on his arm. "To get weapons." And to save Ozzie.

Because the other possibility I couldn't bear to think about.

CHAPTER 35

Ozzie

S hards of window glass sprinkled around me as I dove off the couch. My phone flew from my hand, landing out of sight.

Momentarily stunned, I laid on the floor for a second to get my bearings.

What the hell just happened?

More glass shattered and hit the floor, but that sounded more like someone clearing what was left from the window frame.

A string of curses flew through my brain.

Turner had decided not to wait for me to figure out who was in the footage. But he'd been a few seconds too late. The rendering on my software finished moments before he shot out the window.

Think, Oscar!

Boots crunched on the glass.

Fuck! I was out of time.

My gaze zeroed in on my gun. It was on the table beside the couch.

Just out of reach.

Three shots blew through the back of the couch, the bullets impacting the wall several feet to my left.

My heart hammered in my throat as I flattened myself to the floor.

"I know you're here, Oscar. I saw you through the window. You'd be dead if you hadn't moved." Footsteps came closer.

It was now or never.

Muscles tensing, I steeled myself, blanking out everything from my mind. No fear. No second-guessing. It was action, or I was dead.

I sprang to my knees and dove for my gun.

Bullets splintered the floor right behind my feet as I rolled away from the couch and behind my large leather recliner. I yanked the weapon from its holster and fired two quick shots in his direction.

I heard a thud as he dove for cover.

"You really shouldn't have done that. You're just making it harder on yourself, Oscar."

I barked a short, mirthless laugh. "Sure. If you say so."

"I do."

Two more shots ripped through the recliner's back.

I folded myself even smaller and edged as far to the side as I could. I needed better cover. Lifting my head, I gauged the distance to the kitchen. The island would provide not only cover, but I could skirt around it and get on his other side.

Shifting to the balls of my feet, I adjusted my grip on my gun.

Sucking in a quick breath, I pushed off. Arm extended, I fired three shots toward him as I dove.

A hot breeze whizzed past my neck and the corner of the island base splintered, but I made it past the wall and now had the fridge blocking one angle and the island another.

"You should have charged Warren. He was the perfect fall guy. Plus, he's an asshole. He treated Marie like shit."

I pressed my back to the cabinet as I scurried around it. With a moment to collect myself, I removed the two extra magazines from my holster and stuffed them in my pocket. I still had eleven shots left before I needed to reload.

Drawing in a deep breath through my nose, I slowly let it out, forcing my emotions to calm. Letting the adrenaline and fear rule would get me killed.

I turned my head, listening, but the room was silent. That wouldn't do. I needed to know where he was. "Why did you do it, Gabe?"

"Because she was no better than the jackass she married. She still intended to leave. Even though she was divorcing him, she still wanted to move back East. Said she was done living her life with someone else in mind."

Bingo! With his words, I pegged his location. He was against the wall, sliding along it toward the kitchen. To come in, he'd be exposed when he got within a few feet to round the corner.

Gabe snorted. "That didn't stop her from wanting to spend as many nights together as we could until she left." A moment later, I heard the scuff of his shoe on the floor.

"So, what? She called you over and before she could seduce you again, you stabbed her?" I shifted into a crouch, moving further away. I would get one shot at this. There was nowhere else to hide. He'd cut me off from the rest of the house and the back door was locked.

"No."

I frowned, but stayed silent, not wanting to give away my position.

"My plan was to move with her. To get a job there and do my best to convince her we belonged together. But she just... wouldn't... *listen.*" He shuffled closer.

I shuffled further away.

"Grace didn't like my plan."

Grace?

My eyes widened. The last few pieces of the puzzle clicked into place. The woman Savannah saw fleeing the fire. It was Grace.

"And you know? She was right. Hers was so much better. Except we didn't count on Warren being so adept at hiding. He's really not that smart."

Turner's boot hit the floorboard at the edge of the kitchen that always squeaked. I tensed.

"And you. We didn't count on *you*."

Ears open to the sound of the smallest movement, I slid around the side of the island, rising just above counter height to fire two shots as he lunged into the kitchen.

The first bullet missed, but the second hit him in the left shoulder, spinning him to the side. I fired a third and struck him in the chest.

His hand went slack, and the gun slipped from his fingers, hitting the floor with a clatter. Blood welled from the wound near his sternum, and he crumpled to his knees. The cabinet caught him as he tipped sideways, and he slouched against it.

"Oscar!"

Ellis's distant shout carried through the broken front window. I ignored him and moved toward Gabe Turner's still body. With my foot, I kicked his pistol away. It skittered over the wooden floor and smacked into the cabinet baseboard behind me.

Using one hand, I checked his pulse. It still beat weakly beneath my fingers, but his chest no longer rose and fell.

"Oz!"

Ellis's voice was closer now. At the window.

"I'm in the kitchen," I called back.

Glass crunched and a soft curse floated through the air.

Laying my gun on the counter, I shifted Gabe onto his back and started chest compressions.

Blood oozed from the wound on his chest and poured over my fingers.

"Holy shit. Jesus Christ, Oz, are you okay?"

"Yeah." I glanced up. "Call an ambulance. Where are Claire and Mina?"

"Outside." He pulled out his phone. "I made them stay in the truck. They're both armed. Your girl's got a nice hunting rifle collection."

I could see that by the one hanging over his shoulder. "After you call for help, go back out and get them. We need to stick together. This isn't over yet."

CHAPTER 36

Claire

I clutched the door, leaving nail dents in the leather as I stared out the windshield of Ellis's truck at the broken front window of Ozzie's house. My other hand clutched my Mini-14 rifle. I wanted to run in there and help, but Ellis told us to stay in the truck. That we could make things worse since we didn't know what we were doing.

He was right, but that didn't make waiting any easier. Especially since we heard gunfire when we arrived.

But it was quiet now.

"This is ridiculous," Mina growled. She leaned forward from the backseat to stare through the windshield. "Is he okay or not? We haven't heard any more shots since Ellis went in. Why hasn't he come back out to tell us if Oscar's okay?"

Why, indeed? It had only been a minute, but he should be able to assess the situation quickly and pop back out to tell us everything was all right.

Or he was a hostage now and couldn't.

I glanced back at my friend, holding her gaze in the truck's dim interior. The same desire to go in blazed in her eyes.

That was enough for me. "Let's go." Turning away, I yanked on the door handle.

Mina climbed out the rear door and we met in front of the truck.

"So, how do you want to do this?" Mina asked. "Do we go in through the window, like Ellis?"

"Probably, but we need to approach with caution. If Officer Turner has them both as hostages, I don't want him to see us. We might be their only chance." I refused to consider that Ellis might be the only hostage. That he'd walked in to find his brother dead.

Nope.

Not a possibility in my mind.

Sticking to the snow so our shoes wouldn't make noise on the concrete path, we headed for the house, rifles tucked into our shoulders but pointed down slightly.

I glanced up the street, looking for what, I didn't know. A neighbor who could call for help, maybe. Ellis was the only one with a phone. Mina's was on the counter at my house. Mine was on the coffee table. We'd left in such a rush, neither of us grabbed them.

Movement in a white SUV parked in front of the neighbor's house drew my attention. "You see that car? The white one?" Using just my eyes, I gestured toward it.

Mina took a quick glimpse. "Yeah. What about it?"

"There's someone in it."

"It's probably a neighbor who's scared shitless. It's not every day gunfire erupts next door. And definitely not at the cop's house."

My lips flattened. Maybe.

"Freeze."

I jumped, but stopped, and turned toward the female voice from the side yard. A woman in a maroon stocking cap and black coat and leggings aimed a pistol at us. "Put your guns down."

Oh, hell no. My grip tightened.

The tip of Mina's gun dipped, and she squinted. "Grace? Is that you?"

Snow crunched softly under the woman's boots as she stepped forward, bringing her features more into the glow from the streetlight, and I recognized her. Grace Alonso was a teacher at the school. I'd seen her in The Cozy Cup too.

"Hello, Mina." Grace offered her a sad smile. "I'm sorry to involve you in this. You picked a bad night to visit your friend."

The frown on my face deepened with every word. What was she doing here?

Then it clicked. Sometimes it paid living in a small town.

Grace Alonso and Officer Gabe Turner were siblings.

My eyes widened as it all came together in my mind. "Oh my God. You're the one who torched my office. Your brother was Marie Hammond's lover."

"And that's why I set the fire. You're too clever, Claire. Unlike my damn brother, who can't remember to pick up after himself," she growled through clenched teeth. "Those pictures you took of Marie's house needed to be destroyed before you could make the connection to him."

"The shirt on the hamper," I said, hoping to keep her distracted. She hadn't told us to put our rifles down again, and I wanted to keep it that way. "It was your actions that made us think harder about what I had that the killer wanted. If you'd left it alone, we probably wouldn't have known."

"Lies!" Grace shifted her stance. "Eventually, the truth would have come out. Because Gabe's an idiot!" The gun wavered in her hand.

I tightened my grip on my rifle and cast a quick look at Mina from the corner of my eye. Her rifle rose fractionally.

"I had this all planned," Grace continued. "Down to the last detail. And then Gabe had to screw it all up and sleep with her one last time. He told me they were through. That when she told him they were going to Boston to look for a house, he knew she was serious about leaving, and he ended things. But he didn't! He took what that whore gave him and left his shirt behind. It wasn't until after I stabbed the bitch that I learned what he'd done. I found it cleaning up."

Grace murdered Marie?

"It was the perfect plan. Marie died. Then, eventually, the cops would find Warren dead in the backyard of his house, with a letter in his pocket that said he couldn't live with the guilt or without her. It was all supposed to be wrapped up with a neat little bow. Then Gabe could move on." Her hand shook and her cheeks flushed as anger blazed in her eyes.

"It wasn't supposed to be like this. I didn't want to kill her. Gabe was supposed to let her go, but he…just… *couldn't*. He wouldn't have been happy on the East Coast. This is his home. So, the bitch had to die."

Boy, but was she delusional. Who murdered their brother's girlfriend so he wouldn't move away or pine for her?

A siren sounded in the distance.

Finally! Relief flooded my veins, making my limbs a little heavy.

Grace's eyes darted toward the sound. "Dammit! Stupid, nosy neighbors. This is Alaska. People shoot guns."

Not inside houses, they didn't.

Her stance shifted and her expression hardened. "I'm sorry about this." The gun in her hands swung toward me.

I saw the decision in her eyes before her body acknowledged it.

She was going to shoot me.

Except I had no plans to die tonight. I—hopefully—had a man in that house who I planned to hold close for many years to come and a long life left to live.

This crazy woman wasn't going to take that from me.

Years of hunting had made me an excellent shot. From this

distance I knew I couldn't miss. Before she could pull the trigger, I took aim and fired.

CHAPTER 37

Ozzie

"What the fuck was that?" My head came up at the crack of a rifle outside.

Ellis froze, still on the phone.

I scrambled to my feet, knowing Claire was out there. "Take over."

"Hell no. He's already dead." Ellis hung up.

Most likely. My aim had been true. Picking up my gun, I ran around the counter and into the living room to the busted-out front window.

Cautiously, I peered out.

The driveway and front yard were empty, but movement and raised voices under the tall pine in the side yard caught my eye.

"There." Ellis nodded in the same direction.

"Yeah."

Sirens blared and bright red and blue lights lit up the street as Riggs's truck came roaring around the corner.

No more shots rang out, and whatever it was going on under that tree, it wasn't focused on the house or the street.

"Come on." Head on a swivel, I stepped through the window.

Turning right, I jogged through the yard and around my truck.

Riggs rocked to a stop at the end of the driveway and got out. His flashing lights lit up the area, and in the strobing glow, I saw three figures in the snow flailing about.

"Dammit, they were supposed to stay in the truck." Ellis started forward.

I couldn't make out who was who in the wild lighting or from this distance, but I could tell it was at least two women by the sound of their voices and their slighter figures. One voice rose above them all with a cry of pain.

My heart stuttered, praying it wasn't Claire.

Speeding up, Ellis and I reached them in seconds. I paused for a moment, taking in the fracas.

Mina lay over a pair of black-clad legs—a woman's legs—holding them down. Claire was sprawled over the woman's back, holding one of her hands wrenched behind her back. Blood dotted the snow on the woman's other side and three guns—a pistol and two rifles—were scattered on the ground just out of everyone's reach.

"Claire! Mina!" I dropped to my knees beside Claire and took hold of the woman's arm.

"No!" The woman shrieked and bucked.

Ellis stooped beside Mina to help her.

The woman turned her head, her brown eyes spitting the fires of hell at me.

Grace Alonso.

She shrieked again and tried to pull her hand away.

I clenched my teeth. Once again, I didn't have any handcuffs on me.

"Quartermaine!" Riggs jogged over, kicking up snow.

"Do you have cuffs?"

Metal clacked together as he pulled them from his belt. Coming around Grace's other side, he reached under Claire, who moved back to give him access.

The bracelet clicked as he locked it around Grace's wrist.

"Be careful with her other hand. It has a hole in it." Claire sat back on her haunches and swiped the hair out of her eyes.

Riggs picked up Grace's arm, bending it back, and the woman howled again with pain. He locked the cuff around her wrist, which was coated in blood.

"What happened?" I looked up from the sight with a frown.

"She had a gun." Claire brushed some snow off her top. "I shot it out of her hand."

"You—" The words wouldn't come out. She'd shot a handgun out of someone's hand? "Why didn't you aim for center-mass? Was she trying to shoot you?"

"Yes. But I didn't want that on my conscience." Her mouth twisted, then her expression hardened. "Besides, I want her to pay for what she did. Death is too easy."

"What she did?" A sinking feeling filled my stomach.

Claire nodded. "Grace killed Marie. Her brother just covered it all up. She set fire to my office too."

"You can't prove any of it!" Grace wiggled beneath me but halted with a moan. "I didn't say shit on the record."

"Maybe not," Riggs said, locking her handcuffs so they wouldn't tighten anymore on her. "But after all this, I can get a bunch of warrants for all kinds of things." He rolled up onto the balls of his feet and hooked a hand under her arm.

Ellis and Mina got up, and I grabbed Grace's other arm, helping Riggs get the woman to her feet.

An ambulance turned the corner, killing its siren as it approached.

Riggs glanced at me. "Where's Turner?"

"Inside." My gaze flicked to Grace. She didn't know I'd killed her brother.

She turned her head to look at me, still glaring daggers, but she must have seen something in my eyes. The fire leached from her expression and a hollowness appeared in her cheeks as horror took hold. "No," she whispered. A glare formed, bringing her brows down to a point. "No!" she screamed and jerked against Riggs's hold.

"I'm sorry, Grace." I wouldn't fill her ears with a line like, "I had no choice." I didn't, but she wouldn't care. Someone she loved was dead. It didn't matter that he attacked me. To her, it was my fault, and it would always be my fault.

"No!" She screamed again. "You bastard!" Riggs firmed his grip and started her toward the ambulance. "Oh, you better hope they lock me away for the rest of my life. I will *murder* you in your sleep if I ever get out."

Stumbling over her feet and still struggling with the chief, she continued to shout threats and call me names as he hauled her away.

Sorrow twinged in my chest. For her and for Gabe. It didn't need to end this way. No one needed to die. They'd made a choice and so had I.

Mine had been to live.

"Oh! Ozzie!" Claire fell into me, wrapping her arms around my neck.

I buried my face in her hair, breathing in her sweet scent. It felt so good to have her in my arms. "You okay, honey?"

She nodded against me. "I'm fine. Everything is okay now." Leaning back, she framed my face in her hands, searching my gaze. "I'm so glad you're all right."

"Same, sweetheart." I palmed the back of her head and gave her a quick, fierce kiss. Just enough to make my brain believe she—this—was real, and I wasn't lying on my kitchen floor, dreaming about her as I bled out.

"Oz. Man." Ellis's hand landed on my back.

I let Claire go and turned to hug my brother. Tears pressed at the backs of my eyes, and I hugged him harder. "Thank you." When I decided to come to Alaska, forging a stronger relationship with Ellis was the driving factor. We were each other's only living relative. To think I could have lost him or he could have lost me was as unfathomable and as painful as the idea of losing Claire.

"Can we not do that ever again?" Ellis eased back and gripped my shoulder.

Huffing a quick laugh, I agreed. "Never."

CHAPTER 38

Claire

F*our weeks later…*

THE CLAMMY SHEEN OF SWEAT DAMPENED MY PALMS, AND I swiped them down the sides of my jeans. My heart thrummed in my chest, flapping like a butterfly caught in a windstorm.

Why was I so nervous? It wasn't like he'd say no.

At least, I didn't think he would. That was the whole reason I was asking. If I thought he'd turn me down, I would keep my mouth shut.

But I was still nervous. It wasn't every day a woman asked her boyfriend to permanently move in.

Since the incident at his house with Grace and Gabe, he'd been staying with me. At first, his house was a crime scene. Plus, there was a gaping hole where the window used to be. Not to mention the damage to the flooring, walls, and cabinets from the bullets.

The police spent over a week collecting evidence from Ozzie's house and holding the scene until they were sure they had what they needed. He couldn't do anything except board up the window until then. It had about driven him insane to be put on administrative leave and completely sidelined from the investigation, but Riggs and the state patrol officers who came in to assist were adamant he stayed away.

But the ball was rolling now. He'd been cleared of wrongdoing in Gabe Turner's death and taken off of leave, but he was still out of the loop on the case.

As far as the house went, over the last couple of weeks, he'd met with insurance adjusters and contractors to start the restoration process. It would be at least another month before he could move back in. Even then, it wouldn't be finished.

So, I had a plan.

I touched the blue and silver wrapped package on the counter. It wasn't anything fancy. Literally a piece of paper I put in a box and wrapped. But it was arguably one of the most important pieces of paper of my life.

I glanced at the clock on the stove. Five-twenty-three.

Where was he?

Before he left this morning, I asked if he thought he would be on time for dinner tonight. That I had an elk roast to use up, and it was better right out of the slow cooker than reheated later.

He said barring a case coming in last minute he didn't see it being a problem. Then he promised to call me if he would be late.

The clock ticked over to five-twenty-four.

He was late. I couldn't leave the roast in the slow cooker on warm for much longer. It would get too dry.

I huffed.

Relax, Claire. My rational mind poked her head out and rolled her eyes at me. *He probably had to finish a report and didn't think it would take long.*

I knew that side of my brain was right, but it didn't make waiting any easier.

Rather than stand around clock-watching, I decided to set the table. We usually just grabbed plates from the cupboard and dished up our meals right from the pots and pans on the stove. Tonight, we'd be fancy. I even found a couple of placemats.

Carrying my load to the table, I set the mats in front of the chairs we usually sat at, then put the dinner plates on top. Silverware went down next on top of folded napkins. They were paper, but it would suffice. We weren't *that* fancy.

With the place settings out, I stepped back and assessed the table. Did I want to add candles?

No. That would be overkill.

But we did need wine and drink glasses.

Spinning around, I took two steps toward the kitchen when the front door opened. Pebbles barked and ran for the door.

"Hey, it smells good in here," Ozzie called.

Changing course, I stepped further into the room so he could see me and smiled as he came into view. "Thanks. I just set the table. Everything's ready."

He arched an eyebrow as he shrugged out of his coat. "You set the table?"

"I was feeling a little posh tonight."

He hung up his jacket with a chuckle, then gave Pebbles a scratch before he walked closer and gave me a kiss. When he pulled back, he frowned slightly. "What's the matter? You feel a little tense."

Knowing he wasn't wrong, I didn't deny it. "Come here." I took his hand and led him to the kitchen.

"Claire?"

I could hear the question in his voice, but decided to let the gift I wrapped speak for me. Letting go of his hand, I scooped it off the counter and held it out to him. "Open this."

Ozzie frowned at the box, then gave me a curious look,

but he took it. "What's this for? It's not my birthday. Or Christmas."

"Just open it." I waved a hand at the present, catching my bottom lip between my teeth as nerves took hold.

Brows still drawn together, he turned it over in his hands to find the seam in the paper and ripped it open. Holding it against his chest, he tugged the lid off the box and tucked it under his arm before moving the tissue paper out of the way.

He lifted out the change of address form, then looked at me in utter confusion. "A change of address form? What's this for?"

I clutched my hands together in front of me to keep from fiddling and let my lip slide free. "So, I thought you might want to fill that out and make your presence here permanent."

The look of confusion on his face went through several phases as he worked through my statement. Finally, it landed on one of confused hope.

A bit of my nerves melted away.

"You want me to move in for good?"

I nodded. "I know we haven't talked much about the future, but these last few weeks have been some of the best of my life. I love having you here, and I can't imagine you going home."

Ozzie put the paper back in the box and set the lid on top before reaching around me to set it on the counter. He took my hands and tugged me closer until our shirts brushed. "It's been in the back of my mind for close to two weeks that I needed to find a way to make our living situation permanent. I don't want to go home, either. I'm already home, Claire."

The last of my nerves took flight, floating away on a wave of hope. Intense love for this man warmed my chest. "You are?" My voice came out on a rough whisper.

"I am." He let go of my hands to frame my face. "I've been holding onto these words about as long as I've been here, telling myself it's much too soon to feel the way I do. Except I realize now the time doesn't matter. When it's right, it's right. I love you. I think I have since you came running down the sidewalk in your blue robe and hot pink slippers, chasing Pebbles."

A watery laugh bubbled out. I slid my hands over his. "Same, Detective. Same. I love you too."

The smile that split his face was nothing short of pure joy. My own felt stretched to the max. But he quickly stole it away with a kiss that seared me to my toes.

I still had one question, though.

Easing back, I looked up at him. "If you were planning to make our living situation permanent, what's the plan for your house?" There were still repairs to make. Even if he planned to sell it, they needed to be done.

One side of his mouth lifted. "I might know a certain Coastie turned fisherman who's still looking for a house to buy."

My smile bloomed once more. Ellis. "I think that's a wonderful idea." Ozzie wasn't the only Quartermaine I'd gotten to know in the last month. The more time I spent with Ellis, the more I appreciated his brand of humor and the bond the brothers shared.

Ozzie wrapped his arms around my waist and lifted me off my feet. "Me too. So, how long will dinner keep?" he asked a moment before he kissed me again.

My joyful laugh died in my chest as need took hold.

Dry elk roast wasn't *that* bad.

～

About the Author

Ashley started writing in her teens and never stopped. Her first novel, Smoky Mountain Murder, came out in 2016, and she has since published two more series and has plans for more. When not writing, you can find her with her nose stuck in a book or watching some terrible disaster movie on SyFy. An avid baseball fan, she also enjoys crafting and cooking. She lives in Ohio with her husband, two kids, three cats, and one very wild shepherd mix.

Website: https://ashleyaquinn.com
Facebook Reader Group: facebook.com/groups/
349932159616427

goodreads.com/ashleyaquinn
amazon.com/Ashley-A-Quinn/e/B07HCT4QST
facebook.com/ashleyaquinn.writer
instagram.com/ashleyaquinn.writer

Also by Ashley A Quinn

The Broken Bow

A Beautiful End

Wildfire

In Plain Sight

Close Quarters

Scorched

Light of Dawn

Pine Ridge

Sweetness

Loner

Shark

Katydid

Homespun

Foggy Mountain Intrigue

Smoky Mountain Murder

Smoky Mountain Baby

Smoky Mountain Stalker

Smoky Mountain Doctor

Smoky Mountain K-9

Smoky Mountain Judge

Prequel to Wagner Brigade

Stranded with Ezra

Wagner Brigade

Ford's Fight

Dean's Dilemma

Jordan's Journey

Sam's Salvation

Asher's Assignment

Max's Mission

Parker's Landing

Midnight Secrets

Book 2: Coming December 2025